SNOWS OF ATURIA
THE DARVEL EXPLORATORY SYSTEMS

S.J. SANDERS

©2021 by Samantha Sanders
All rights reserved.

No part of this book may be reproduced or transmitted in any form or by any means, electronic or mechanical, including photocopying, recording, or by any information storage and retrieval system, without explicit permission granted in writing from the author.

Cover art by: Pierluigi Abbondanza
Artist websight: abboart.com

This book is a work of fiction intended for adult audiences only.

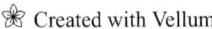 Created with Vellum

CHAPTER 1

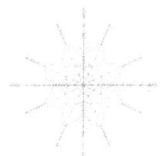

*V*anessa frowned as she eyed the dress that had been packed for her. Gossamer sheer with a subtle sparkle when the finely woven fabric caught the light, it had her mother's touch all over it.

A pained groan escaped her as she rummaged through the bag and saw that half of her cozy sweaters and knit leggings had been replaced with similar clothes. Elegant blouses, silk skirts, and a couple of pairs of expensive slacks had been ill concealed beneath a couple of thick sweaters.

She sighed and stuffed it all back into the bag, not caring that it was going to wrinkle. She had absolutely no intention of wearing that silly dress, or anything of the selections her mother had smuggled in.

Damn it!

She had *told* Natalie not to let her mother touch her bags while she was running last minute errands, but clearly Desiree had gotten her way, as usual, and had managed to make a few switches. Each of them entirely impractical for a writer's retreat at the cabin she had reserved.

The intercom overhead dinged, and she smothered a groan.

She had only been awake from stasis for an hour. Who could possibly need to talk to her now?

"...Yes?" she reluctantly answered.

There was a pause and a throat cleared with a hint of censure before the captain's deep voice filled the room.

"*Miss Williams*," he growled in a tight voice, "we've received an intergalactic comm for you from Earth."

Oh no.

She squeezed her eyes closed. No wonder he sounded peeved. The starcruiser, *Anointed,* strictly forbade comms after leaving the Sol system. There was only one person who could have managed to get through: Desiree Williams. No one said no to her mother, as evidenced by Vanessa's current wardrobe. She had left Earth to escape her mother's matchmaking machinations. She was the last person Vanessa wanted to talk to on what was supposed to be her vacation, but she had played this game enough with Desiree to know that she had no real choice in the matter.

"My apologies, Captain," she sighed. "Go ahead and put her through."

"Thank you," he replied, almost sounding sympathetic. "I'll patch her through immediately." He hesitated before muttering a hasty "good luck," and then the comm clicked and his voice was replaced by a feminine shriek that made Vanessa wince.

"Darling, thank goodness! I've been so worried!" her mother wailed.

Vanessa raised an eyebrow—not that her mother could see since the comm was a direct line voice communication—and wiggled out of the wet fabric that had covered her during stasis.

"I don't know why you would be so worried," Vanessa said as she stepped into a pair of warm leggings. "I know that their policy makes them send message alerts to family when we're awakened during approach. You should have been notified immediately."

"Oh, *that*. You know I don't trust such things! Why, anything could have happened... *pirates*, even!" her mother gasped, and Vanessa imagined her mother clutching her heavy ropes of pearls close to her chest as she fanned herself with her silk handkerchief. She freely rolled her eyes for a change and plucked up a beautiful deep green angora sweater and pulled it over her head. Enclosed in the softness, she was finally starting to feel warm again.

"Mom, we both know that automated alerts would have been sent out with specific codes and evac coordinates in the case of any crisis. Pirate attack is on that list."

Desiree gave an unhappy harrumph. "Well, when are you planning on coming back? Six months is a long time to travel, darling. With travel time alone, you'll be gone for a year!"

"Yes, Mom, but we talked about this—remember? I really need a good three months to have some peace and quiet to work on my book. I have a six-month visitor visa to the human colony on the southern continent of Aturia and plan to make as much use of it as I can. I promise I will let you know as soon as I'm ready to come home."

"And I suppose there is no talking you out of this insanity?"

"I am my mother's daughter," Vanessa quipped, knowing that it would make her mother laugh.

Despite her tendency to be overdramatic, Desiree was well aware of her faults and acknowledged them with humor while, at the same time, not changing a single thing about them. She claimed that they gave her character, and Vanessa's father did seem to love those same little quirks. Her mother might drive her to distraction sometimes, and hovered way too much over her only child, but Vanessa never felt any lack of love from her parents.

"Oh, very well, since you insist." Her mother sighed. "Cary is just going to have to wallow in misery until you get back."

Vanessa threw back her head and groaned. "*Mother*, not Cary."

"What's wrong with Cary? He's a perfectly sweet young man, good looking, and very talented. He's rising in the vids as we speak if you would ever pull your attention away from one of the books on your datapad to pay any attention. Most importantly, he really thinks you're exactly what he's looking for in a wife. It really is a good match, darling." Her voice dropped a bit. "And it's not like you have a lot of offers as of late."

She meant ever since Vanessa dared to turn down her last proposal three years ago, just before turning thirty. Although she was successful with women readers on Earth and throughout the colonies, she was no longer a fresh-faced young woman of status. Although most actors belonged to the lower pleasure arts class, only those who were truly successful belonged to the greater arts and entertainment strata. Vanessa was born into it, as was Cary, which meant that they had the best arts education that money could buy.

"Cary is nice, but he's so boring," Vanessa replied. "I'm actually okay being on my own. If love happens to come along, then great! But I don't want to settle for someone who looks good on a data record but does nothing for me."

Her mother's disappointed sigh was audible. "I know, Nessie," she said, making Vanessa cringe at the pet name, "but I don't want you to end up all alone. I won't be here forever... and I wouldn't mind grandbabies to spoil, since we're being perfectly honest."

Nose wrinkling, Vanessa muttered the foulest curse she could think of under her breath.

"Did you say something, Nessie?"

"Sorry, just thinking aloud. I'll try harder when I return, Mom. Maybe one of those matching agencies you're always talking about. But no promises," she interjected at her mother's excited gasp. "I'm not going to just get hitched to whomever I'm matched with either. This has to be all or nothing."

"Of course, darling!" her mother trilled.

She suspected that her mother ignored about half of what she just said, but that was a battle for another day. Glancing down at the time on her comm band, she winced. She needed to hurry and wrap this up before she delayed the shuttle.

"Mother, I really need to go. My shuttle is departing for the surface in about forty minutes. I really can't hold them up."

"Nessie, you are a Williams, dear. Not only our daughter, but well known in your own right. You know very well that they'll wait for you without complaint."

No complaint that Vanessa would hear, anyway.

"Yes, but it's rude to keep people waiting, as you've often told me when we've had to go to social functions," she reminded her mother cheerfully. "Have a great time preparing for the Midwinter Feast," she added.

"It won't be the same without you, but I'll try. Daddy gives his love. Comm us as soon as you're settled," her mother said, making kissy sounds into the comm. "Bye, darling."

"I will. Bye!" she assured her, nearly sagging with relief when the comm terminated.

Running a weary hand through her long brown hair, she glanced at the time again. She had just enough time to grab her belongings and head toward the docking bay. Scooping up her coat, she tossed it over her arm and rushed over to pick up her bag just as her comm alerted her to proceed to docking.

The departure crew was waiting for her when she walked into the bay, the heels of her boots clicking in a sharp staccato, announcing her presence. At her punctual arrival, the tension drained out of them, and they nodded politely to her with cheerful smiles as they opened the shuttle door. She returned their smiles and ducked inside, pleased with the cheerful cherry red padded interior. She hadn't noticed that they had followed her inside and departed for their assigned stations until the pilot's voice greeted her through the comm system.

"This will be a bumpy descent, so get fastened in good and tight, Miss Williams. It looks like we have a bit of weather below."

Vanessa sat down and strapped herself into the harness tucked discreetly into the sides of the chair as she frowned up at the comm.

"Is it safe?"

"Don't worry. It's no worse than we've descended through before. Just some upper atmospheric winds and snow as we get lower. Once we get on the right flight path, we can head to the southern continent without a problem. Just hold tight."

"Okay," she mumbled, her fingers curling around the edge of the seat.

The rumble of the shuttle's engine and the heavy grind outside of the docking bay opening into space nearly drowned out the voice on the comm. Going back and forth on the shuttles between starcruisers and planetside was always frightening, but there was no avoiding it. The cruisers were too large to land and take off from a planet. Old starships had once been rocketed up from earth, but now the enormous cruisers, traders, and fleetships were all built in space. Shuttles were a necessary way to travel.

Vanessa swallowed back her nausea as the rumble around her grew louder, focusing on the voice of the pilot overhead.

"Disembarking *Anointed* in five... four... three... two... one."

CHAPTER 2

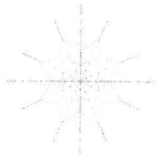

*J*or'y flexed his wings as he stared out of the tall southern window of his home, his mood pensive as it had been frequently as of late. Fluffy white snow crystals drifted down from the sky, but he knew that the sedate peace wouldn't last. The storms this winter were going to be bad. He could feel it in the marrow of his wing base.

Perhaps more of his kind would have recognized the instinctive warning signs of bad weather if it hadn't become fashionable to dock their wings and adapt to the "civilized" city life that had come with the arrival of humans, bringing with them the advances of the Intergalactic Union two generations ago. Their entire way of life had been changed... and not for the better, in his opinion.

Reared by his proud grandsire in the mountains of the eastern continent, Jor'y had been raised to respect Aturian ways. Unlike many of his peers in the cities with whom he was forced to deal for business, he clung to tradition like most outer rim males of their planet. He kept his broad, feathered wings, and even the plume of fine feathers that filled out the lower length of his tail that were barely thicker than the long wispy feathers that grew from his head.

Although his business associates and the occasional human he met did not bother to hide their contempt, he was proud of his feathers and his ability to fly as nature intended. He had still been young when he learned of the horrors his species inflicted upon themselves. He had trembled beneath his grandsire's wing for two days after coming across a "health vid" that demonstrated how the urban Aturians were having the tiny cuticles of their infants' tail feathers removed, and around the same time they severed the delicate, featherless wings. Body feathers were otherwise lasered off whenever they made an appearance.

For health. That was how it was being pushed onto their people. Feathers were dirty, susceptible to pests and disease that could potentially cause wing rot, so the medics considered amputating the wings and defeathering the tails to be the most sanitary actions. In collaboration with off-worlder medics, of course. Flightless human colonists, and the few other alien visitors that they had, were frightened by Aturian wings and had been the first to call them unhygienic and a threat to community health. It was only a short hop from there to becoming uncivilized, inconsiderate—wings and feathered tails required more space and were seen as unnecessary as Aturians adopted the use of shuttles and flyers to travel.

Jor'y sneered. Those shuttles would not do them any good in the storms that were coming. Nor would they find extra warmth with the comfort of feathers.

He stroked a hand over the fine feathers that ran over his neck and shoulders like a collar brushing over the top of his pectorals. While it formed a thicker ring of slightly longer feathers circling his neck, those on his neck were smaller, like a fluffy down, but provided a comfortable barrier that kept him warm. From below the collar, the downy feathers thinned to show the rough purple skin that covered the rest of his body.

He glanced down at his broad chest visible in the deep V at

the front of his knee-length robe. It was vanity, but the large, muscular chest was another thing that the mutilated members of his species lacked. The females were not so aggrieved over it, but, despite the fact that they would not foul their nest with his presence as a mate, there had been more than one admiring look cast his way—and more than one jealous glare from rival males. His tail rose behind him, the long, thin feathers fanning out as he stretched them to work loose some of his annoyance.

He was tired of the offers to pleasure join. There was nothing wrong with it. It was a method for revitalization and restoring one's energy, even if it was addictive to some of those who were unmated. Recently, however, he had refused all offers because he wanted a mate and to breed offspring. Not to merely pass a few hours in the company of a female looking for a momentary thrill, to exchange energies. He wanted to find his a'talyna, a female compatible with his energy and heartsong.

His ear twitched at a scuffing sound behind him, and his nostrils flared. *Ah*. His assistant—and friend, he had to acknowledge, even if the male annoyed him in equal portion to his skill at his work.

"I'm going to leave now, Jor'y, before the weather worsens, unless there's anything else you need?" the male said in a low voice.

Jor'y glanced over his shoulder, his eyes narrowing slightly on Vi'ryk, noting the way the wings lay restless against his side.

"A wise decision. You do not wish to be caught flying home when the weather breaks," he rumbled, one of the claws of his toes clacking in a thoughtful beat against the stone floor.

The movement sent the gold hoop bracers around his foot jangling, but he ignored it. It was merely an annoying nervous habit when he was restless. This weather, among other things, fueled his poor mood. He was certain that Vi'ryk was feeling similar effects since he wasn't able to keep his wings flat at his sides. At least the male had a mate to go home to, the fortunate prick.

"It will be a bad one, I suspect. It will likely snow us all in," Vi'ryk murmured. "You should know that I have canceled all of your appointments for the morning."

Dipping his head in acknowledgment, Jor'y grunted deep in his chest, wordlessly communicating his appreciation.

"Make sure that they are cleared for the week. This storm isn't going anywhere soon," he muttered.

"You feel it that deeply?" Vi'ryk cocked his head curiously. "There is no indication on the weather system scanners."

He nodded and the male immediately turned his attention to the datapad in his hand. They both knew just how unreliable the scanners were. They did fine for issuing immediate alerts to the populace, but the weather on Aturia was too unpredictable for them to be dependable. He could feel it, though. It was an instinctive thing buried deep within his bones, bred into him over generations, ever since his ancestors were selected as the valmek. The duties of the valmek had been passed down to him fifteen revolutions ago when he demonstrated the instincts and aptitude for it and his own sire had welcomed retiring from the role. As such, Jor'y was the guardian of the valetik, the extended family grouping to which he belonged.

His strength and guidance were depended on, especially in matters such as these. His warning of the storm would be heeded.

"Done," Vi'ryk announced. "I have also sent out alerts to the valetik so that everyone is advised to stay close to home. Is there anything else you require?"

Jor'y shook his head, his gaze remaining fixed on the snowy mountains. He sensed his assistant's hesitation.

"Is there something on your mind Vi'ryk?" he grumbled.

"Actually, if I may speak freely…"

Jor'y snorted, casting a glance at the male lingering behind him. "When has that ever stopped you, my friend? Go ahead."

A chuckle escaped Vi'ryk. "Fair enough. It's just that… everyone is concerned," he managed tactfully. "You are not a young male anymore. You have no heirs to train to take your place, and you were your sire's only offspring. Our people look to you for protection and leadership, and some worry that you have yet to take a mate."

"You speak as if this is a simple matter," Jor'y growled, his forecrest rising slightly as his crown feathers puffed up in agitation. "I am a busy male, and it is not as if unmated females are plentiful among the outer rim valetiks." The fact that many of the younger females had chosen to leave the valetiks and undergo the necessary surgeries for a more comfortable life in the cities did not help matters. "We both know that within the cities there are not options," he added bitterly.

"There were some females who indicated interest a few rotations ago," Vi'ryk reminded him.

The male knew exactly why Jor'y had not chosen either of them, and had agreed, at the time, with his decision. Jor'y had a difficult time feeling any kind of interest in those females, and even more difficulty in trusting them with the welfare of his valetik.

"I would not to do that to my kin," he grated out, his wings squeezing closer to his body with his mounting annoyance.

"And that is why the valetik loves and respects you. You put us before your own loneliness."

"Hardly a sacrifice in that case."

"But still," Vi'ryk interrupted, smiling, "we would like to see you with a female. Any female. I doubt anyone would even object if you flew south and kidnapped one of those soft-skinned humans," he laughed.

"I do not think the human colony would find that as amusing," Jor'y replied, the corners of his mouth tilting up.

"As if they know one Aturian from another," his friend scoffed. "All they would see is some barbarian outer rimmer and cry to the planetary government. And what could they do? They cannot even enforce the ridiculous human laws regarding interspecies pleasure joining. Or manage to remove the vids," he chuckled.

Despite his refusal to entertain Vi'ryk's suggestion, Jor'y's mouth went dry. He had seen some of the so-called "illegal" vids. Despite being classified as illegal to satisfy the human colonists, the vids were easy to find and purchase without any repercussions. Although the male and female Aturians in the vids had been disfigured as was now socially the norm, even he had been entranced by the highly erotic pleasure demonstrated by the small, soft human species.

He wouldn't stoop to anything as dishonorable as kidnapping anyone, but to have a soft, expressive female under him was tempting. The only thing that soured that fantasy was knowing how humans would react to his feathers. He would not see such loathing and disgust in the eyes of any female he sought to mate. His heart wouldn't be able to bear it. Nor would he disfigure himself for any mate. Not for an Aturian female or a human.

Vi'ryk cleared his throat. "As for the Hashavnal…"

"No."

The male sighed. "Jor'y, the valetik expects it. And we are to have visitors in attendance."

Visitors? That was the first Jor'y had heard of it. He cast a questioning glance at his friend, and the male shrugged his wings apologetically.

"It is on request from the Aturian government. Darvel is seeking to open further trade with the outer rim and so we are expected to host a small delegation during the event." He winced. "They will be your guests."

Jor'y froze, his eyes widening for a moment before he dropped his head and gave a vicious curse. Vi'ryk, despite his more mellow disposition like most Aturians, did not attempt to comfort or placate him to defuse the hostility brewing within Jor'y. Instead, the male's eyes glittered with appreciation at the just venting of the anger and frustration on behalf of the valetik. These reactions were depended on from him in the face of potential hostility.

"Why was I not informed of this earlier?" he demanded.

The male's mouth twisted. "I was just informed today. I know that the valetik will be thrilled to have visitors during our sacred Hashavnal." He cocked his head again. "Do you suppose the storm will have passed by then?"

Jor'y grunted again. "Yes. The Hashavnal is half a cycle away. This storm shall have us snowed in for a while, but we should be ready to accept guests by then."

Unless something changed. He would make sure that the valetik had plenty of warning, but communicating that to the humans could prove a difficulty.

"I will let my Ama'ri know. You know how much she enjoys this time of the revolution."

"Perhaps it will at least be enough to distract everyone from concerning themselves with my mating," he muttered.

His assistant glanced at him with an amused expression. "I would not depend on that," the male advised with a huff of laughter. "If anything, the females will be looking at the delegation all the more closely in hopes of finding a female among them for you."

He shuddered. The last thing he needed was the females arranging a mating for him with some poor unsuspecting offworld female.

"It might even be a good thing if you can't be persuaded to find one yourself."

"Get out. I do not know why I made you of all people my assistant," he growled.

"Because I am not intimidated by you and put up with your growling," Vi'ryk observed, a grin stretching across his face. "Face it. For an Aturian, you are not an easy male. Your sire and grandsire should have had whole broods to fill this estate, just to give you someone to fight and bicker with. Your kind is not meant to be so alone up here. Since that is not the case, you are stuck with me."

He was not wrong. The same genetics that made valmeks superior leaders and protectors heightened their aggression. The valmek estate was intended to be filled with warriors to protect the valetik, but battles that broke out around the time of the human colonization thinned their numbers drastically, and his grandsire had ceased to reproduce after Jor'y's grandmother died. With his parents dying prematurely, with only one young offspring between them, and the last of the elder generation dying away, the estate was hauntingly empty. That Vi'ryk willingly endured his company day after day hinted at least a drop of valmek blood somewhere in the male's line.

Or just incredibly strong bonds of friendship. That alone was something.

Jor'y snorted but not without amusement, flicking a wing at the male. "Go home to Ama'ri and give her my greetings. Be sure to keep her indoors and warm, my friend."

Vi'ryk nodded, his expression turning firm. "That I shall. She will fuss at being confined inside when there is much to be done around town, especially with the news of the delegation, but I will not risk her going out if it will be bad as you say." His expression turned concerned. "Be sure you remain indoors and warm too, Jor'y."

Grunting, Jor'y waved the male off. The hesitation was only brief before his friend nodded and left, his claws clicking on the stone floor on his way out. Silence descended quickly on the heels of his departure, emphasizing every little creak of the ancient building. Although it had been upgraded with tech, the stone walls and wooden beams held history that seemed to speak the loudest when he was alone.

As he was too much of late.

He sighed. Vi'ryk was not wrong. He needed a mate. He needed someone to help beat back the emptiness and loneliness of his position. He needed heirs to protect the future of his valetik. More than all of that... he needed a companion. *Love.* He needed to rediscover the joy that seemed to dwindle more and more every revolution.

He flattened a hand against the window in front of him, his black claws splayed wide.

Where are you, my mate?

A bark of self-deriding laughter left him, and he shook his head. What he needed then was to prepare for the storm. It was already beginning to pick up. Although he knew that Vi'ryk had sent warning to everyone's comms, he should make another announcement just in case. He began to let his hand drop away from the window when a flash of light appeared over the northern mountain range, lighting up the sky with a brilliant flare. He squinted at the intense light that seemed to get only brighter as it fell until it suddenly banked.

Dread crawled over him making his wings quiver. That was no meteorite falling. Someone had crashed. He did not know who, but at that moment it did not matter. He could not, in good conscience, abandon anyone to the appetite of the storm moving in.

With a snap of his wings, he turned away and hurried from the room. He only hoped that he would be in time.

CHAPTER 3

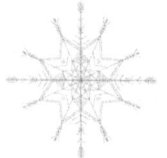

Vanessa slowly sat up, shivering. Her head hurt something awful, and the cold penetrating the shuttle was burrowing deep through her layered clothes.

How can anything be this cold?

A large figure dropped down into the chair beside her, and Vanessa glanced up to meet the concerned dark brown eyes. Thick black eyebrows furrowed as he reached forward and gripped her shoulder with a warm hand. Tackert. He had sat across from her during the flight down and introduced himself as Michael Tackert. Her eyes stung with tears, grateful that she wasn't alone. If only she wasn't so damned cold. He didn't seem to be cold at all, but then crew members were wearing those nifty TRSs.

Damn. She'd never been more envious.

"Are you all right?" he asked. He had to shout to be heard over the wind whistling through the enormous tear running along one side of the shuttle.

She nodded, her teeth chattering. "Just c-cold," she replied, her arms hugging the front of her body.

His lips pinched together with worry, and he gave her

shoulder another squeeze. "I'll find the emergency pack and get out a blanket for you. Stay here."

Reaching up, she grabbed his wrist before he could leave. "Is e-everyone else o-okay?" she asked through her chattering teeth.

He gave her a small smile and nodded. "Just a bit banged up, but we all made it. The rest of the crew went outside to set up a beacon device. We just need to hang in there until someone comes to get us. Everything is going to be okay," he assured her.

"O-okay," she whispered, her eyes following him as he walked away at an angle with one arm braced against the wall to accommodate the tilt of the shuttle.

Approaching a wall near the pilot's seat, Tackert withdrew a black duffle bag from a compartment and set it at his feet to unzip it. It only took a few minutes of rummaging around in it before he fished out a metallic square. He quickly unfolded it to reveal a large emergency blanket, which he draped over one arm before bending to rezip the bag. Standing, he shouldered the bag and made his way back to Vanessa. Plunking the bag in one of the nearby seats, he wrapped the blanket around her.

It was warmer than she expected. She immediately burrowed into it and gave him a grateful smile. "T-thank you."

His smile widened a bit, showing straight white teeth, and he nodded. "You're welcome. Just stay put now and rest. You've got a nasty bump on your head there. Someone will be out to retrieve us soon."

"Don't go making promises, Tackert," another sighed as he ducked inside. His cheeks and nose were already chapped and bright red from the cold. He gave her only a brief glance before directing his attention solely to the man in front of her. "The storm is picking up, and somehow our navigation got screwed up from some sort of atmospheric interference enough that we're nowhere near the southern continent. The lieutenant isn't sure where we are, since we can't get a lock on anything familiar out there." He hesitated, giving her another glance before lowering his voice and drawing Tackert over a short distance away, but not enough that she wasn't able to just barely make out what he said. "We aren't even sure if there are any settlements around here. He thinks we may be in the outer rim."

"Fuck," Tackert groaned. "What's the plan, then?"

The other man shrugged. "Hunker down and do whatever we have to in order to survive. We've got enough rations stored for a few days but after that... I don't know. We're up in the mountains, and that seems to be causing some signal interference. If help doesn't arrive, we might have to start making some hard decisions to keep our crew alive."

Tackert sighed but didn't disagree. He gave a reluctant nod, and they stepped out of the shuttle, their voices lost to the storm.

Vanessa didn't need to hear any more. Her heart chilled, her eyes widening even as she ducked her cold face lower into her blanket. She tried not to cry, not wanting icy tears freezing to her face, but that didn't make reality any less terrible. If help didn't come, they would have to try to make it on foot so that they didn't all starve to death. There was a chance of all of them making it—except her. She didn't have a TRS, and without one there was no way she would survive the brutal cold to walk even a handful of miles.

If a rescue team didn't arrive, they would be forced to leave her to die in the mountains.

After all the characters she'd brutally killed off in numerous ways, there was a certain irony to the fact that she would be meeting her own end similarly. Didn't she once have someone die from exposure? She laughed weakly.

She leaned her head back against the wall and closed her eyes. Her head was starting to hurt even worse, and exhaustion had crept in. She considered taking a little nap to escape the miserable cold when a startled shout from outside made her eyes snap open.

Suddenly the crew poured back into the shuttle, their booted feet clomping heavily, half-skidding on the melted snow. They shouted to on another, grabbing blasters as they hunkered down, their eyes fixed on something outside beyond her field of vision.

Tackert dropped beside her, his blaster raised, and she gave him a worried look.

"What's going on?" she whispered.

He shook his head, his mouth tightening as fear flickered in his eyes. "Something is out there. Something fucking big."

"Shit! It's coming right for us!" another shouted, the end of his blaster shaking only very slightly as he kept it aimed. He cut a quick glance to the man at his side. "Stephens, do we have a lock on it?"

The man beside him, she guessed Stephens, glanced at his comm and shook his head. "The shuttle is toast. My comm uplinks aren't even registering this thing. I can't get a lock."

"Fuck!"

Vanessa leaned forward, squinting as she attempted to peer between the men pressed tightly in formation in front of her. Something clattered to the floor, and Stephens cursed. He ducked to pick it up, and the outside world suddenly opened up to her. She was able to see the craggy, snowy landscape stretching out beyond the gaping hole.

Snow blew down hard, obscuring almost everything except the nearest icy gray stones jutting up from the drifts like jagged teeth. Two phantom white blotches fanned wide, and her breath caught in her throat. They were wings, each possessing two sets of dark, claw-like "fingers," a set at the wing joint and another further down. If not for their dark color against the rush of white, she wouldn't have been able to make them out, and even then it was only just barely.

The massive purple body and whipping feather tail that came into view grabbed her attention more vividly. Vanessa gaped, unable to comprehend what she was seeing. She had never even bothered to look into what large predators existed on Aturia. She was supposed to be in her cabin on a mild continent colonized by Darvel Exploration Corporation. It was supposed to be safe.

Whatever the creature was, it was also clearly intelligent. The moment the targeting beams of the blasters fell on it, the creature gave a terrifying snarl. She was stunned, however, when the snarl quieted and a deep voice growled at them, perfectly audible despite the wind.

"You test my good will, humans. Put your blasters down before I leave you up here to freeze."

Stephens straightened, once again blocking her view. With all of their backs turned to her, she had no idea what thoughts might be going through their minds, but she could see the explosive device clenched in his hand. Her mouth rounded in shock. *That* was what he had dropped! Thankfully, Stephens didn't seem inclined to use it at the moment. He lowered his arm to his side.

"I am Mitchell Stephens of starcruiser *Anointed*. Identify yourself!" he shouted.

His demand was met with another snarl, this one sounding more exasperated if she wasn't imagining things.

"I am Jor'ytal of Mirfal valetik."

"All right Jor… ytal. What is it you want?"

There was a pregnant pause, and Vanessa could almost swear that she could see the shadow of his head tilting. "You have crashed in my territory, and so I am here. Now do you require assistance or not?"

"You're Aturian?" another called out warily. He cleared his throat when his question was met with silence. "My apologies. I'm Jeremy Fowler, Communications."

"I am," came the growled reply, their would-be savior rapidly losing patience.

Stephens shook his head. "Bullshit! He has wings! And that tail…"

"He's an outer rimmer," Fowler shot back. "They don't look like the civilized ones. We might be able to trust him anyway, but I don't know for certain."

Vanessa stifled an annoyed grunt and pushed forward, brushing off Tackert's attempt to grab ahold of her as she squeezed in behind them to glare at Fowler. A man with a bright shock of ginger hair just barely visible and stubble on his cheeks blinked at her in surprise.

"Look, I appreciate that you're trying to lookout for everyone's safety, but I will freeze or die of hypothermia if I don't get out of here, so at this point I don't care if he's Krampus himself descending upon us with chains and whips as long as I get somewhere warm."

"You have a female with you?" the Aturian growled, making all the men around her stiffen.

"What's it to you?" Stephens shot back.

"You are putting her life at risk with this foolishness," the alien snapped. She swore his neck craned, but his height was impressive enough that he might have just straightened. She had the distinct impression he was looking for her. "Come out, female, and I will take you to safety."

"Wait." A man stepped out of the pilot station, his mouth pressed into a grim line, his arm shooting out to block her from stepping out gratefully to the stranger. His assessing gaze roved around the group, obviously putting everything together between what he had overheard in the cockpit and what he could see before his eyes. "I am Lieutenant Vincent Carthy, and I'm in charge of this unit, sir. I appreciate your concern and have to agree with you." He cast her an appraising look. "Our comms are fried, and the shuttle is dead. I can't get the engines back online and have been told that the beacon signal isn't getting through.

We can't get ourselves to safety, much less her." His lips tightened, and he shook his head. "I acknowledge that she's not in a position to survive long out here, but, as we are entrusted with her safety, I can't just release her to your custody. We will go with you, but only together. Not a single member of this unit or our charge will be made unnecessarily vulnerable by going alone."

The alien stepped back, and Vanessa's heart jumped into her throat, terrified that he might leave. She began to push against the restraining arm when the male spoke.

"Very well. I shall return with aid. Remain here."

Wings spread and a thunderous clap filled the air as the snow whirled for a moment and then he was gone. Vanessa stared at the space where the Aturian had been, her heart plummeting.

"He said he was returning with aid," Tackert said behind her quietly as he tugged on her arm, pulling her back out of the cutting wind.

She nodded and pulled her blanket higher as she sat heavily once more in her chair. She was starting to shiver again even with the blanket protecting her.

"He'll be back," she whispered in affirmation, hoping with everything she had that it would be true.

Fowler snorted and dropped into the chair at the other side of her, shaking his head. "No doubt about it. For whatever reason, whether we can trust his intentions or not, I just know he'll be returning for you, since you made yourself known. I hope we don't end up regretting it."

Stephens muttered in agreement, but Carthy frowned at them, shouldering his blaster. "Miss Williams may have forced our hand, but we didn't have any real choice in the end. She was correct that she wouldn't be able to survive long here. It's necessary to get her to safety as soon as possible."

"Even if it means risking the rest of us. We have no idea what they do with strangers out here, and no one knows where we are."

Fowler swiped a hand down his face with a sigh. "Don't mind me. You're right, this is the only option. Our chances of hiking out of here, even with the TRS, were shaky at best."

"Fuck." Stephens sighed. "Okay, let's get all cozy and try to keep Miss Williams as warm as possible. Who knows when that scary asshole will return?"

"That's the spirit, Stephens." Carthy chuckled. "Detach two of the seats from the side that has been punched through and drag them over here. The emergency kit should have a small space heating unit we can set between us. It will have enough charge to keep going for a few hours. Between that and the heat generated from our bodies pressed together, we should be okay for a little while."

Tackert gave her a comforting smile as he stood. "See? I told you everything would be okay."

As she watched him join the others pulling up the seats while Carthy busied himself with setting up the heating unit, Vanessa tucked her nose once more beneath the blanket and prayed that it wouldn't be too long.

She hadn't been joking when she said she would go with the alien regardless of who or what he was. In her mind, he was salvation. He was already her hero, regardless of what sort of monster the men were afraid he might be. She didn't know enough about Aturians to even be able to guess what differences lay in an outer rimmer, but she couldn't deny that she was curious. Blame it on being a writer, but she couldn't wait for him to return so that she could finally get her first real look at her rescuer.

CHAPTER 4

Wings tipping into another air current, Jor'y headed directly for the valetik's town nestled in the valley below. He hated to rouse any of his brethren in assist him when the storm was already descending, but he had little choice. There was no way he could safely move all the humans alone, and they were determined not to let him remove the most vulnerable one in their company without their protection. It was perhaps honorable that they wished to protect her, if also foolish. Still, that meant that he would need assistance, especially since the one flyer that their town possessed for transporting goods wouldn't make it in through the storm.

Only an Aturian, bred for their planet's harsh climate, could fly in this weather. And even they had their limits. Fortunately, it was still early and the full fury of the storm had not yet arrived.

Circling as he descended, Jor'y located Vi'ryk's home. He hated to disturb the male so soon after giving him leave for the evening, but he trusted his friend's input, and Vi'ryk would better know which males to call on and was among the stronger flyers in the valetik. His friend would be needed for this rescue. His target located, Jor'y folded his wings just enough to allow himself to descend. The ground sped toward him, and his wings flared wide to slow his drop at precisely the right moment, his body bending so that his clawed feet hit the walkway in front of the house.

He didn't feel any chill from the already accumulating snow any more than he had on the mountain thanks to the downy feathers that started mid-calf and thickened around his feet to provide a warm waterproof barrier against the icy cold. With barely a pause to adjust his balance, he strode forward. The door swung open at his approach, and Vi'ryk stepped out, his wings shrugging and stretching as he gave Jor'y an annoyed look.

"Jor'y? You got here quickly. I received your comm and alerted three other males to accompany us into the mountains like you asked, but you explained nothing," Vi'ryk growled as he descended the shallow steps that kept his house above flood level during the melting season.

"They are coming?" Jor'y glanced around impatiently.

His friend nodded. "They will be joining us at any moment. Not to be disrespectful, but what's going on?"

Jor'y fluffed out his wings, his jaw clenching as he continued to scan their surroundings for any sign of the approaching males. "A shuttle went down in the mountains. I went to search for survivors, but there are too many to carry at once, and they refuse to be separated from their most vulnerable member… a female."

"A female is stranded in the mountains?" Vi'ryk asked, his wings fluttering around him anxiously.

Jor'y's jaw tightened as he battled back a wave of fury. He glanced over at Vi'ryk. "Comm the males and tell them to hurry. We must leave now. I have the impression that the female was not as well protected as the males around her. I cannot rest until she is safely within the estate walls." He paused, his feathers bristling at the unbidden thought of any of the males attempting to warm her with their wings or feathered scruffs. He had barely caught a glimpse of her, her face unnaturally red, likely from the frigid temperatures, but there was something about her in her most vulnerable moment, an underlying strength and perseverance, that called to him. "Tell them that the responsibility of the female is mine. I will see to her care personally."

Vi'ryk raised a feathered brow.

"Not for the reason you are thinking," he growled. "I have no intentions to steal the human. I merely feel responsible for her welfare, and it is the most practical solution. I can best protect her and keep her warm, given that I am larger, stronger, and have fuller plumage."

"As you say," his friend replied cryptically as he sent instructions through the comm on his wrist, rousing Jor'y's annoyance further.

A growl rattled out of him, which seemed to amuse the male, but it silenced at the immediate swell of relief that filled him as three strong males flew into view over the top of the neighboring buildings, their white wings spread wide. Jor'y didn't wait for them to land. There was no time for it, and with his instructions relayed over the comm, it was unnecessary. With a leap and a powerful flap of his wings, he rose into the sky, Vi'ryk following close behind him as he immediately sped back toward the mountains... and the female.

If the approaching males were surprised at his sudden departure, they did not show it. The Aturians merely swooped through the air and dropped into formation behind him. The brisk beat of their wings sounded above the wind, cracking not unlike thunder. In the old times, before the colonization of their world, a formation of guardians would have been enough to instill fear into hearts, and inspire hope for any injured, stranded, or lost. He wanted the female to feel hope when she heard their approach. Despite their small number, there was no missing it.

Keeping a punishing pace in hopes of outrunning the worst of the storm, they flew higher into the mountains. He knew that it strained the males in his wake, but still he pushed them, his eyes scanning the storm. When at last the half-buried shuttle came into view, he exhaled in relief and dropped down to it. He was not surprised to see the red glow of several blaster targeting systems snap up toward him and then separate in a confused rush. He trusted that the humans would not be so foolish as to fire on their rescuers.

Although no blaster fire came, the lasers remained locked onto them as they landed with echoing whomps in the deep snow. Slowly, Jor'y straightened from his half-crouch, the feathers on his feet creating a broad enough padding with his large clawed toes that he didn't sink as he strode forward. He kept his pace easy so not to frighten the humans. The humans stared out at them, their faces still rigid with suspicion as they clustered around the female and kept their weapons trained on them.

A few of the males behind him, despite their typical easy natures, growled at the sight, especially when one of the targeting lasers rose to his chest, but he lifted a hand to silence them. He didn't want to trigger any tensions that could result in injuries or loss of life.

"The humans would not be so foolish as to fire on their only hope for safety," Jor'y reminded them.

As if on cue, one of the humans shuffled forward warily. The male he recognized as Lieutenant Carthy, the one who claimed to be in command.

"Is this the rescue party?" the male shouted over the wind.

He inclined his head. Unlike the smaller human, he didn't need to raise his voice so much to be heard. "It is. We will get you to safety. From this moment on you are formally under my protection and shall remain so until we can hail the southern continent."

The male drew in a deep breath and nodded. "And you are the one in charge around here, correct?"

"I am the valmek," Jor'y affirmed. He raised his head to the wind, the fine feathers on his crown puffing out, and frowned. They would have to make this quick. The storm was gaining strength sooner than he had estimated. "We must make haste. Give me your female. I will personally assure her safety. My males will transport each of you."

"Shit, we're going to be carried flying down the mountain?" One of the other males, Stephens, stared fearfully out at them, his throat working. "I thought we would have a flyer."

Jor'y snorted derisively. "You have the best flyers in these mountains. No flying machine would make the flight that we have been designed by the gods for. But even we are not gods ourselves. Our window of escape is closing as we speak. We must make haste."

Carthy nodded and glanced over at the male beside him. This male, with his darker complexion did not look as pale and red as the others, his dark gaze assessing.

"Tackert, bring Miss Williams up," Carthy ordered.

The male nodded and stepped back, disappearing into the ruined remains of the shuttle and reemerging with a much smaller figure beside him wearing bulky layers and some type of metal cloth wrapped around most of her. All except those warm brown eyes that immediately found Jor'y.

Tackert bent and whispered something to her as he gestured to him. To his relief, the female did not balk. She nodded, her gaze never leaving him as she started through the snow. He noticed immediately how woefully disadvantaged she was. The moment she stepped out of the shuttle, her small, booted feet began to sink, plunging knee-deep. He frowned at the sight. She was going to get soaked. He could already see her body shivering harder as she made her way toward him. He wanted to stride forward and just scoop her up, but he forced himself to wait calmly as she came toward him as not to frighten her. Although she was wary, there was a measure of trust in her eyes that he did not wish to see extinguished.

Stopping just in front of him, she tilted her head and smiled up at him, her lips rising just above the protective level of her wrappings.

"Hi there, I'm Vanessa Williams. You're Jor'ytal, right?" Her pronunciation was terrible, but her voice was soft and sweet and made him want to wrap his wings around her so he could keep her tucked against him.

He inclined his head and stretched a hand out to her. Electricity shot through his arm at the soft touch of her palm against his, and he hissed deep in his throat. Her eyes widened, and her muscles tensed as she prepared to jerk her hand away. He closed his fingers first, capturing her hand within his.

"You are safe. Come, Va'nessa," he rumbled, slowly drawing her toward him, his wings cupping protectively.

Her giggle was nervous, but she nodded as she allowed herself to be pulled into his embrace. "Okay then. I guess we're going flying now."

"We are. Do not fear."

She angled her head up, looking him in the eye. "You won't let me fall, will you?"

"Never," he growled.

Her face lit up with a broad smile, and then she did the most marvelous thing. She ducked her head against his collar of feathers, pillowing her face in their softness like a female taking reassurance and comfort from her mate. The sight did something strange to his heart. If he had not already been entranced with her, he would have found her enchanting now.

Crooning low in his throat, he wrapped his arms around her, drawing her up against his chest more firmly. From the corner of his eye, he could see the other humans approach his males, their bearing stiff as they allowed the Aturians to wrap their arms around them in an attainable grip. Vi'ryk cast him an exasperated look as he carefully adjusted his grip on Stephens, who appeared to shrink away from the male's touch.

Jor'y huffed in amusement and turned away, orientating himself in the direction of his estate. Clutching the warm feminine bundle close to him, he allowed himself a moment to draw in her sweet perfume as he spread his wings wide before launching them into the sky.

Although distantly he heard a few masculine shouts, he was proud and very pleased that his female did not scream or cry. She gave nothing but a small gasp that dissolved into an awed sound. Every now and then when he was required to drop suddenly or take a turn so not to fight against the wind, her little tantalizing gasps reached his ear and made his blood ignite, fueling his imagination with other ways he could make a female gasp in his arms.

It was entirely inappropriate. It was contrary to everything he had been taught at a young age of how a valmek was to behave around females or anyone in need of his strength. She gave no indication of interest in mating, but some part of him was fixating on her, and by the gods, he enjoyed it.

CHAPTER 5

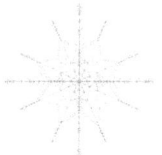

With her body pressed firmly against the large frame of the alien carrying her, surrounded by his incredible heat, Vanessa had spent their flight through the mountains in a languid state. Half-asleep, she had clung to him and enjoyed the warm, spicy scent of him not unlike a pleasant, mulled wine mingling with an unfamiliar masculine musk. Paired with the fact that his body seemed to emit more heat than a human, and that her cheek was nestled in the softest, warmest downy feathers that covered his upper pectorals and thickened into a luxurious collar, she had no interest in looking around until his wings dipped in descent.

Curiosity being the bane of so many writers, she abandoned that warmth to crane her neck just enough to watch with interest despite being immediately hit in the face with a frigid blast of air that threatened to steal the breath from her lungs. The stinging sensation of the cold against her skin was just barely tolerable for a short amount of time. Enough time that she was able to watch as the mountainside and valley below them came into sharper detail as they dropped from dizzying heights.

Her eyes widened as a large gray shadow just above the valley became more defined, emerging from the swirling snows. She was looking at an actual castle! There was no mistaking what it was. No fewer than six impossibly tall turrets jutted up into the sky from a massive walled structure that seemed like it was carved out of the rock itself. Not an impossible feat to be sure, since there were civilizations in Earth's own history which had accomplished similar works. But seeing it in person, half-covered in snow yet lit from within with the warm glow of lights, was awe-inspiring.

She had thought that a cabin on the southern continent would have been a pleasant retreat to inspire her imagination, but if this was where she was going to spend a few days while awaiting transport, she had no complaints. It was just the sort of fuel her imagination craved. She wanted to ask her rescuer a million questions, but the whip of air made conversing difficult, and the cold temperatures eventually forced her to tear her gaze away from the beautiful sight to press her face once more into the warm feathers.

From the corner of her eye, Vanessa watched as white wings folded, and her fingers dug into the feathers along his collar as he suddenly plummeted. Pressing her face against him, she just barely held back her shriek—or maybe she didn't. She couldn't really tell with the wind whistling in her ears from their rapid drop, made even worse when her hearing became muffled for several seconds before her ears uncomfortably popped.

Her rescuer's body suddenly contorted around her at an angle that practically enfolded her within his large frame as he dropped his legs. It was the only warning she got before the landing jolt slammed her head against the bottom of his jaw.

"Fuck!" she hissed, slapping a hand up protectively over her head even as the male snarled a low curse.

He stiffened when her fingers encountered a protruding horn-like spur at the corner of his jaw. She was relieved that she hadn't hit that part of him because she was certain it would've done some damage. Nearly as large as her thumb, she noticed that it had a slight curve to it as it came to a point. A rattling croon rolled through his chest, his throat vibrating hard enough that she could feel it even through her fingertips where she touched the large spur. She yanked her hand away, her face flooding with embarrassment.

Vanessa swallowed a groan. What had gotten into her? For all she knew, the alien could have taken that as a sexual come-on. That was the last thing she needed. She spared a covert glance, eyeing the men who were carefully deposited around her on what looked like a massive extended balcony. No one seemed to look her way, or even notice the sound coming from the male holding her. Well, no one human, anyway. One of the large males nearest to them turned his head, the long wispy feathers on his head raising slightly as he looked at the male holding her before turning a speculative gaze on her.

The narrowed amber eyes almost had her ducking her face back into the feathers. She probably would have hidden within them if not for the fact that the male was still crooning at her in a strange, repeating sequence of two reverberating notes, and she wasn't sure if that would cause further confusion. Instead, she gave his chest a pat, indicating that she wished to be put down.

Jor'ytal's beautiful, gold hawk-like eyes blinked down at her before she was slowly lowered to the stone floor, his croon only growing louder.

"Thank you," she mumbled, flushing further with embarrassment as she felt several more pairs of eyes turn toward them.

She immediately dropped her gaze to look at the balcony beneath her feet. Although windswept, the bare stones had several areas crusted with ice that grew even thicker toward the edge where the balcony was enclosed by an elaborately carved wall. Rivers of ice seemed to drip off the carvings, making the crouched winged figures adorning them appear almost monstrous.

A shiver ran through her, and she stepped away, turning toward the light she could see coming from the narrow windows on either side of a massive pair of wooden doors. Not a drop of light spilled out from around the doors, giving her hope that the interior would be pleasantly warm rather than drafty. She took a step and slipped, only to be rescued once again by her alien and pulled up securely against his body. He regarded her silently, his strange croon disappearing. His feathers fluffed out and his mouth curved downward with disapproval as his fingers tightened around her arm where he gripped her. One wing dipped, curving around her in a wall of white feathers.

"Stay with me. You are not made for our world and are as helpless as a youngling," he remarked in a deep, rumbling voice.

The observation stung a bit until she looked down at his feet. She noticed then that the aliens had little trouble clinging to the stone and ice with the strong hooked claws on their toes, the dark claws stabbing out from the tufts of feathers on their feet. She supposed that the comparison was apt since the Aturians had an advantage that she and the other humans lacked. Not that everyone seemed willing to acknowledge the fact. She could hear the curses that came from one of the men as he stubbornly tried to walk by himself repeatedly only for his boots to skid uselessly on the ice.

Absently, she wondered who it was. The low muttering wasn't loud enough for her to identify his voice and the heavy snow made it difficult to visually differentiate between the men. Certainly not enough to identify the man standing with his arms flung from his sides and his legs braced as he attempted yet again to walk unassisted.

She rolled her eyes and turned away from the sight. She wasn't too proud to accept help to keep her from falling on her ass. It just meant getting inside sooner. If they had to cling to the aliens for assistance, then so be it. She was glad to see that most of the men were on the same page as they clung to the muscular arms of aliens holding them up as they were escorted toward large doors that opened automatically at their approach.

The swirling snow that obscured so much of her vision cut off the moment she was led inside, and Vanessa gaped at the beautiful interior. Smooth stones covered the walls and floors, and numerous sconces lit with artificial light brightened the warm interior. Although there was minimal decor in what she perceived to be some sort of entry way, what she did see was vibrant in color thanks to the large viewscreen that filled most of the wall. It cycled through beautiful images of the region filled with exotic wildlife. Although it was wintertime, they gave her a hint of the planet's beauty as she was steered past and into a long hall.

To her surprise, the male holding her didn't release his grip on her arm now that they were indoors. Nor did he drop the large wing that still bowed around her side as he led them into a large room filled with numerous overflowing shelves and dominated by a large hearth despite the castle's modern conveniences. A fire roared inside of it, and although she knew it wasn't responsible for the warmth, it was a wonderful sight. There were several large chairs set near it, and the shelves were filled with angular metal and wooden cases with blocky alien script that could have been books, giving the room the cozy feel of a study, something only the wealthiest could afford. Her parents had a study in their home, but it paled in comparison to this one. The one thing that didn't quite fit was the one wall that held a long-range comm system. Its viewscreen took up much of the wall.

A map filled the screen, shifting in perspective every couple of minutes, often bringing up close-up views of certain areas. To one side, more of the blocky alien script slowly cycled like a series of updates. She peered at it curiously, her attention dragged away only when the male beside her spoke, his deep voice stirring a mortifying thrill in her blood. A quick glance around informed her that most of the alien males had left, except one who continued to look her way every so often.

"Your approach over our mountains occurred at a bad time. It was a foolish point of entry through our airspace. The storms here are highly unpredictable to most technology during winter, but we were fortunate to get to you in time, especially since you had a vulnerable female with you," the male beside her rumbled, his brows slanted down in a perturbed glower. "Rest assured that as soon as the weather permits, though it may be several days yet, we will get a comm out to your human colony base to retrieve you. Until then, you are my guests in the comfort of my estate."

Several days in a beautiful castle? Vanessa nearly wiggled with excitement. This definitely beat the hell out of her cabin retreat. She couldn't wait to pull out her datapad and get to work!

Carthy removed his helmet, melted snow running off of it onto the stone floor, and nodded. "We are grateful for the assistance, Jor'ytal, and for the accommodations while we wait. Your criticism is certainly valid given that we did not accurately factor in storms. Truthfully we did not see any indication of one brewing."

"You would not," Jor'ytal grunted. "The storms come up too quickly to accurately predict and track and are merciless. Travel is discouraged during the winter for this reason." His eyes narrowed. "Were you not aware of this? It is something that has been explained to Darvel many times."

The muscle in Carthy's jaw jumped and Vanessa winced. They hadn't been prepared at all.

"No sir, we were not aware of that fact. We accepted the transport with the understanding that it was the most direct route to the southern continent. Had we been made aware of the threat of unpredictable winter storms, we would have not accepted the transport. We would have rerouted through the capital at Darvel's expense." He glanced fleetingly at her. "No disrespect meant, ma'am. The trip from the capital by private charter would have taken a few extra days but that would have been preferable to putting you and my crew at risk."

"None taken, I assure you," she murmured, her irritation rising at Darvel. *Cheap bastards.*

Carthy's chin lifted. "We will, of course, relay all of this to our superiors. Aturian hospitality is widely known and appreciated."

Jor'ytal, inclined his head before glancing at the other Aturian.

"Vi'ryk, I know you are eager to return home, but will you please alert the staff to make up rooms for my guests?"

The male grinned easily, displaying sharp teeth. "Already done. A wing has been prepared for the males. I can escort them on my way out."

Vanessa didn't miss the frown that creased Carthy's face. "What of Miss Williams? I have to insist that she remain close to us."

Both males whipped their heads toward him, their feathered crowns fluffing out in a way that was definitely *not* happy.

"You would insult a female guest of this house?" the one called Vi'ryk asked, his voice rolling with a subtle growl. "Unmated female guests have their own wing to give them peace from the uninvited attention of males."

Carthy's scowl deepened with obvious objection as tension within the room rose. Vanessa eyed both parties warily. Even though it was Vi'ryk who spoke, Jor'ytal's eyes were narrowed on Carthy with such raw hostility that everything seemed like only a breath away from blowing up. The last thing they needed was a huge incident with their hosts due to an unintended insult. As much as she was grateful for the fact that he was looking out for her, she actually wasn't worried about being separated from the others. She had heard that the Aturians took protection of the female members of their society very seriously, and while she never would have imagined that it extended to guests, that alone made her confident that she had nothing to fear in her own wing. If it avoided a conflict, all the better.

Speaking quickly, she drew everyone's attention to her before the impending argument could break out. "You know, that sounds lovely! I really could use a nice quiet space to rest. Thank you," she said, projecting as much as genuine warmth into her voice as possible.

Carthy's scowl eased slightly as he glanced her in surprise. No doubt he expected her to pitch a fit about not having a guard nearby. Her mother would have. "Are you certain? I'm sure one of my men can double bunk with you so that you have round-the-clock protection…"

The barely audible hiss of the male beside her sent a shiver up her spine.

"No, that's entirely unnecessary," she interrupted. "As much as I appreciate the offer, I think I'll be more comfortable on my own. Besides, I'll have my comm, and it's not like you won't be able to check in with me… like at mealtime or something?"

She glanced up questioningly at Jor'ytal and was relieved when he nodded.

"We will be taking the main meal every midday, and it will be offered at first meal as well for those who are awake. Those who are not, or who wish to dine in the privacy of their rooms, can comm down something to be sent to them at their convenience. You will have plenty of opportunities to ascertain the safety of the female in your guard. Your protection of her in this case is admirable, but unnecessary."

Carthy didn't look completely convinced but, after she gave him an encouraging nod, he dipped his chin in agreement and lifted a hand, silencing Stephens who sputtered just behind him.

"Very well. I hope to see you in the morning then, Miss

Williams," Carthy murmured, inclining his head toward her meaningfully, his dark gaze communicating that she only needed to comm him if she changed her mind. He followed Vi'ryk out, his men trailing after him.

Suddenly alone with the very large alien beside her, Vanessa cleared her throat and gave him a curious side-glance to find him peering down at her, his gold gaze liquid with an unspeakable heat. Her belly fluttered, and an answering heat pooled between her legs. His nostrils flared and his wings expanded, every muscle in his body tensing as if preparing to pounce. Her mouth went dry, her nipples pebbling beneath her bra. She wondered if he would act. The possibility sent a rush of thrill through her. She should have been relieved rather than disappointed when he suddenly stepped back and put some distance between them, his feathers fluffing out everywhere—his collar, crown, and wings—as another Aturian stepped inside.

Smaller and slighter of build, this Aturian was dusky lavender with a bony plating that extended over their nose and brow before terminating into a pair of small, delicate horns. Unlike the other Aturians she had met so far, this one wore a long, embroidered tunic and layers of beaded necklaces draping across their chest. Curious rose pink eyes peered at her discreetly as the Aturian silently stood to the side, waiting for instruction.

"This is Sa'tari. She will escort you to your room," he explained before glancing over at the female. "Be sure to see to Miss Williams' every need, please."

Vanessa was both relieved to be given the opportunity to escape his burning attention and at the same time somewhat disappointed. That gave her pause. For whatever reason, the thought of having him there with her in a bedroom had sent a forbidden rush of excitement through her. It was a good thing that it was Sa'tari and not him escorting her to her room. What she was feeling was illegal. She should have been appalled at her reaction to him. How the hell was she going to hide this secret attraction when once again she found herself blushing?

Sa'tari, fortunately, gave her a friendly smile, her wings fanning behind her slightly as she waved her forward.

"Come with me, Miss Williams," she said in a soft, almost musical voice.

Tongue glued to the roof of her mouth, Vanessa rushed after her. Only when they were out in the hall and away from the imposing alien lord, or whatever he was, was she able to relax enough to speak with the alien chatting animatedly at her as they walked through the halls.

"I do hope that you are comfortable here. It has been a long time since we have had guests, and even longer since any females have visited here. When I was made aware that you were coming, I did my best to make the room suitable. Do not worry, though, I am familiar enough with the needs of your fragile species. I have put you in a suite with a private bath. I figured you could use it after being out there in the cold, especially considering how small and delicate you are."

Vanessa smiled at the friendly Aturian, the last lingering remnants of stress from the day ebbed away. Being called small and delicate when her curvy, solid frame was anything but, teased a smile out of her despite her exhaustion. She supposed that compared to an Aturian, she probably was. Despite how much smaller the female was compared to the males of her species, Sa'tari was still considerably larger than Vanessa. That probably would have made the female frightening, especially with her sharp teeth, if it weren't for the fact that she was so clearly delighted with having Vanessa there.

"Thank you, I'm sure I will. Truthfully, a room with a bath sounds perfect right about now," she agreed as they turned down another hall. "And please, call me Vanessa."

CHAPTER 6

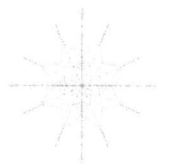

*V*anessa stretched leisurely in bed, reluctant to get up. A sheen of sweat slicked her body, her pulse beating frantically as the fog of her erotic dreams slowly released her mind. Despite the sexual tension crawling through her, she felt completely boneless and content to lay there. After a long, luxurious bath the night before and indulging on the snacks that Sa'tari had left out waiting for her, she had been more than happy to crawl into the enormous bed and drop into a deep sleep where forbidden fantasies came to life. Things that she had not thought of for years, not since reading illicit literature smuggled from one of the colonies as a young woman detailing the sexual adventures of one Miss Celestine—a notorious pirate and, ironically, an erotic author too.

She groaned, slapping a hand over her eyes. It had to be this planet. She couldn't remember the last time she had given any thought to such things. Certainly not since she had become old enough to put aside fantasies of possessive alien mates and had begun enjoying casual relationships with men whose company she enjoyed.

With the muskiness of her slick on her and the tang of sweat on the bedding, she was embarrassed with the idea of leaving the room at all. Besides, the bed was incredibly comfortable. It was all too tempting to just enjoy the remnants of the erotic thrill running through her body, especially considering that the morning light streaming through her window was dim and a wash of white was all that she could see from the snow. The barely audible howl of wind through the thick stone walls wasn't helping matters any.

Groaning, she flopped over onto her side only to come eye to eye with her luggage stacked neatly against the nearest wall. She blinked at the sealed black cases in surprise and sat up. Her vision was temporarily obscured by a hank of dark hair falling over her face, but she brushed it back behind her ear and peered around the room with a frown.

When had that happened? She didn't recall anything being grabbed during their hasty flight from the wreckage.

"Oh, good, you are awake." Sa'tari walked into the room holding a steaming cup that she set on the table at Vanessa's side.

If the female caught or recognized the scent of Vanessa's lingering arousal, she showed no sign of it. Instead, the female watched her with a polite smile, slowly putting her at ease, making her aware of the delicious smell coming from the cup beside her. Turning, Vanessa picked up the cup and inhaled deeply, a small appreciative sigh escaping her.

The smell coming from it was dark and slightly nutty, with a hint of bitter chocolate. Vanessa peered down into the cup at dark brown liquid that on casual inspection was almost reminiscent of coffee.

"What's this?"

"Steamed o'jar. It is a harvest fruit that is dried. We make desserts from it when sweetened, but it also makes a popular morning drink. Jor'ytal believed that you might enjoy it to start your morning."

Vanessa raised an eyebrow as she swished the contents around a bit. It was a bit thicker than coffee, but not too bad. Its alienness made her hesitate, however. She had never consumed anything that wasn't grown on Earth or directly imported from one of their food producing colonies, and even those crops tended to be hybridized versions of their own native crops. Not even colonies ate alien food crops, as far as she was aware.

Sa'tari's eager expression, however, had her bringing the cup to her mouth. The tiniest hint of something minty hit the back of her nose, and she almost moaned as she was seized by the sudden longing for a big cup of peppermint mocha that she would normally be enjoying at home this time of the year. Surely this wouldn't even come close to comparing.

The first sip she took was a tentative one, the hot liquid barely touching her tongue and yet burst in rich flavors that reminded her almost of a sweet chicory coffee, a hint of chocolate, and a strong peppermint aftertaste that had her immediately swallowing another mouthful. The happy moan that left her was embarrassingly loud but made the Aturian grin with delight.

"This is wonderful," Vanessa admitted between deep swallows.

The Aturian gave an approving nod. "I am glad that you enjoy it. I have heard that humans can be fussy about food. The males with you certainly proved as much since they refused to drink anything but water. We are to provide cooked raw foods since that is what they believe to be the most human-safe." She huffed. "Nearly everything we eat has been tested and proven safe among twenty-eight neighboring species, including humans, but we are setting out the requested foods even though it pains the cook to allow it out of the kitchen. Especially around the time of Hashavnal."

"Day of Joy is what my translator is giving me." Vanessa smiled apologetically. "What is that?"

A smile brightened Sa'tari's face as she dropped down on the bed beside her. "It is only the best day of the year. We hold a vigil waiting for the sun to rise. It is a reminder that even in the darkest time eventually must yield. For this reason, we celebrate all pleasures and joys throughout the day after sunrise. Some even begin celebrations early throughout the nightly vigil, but mostly that is the young and unmated." She chuckled with such delight that it made Vanessa smile. "I am not so young anymore, though my mate keeps me plenty busy during the night, but it is the day we all look forward to. Although we have marvelous feasts leading up to Hashavnal, none is better than the feast of the day."

Vanessa smiled and took another swallow of her drink. "That sounds lovely. We have similar winter traditions. My family has a feast that's always too much food. We exchange gifts, and of course my mother must buy the biggest tree to decorate."

The female's head tilted curiously. Leaning forward, her voice dropped conspiringly. "You decorate a tree—for what purpose? Does this have some phallic representation in your culture?"

At the unexpected sexual reference so soon after her own forbidden fantasies, Vanessa inhaled the hot liquid and proceeded to choke on the steamed o'jar. Lowering the cup, she blinked watering eyes at the Aturian as she coughed. "What?" she croaked. "No! At least I don't think so. It's just something we do to celebrate the return of the sun."

Sa'tari's lips pursed, her eyes narrowing in an expression of disbelief. "It seems unlikely to me, but you would know better. Such associations would only be natural. Humans are like Aturians—you enjoy the pleasure of touch just as we do. This is something our species knows, even if officially it is denied. You may deny it too, but I can tell you now that there would not be an Aturian in all of the valetik who would see anything else. Nor would there be a single male who might not offer to celebrate with you."

Vanessa cheeks scorched at the outright implication that she might enjoy sharing pleasure with an Aturian and yet couldn't seem to find her tongue quick enough to deny it before the female chuckled knowingly and stood. Vanessa reluctantly held out her half-full cup, expecting it to be whisked away. To her surprise, the female shook her head.

"Please enjoy the o'jar. I will be by to retrieve the cup later. Morning meal will be waiting on you... unless you would like something brought here?"

Vanessa bit her lip, tempted to ask for a tray to be brought up. A quiet breakfast sounded perfect, but she had little doubt that it wouldn't go over well with Carthy and the other men responsible for their welfare. She couldn't blame them for being concerned and wanting to assure themselves of her safety. She would merely clean herself up. Humans didn't have the sense of smell that many alien species did, but a quick wipe-down should do the job to at least make herself presentable in front of their host.

Still, she couldn't suppress the little groan squeezed out. "No. I better show my face before I start having a worried bunch of men trying to storm the females' wing and upsetting everyone."

Sa'tari's lips twitched with amusement. "It might be wise, then," she agreed. "I believe even Jor'y, though he prefers privacy in the mornings, is joining them for similar reasons."

Vanessa paused over the name. "Jor'y?"

The female nodded. "Our valmek, Jor'ytal."

"Ah," Vanessa murmured. In her mind, his shortened name rolled off the tongue nicely, but she doubted that she would ever have the nerve to refer to him so familiarly. He would just have to remain as Jor'y in her private imaginings. Not that she had any intention of including him in any fantasies if she could help it. It was bad enough that her mind was going where it ought not to when she was asleep. Vanessa wanted to drop her head into her hands as her delinquent mind immediately turned the exact direction that she didn't want it to go as it replayed the chiseled lines of his chest and began to imagine what remained concealed beneath his clothing.

What was wrong with her?

"From what I heard, he seemed particularly eager to join the males this morning, although I doubt that they are what truly motivates him to share morning meal with his guests." Her eyes gleamed with a certain satisfaction that Vanessa didn't quite understand. "No doubt he will be eager to know how you enjoyed your first night here at the estate."

Heat climbed into Vanessa's cheeks as she imagined being pinned by Jor'y's scrutinizing gaze. She immediately brought the o'jar up, hoping that the steam from the cup and its wide ceramic brim would hide the blush a bit. A fizzling excitement spread through her belly, followed by an entirely unfamiliar case of nerves. The safety of the bedroom was looking more and more appealing. It was ridiculous to be so affected by the presence of one male when she'd been raised socializing with attractive and important men and women due to her parents' reputations. Vanessa would never have such draw herself, outside of having a "good" family name, but she certainly had enough experience to not be overawed by a male who was essentially a local alien lord.

Thankfully, Sa'tari didn't suffer from any need to pry. Her smile simply widened before she swept out of the room, leaving Vanessa to enjoy her hot drink in peace. Or what little she was able to enjoy with her mind drifting repeatedly back to her host. No matter how she tried to dismiss her nerves and enjoy the flavors of the o'jar, she was unable to recapture the comfortable feeling that had been present earlier.

Still, she wasn't in any hurry as she sipped from her cup, delaying the inevitable. Once the last drop was swallowed, Vanessa set the cup down and stood, untying the ribbons that allowed the bright pink wrap-style sleeping gown to fall into a puddle on the floor. Frowning at her luggage, she realized that it hadn't occurred to her to ask Sa'tari about it. At least she had her own clothes to wear. As grateful as she was that someone had managed to find something for her to wear last night, the wrap, even drawn at its tightest, had been too large for her. It had been a miracle that it had stayed on as she'd slept. She certainly didn't want any awkward clothing issues to arise when she was in mixed company.

Stepping over to her largest suitcase, she laid it flat and unsealed it, revealing an assortment of sweaters and comfortable leggings and a couple pair of trousers when she required something less casual. She grimaced once again at the silky skirts and blouses her mother had snuck in and scooped them up, practically balling them up in her arms as she carried them to a wooden clothing storage area against one wall.

Built in a fashion similar to old Earth furnishing—a dresser, she recalled—the storage unit was charming and carved with elegant, curving lines and whimsical alien flowers. She paused for a moment to trace her fingers over one large four-petaled flower that decorated one corner, curling vines trailing down the edge of its frame, before stooping over to dump the bundle of unwanted clothing into the bottom drawer and closing it. The sound of the drawer snapping shut was far more satisfying than she expected but soon forgotten as she turned her attention to unpacking what remained of her belongings, locating her sanitizing wipes, cleansing herself thoroughly—especially between the legs to remove every trace of arousal—and dressing for the day.

Vanessa had long ago come to the conclusion that clothes were like armor. It projected the image that she wished to show to the outside world, masking her vulnerabilities. The simple act of wearing her own clean, tailored clothes repaired a lot of the more recent blows to her confidence since her rescue. The deep cream sweater with its scooped neck draped her curvy figure in a flattering manner in contrast to the soft, snug blue leggings showing off her legs. With her brown half-boots completing the look, she felt more like herself as she met her own eyes in the mirror to the left of the dresser—a competent woman in charge of her future who was perfectly capable of meeting anyone, even a powerful alien.

She was a Williams, after all, as her mother enjoyed reminding her. Hiding in her bedroom would simply not be tolerated.

Giving herself a reassuring smile, Vanessa turned and strode out of the bedroom before she had the opportunity to change her mind. She managed to find her way out of the wing only to promptly get lost. Cursing under her breath that she had been in too big of a hurry to stop and plot the route from the datascreen in her quarters, she trailed through the halls until she mercifully located a datascreen in an alcove off a main corridor. To her relief, it responded to her touch, the screen brightening as an AI spoke in the melodic Aturian language.

"Greetings. How may I assist?"

"Route to the dining room, please," she replied, nearly jumping with surprise when a schematic of the castle blew out across the screen in front of her.

Her eyebrows rose, her mouth rounding in a silent expression of awe. The building was a lot larger than she had realized. Her position was a small speck located just outside of the unmated females' wing, which itself was only one isolated corner of the massive structure. That was surprising. Either this place wasn't expected to house many females, or their unmated status wasn't expected to last long.

Rumors of the lusty nature of Aturians and the black market vids that were only to be found out in colony space, away from the rigid controls of United Earth, had her licking her suddenly dry lips. If those rumors were to be believed, she had little reason to doubt exactly why the species didn't have many unmated members.

For all she knew, there wasn't a single unmated Aturian in the entire valley, much less the castle. Her eyes widened, her lust rapidly drying up as she cringed. It was entirely likely that the male who was currently starring in her forbidden fantasies was already mated.

Oh, gods. She forced herself to focus and located the dining area. At her touch, a route lit up, triggering further response from the castle's AI system.

"Would you like to activate guide lights?" the voice intoned.

"Yes, please."

Between two stones beneath her feet, a pink light blinked on, triggering a trail of them heading down the corridor. They were fit so perfectly between the stones that she never would have expected that the tech was installed there. She was impressed.

"Please follow the lit path to your destination."

Her boots clicking on the stone floor, Vanessa hurried down the hallway. She had little doubt that she was already considerably late. She only hoped that her tardiness would not be too obvious. That hope was promptly dashed when she entered the dining room. Four blasters were aimed at their host. It quickly became apparent as to why. The male held Stephens pinned by the neck against a large, formal stone table, his ivory wings outspread as he snarled threateningly at his guests.

Eyes cutting back and forth between them, her mouth dropped open. She had walked in on whatever argument was going on at just the right time. No one had the opportunity to kill anyone—yet. And she wasn't going to be betting on Team Human to have the winning hand here. Not with the enormous bulk and thick, textured skin that covered the alien. Even his teeth were frighteningly huge. To her embarrassment, she gaped at them longer than was necessary until she noticed that one of Jor'y's long, pointed ears twitched in her direction, betraying his awareness of her arrival. Not that it did anything to ease the tension running high in the room. There was nothing but menace on his face as he stared down the group of shouting men who continued to be wholly unaware of her presence.

She loudly cleared her throat.

"Good morning. So, guys, what's going on? What did I miss?" she asked, projecting a pleasant cheerfulness that she definitely did not feel.

If she could narrow down the moment to one prevailing feeling, it had to be dread. Still, she forced a smile onto her face despite the nerves tightening in her belly as every head turned in her direction.

She should have found some reassurance in the relief of her fellow humans, but it was the golden half-feral gaze of the alien that captivated her for some unspeakable reason. It spoke to her of secret yearnings since the dawn of her sexual awakening. Forbidden fantasies of her youth that had remained mostly forgotten until she arrived on Aturia only to plague her dreams. The fact that he could already be mated seemed as inconsequential as the illegal and forbidden nature of her infatuation.

Fuck. She was in so much trouble. And worse was that she couldn't even bring herself to care. Not even when she became aware of the relief of her escorts turning to disgust, shock, and horror to varying degrees. Everything within her seemed to gravitate toward the valmek as his eyes sharpened with a predatory intensity that burned into her—owned her.

Oh, yes, she was in trouble indeed.

CHAPTER 7

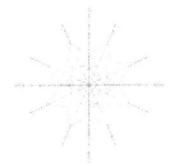

Jor'y stared back at the female, triumph filling him as he saw the first sign of a'talynal, the song of desire, or heartsong, that rose between compatible pairs. Aturians didn't believe in fated mates, but they did understand that certain energies aligned between some individuals better than others, and that those were the best to join with. It could be a rare enough occurrence that many mated the first whom they felt a'talynal with. As Jor'y had only fleetingly felt it once before in his youth for a mated female, he understood that need to claim an unmated a'talynal. Merely by her presence, every hunger within him suddenly sharpened to a ravenous frenzy.

He had felt it stirring in his blood when he had carried the bedraggled, half-frozen female back to the safety of his estate, but it had not bloomed. Instead, the alignment had remained dormant as he had done what was necessary to protect her. Her allure had been nothing more than a curious puzzle at the time that intrigued him. As he had lain alone in his bed that night, he had come to the conclusion that it was due to the influences of the approaching Hashavnal that was timed so well with the start of Aturian mating season, and nothing more.

Everything had changed with just a few softspoken words and the sweet perfume of her scent catching him unaware. Given that he had been distracted due to the aggressive insistence of the humans in his abode, he had little more than a moment to recognize her before his instincts boiled forth.

There was no gentle sweetness of an alignment slowly merging, drawing them together. No, he was cursed—or blessed depending on the perspective—with a full alignment of the heartsong snapping into place instantaneously, an overpowering roar thrumming through his blood. Even now, it pulsed through him in an erotic tempo of heat and desire that overrode Carthy's rapid speech a short distance away. He wanted more than anything to have her caught within his wings, pressed close to him so that he could breathe in her scent and luxuriate in every sensation of her rushing through his body.

His a'talyna, his heartsong mate, was exquisite.

The a'talynal was so strong that he nearly forgot that he was holding the human Stephens pinned against his table until he felt the male feebly struggle beneath his hand. The pale human hand batted against Jor'y's large knuckles.

"Okay, man, I surrender. Want to let me breathe?" Stephens croaked in a weak voice.

Jor'y leaned forward until there were only inches between their faces. He could feel the nervous energy in the air emitting from the other humans, and Jor'y could have sneered at it. He gave Stephens one last snarl in warning before he released his hold on the male. With a pitiful groan, Stephens' hands rose to his neck to cradle and gingerly rub at the bruised flesh.

Ignoring the incapacitated human, Jor'y cast a suspicious look toward Carthy. Although the male's face had relaxed exponentially with Vanessa's arrival, Jor'y was not so foolish to underestimate the one human who bore the most watching. Although

Carthy was too calculating to attack directly as Stephens did, Jor'y noted that the male did not miss anything and would use whatever was at his disposal to accomplish any task that was deemed necessary.

That, Jor'y could respect, especially since he was certain that Carthy, as the leader of his unit, was less likely to react on whim. He was certainly among the most responsive to the interests of the female which elevated him in Jor'y's esteem. He had not only followed Vanessa's lead in regard to the Aturian habitation customs the night before, but, at Vanessa's safe arrival just now, Carthy had the good sense to order the other males to lower their weapons before one of them did something tragically stupid enough to truly inspire Jor'y's wrath. As far as he could tell, the male was both sensible and honorable.

He rather liked him.

Of course, that did not negate the fact that he would still have to monitor him carefully to ensure that he did not interfere with Jor'y's attempts to bond with his a'talyna. Although the estate looked every inch of its incredible age, there had been much work over the centuries to keep it upgraded with technology. He would have no trouble tracking the male's activities even as he dealt with any other ill-thought-out attacks from those under his authority.

It would be a pity if he had to kill him.

Carthy cleared his throat and took a step closer to Vanessa, casting a wary look in Jor'y's direction.

"Ms. Williams, was everything... okay... with your accommodations last night?" The male's query was to the point and quietly spoken, as if wary of provoking Jor'y's anger again.

He knew that the male was gauging his reaction the entire time as the human's attention never truly left Jor'y for even a moment. He returned Carthy's gaze placidly, the tension within him quickly buried beneath layers of cool control. Although valmek passions ran hotter than most Aturians, the peaceable nature of his species had required that he learn at a young age, like all valmeks, how to control all outward signs of anger or hostility. That skill served him doubly now. Especially since he was not legally able to wing clasp his a'talyna as instinct prodded him to in front of these males.

Until she accepted his wing clasp willingly, he had not even a claim of courtship in his favor. As things stood now, his claim on her was about as tangible as the fantasy that had tormented him last night. Even now, it remained at the edge of his thoughts, every touch and the sensation of her warm body drawn tightly to him, open to his pleasure, burned into his mind. Just that quick, all of the desire he had felt during the night as he lay in his nest, tangled in his bedding, threatened to reemerge and crack his composure, dishonoring his station as valmek.

He ruthlessly battled down the hot twisting coils of instinct and lust. In his mind's eye, he saw his a'talyna standing outside on one of the many balconies, overlooking the valetik stretched out down the mountainside beneath the protective shadow of the estate. Woven into her hair, she wore several of his crown feathers, the most perfect snowy white and the most brilliantly hued of his summer plumage that he would gift to her as was custom. They danced in the light wind, fluttering around her face as a stamp of their bond. His breath hitched at the vision, and he mentally held it to himself with unspeakable longing before he managed to wrestle it back down and clear his mind.

This was the now, and, for the time being, he was content just having her there at his side. The smile she offered him before answering warmed him and sent a prickle of pride and approval through him. In her human attire, the strangeness of her appearance was more striking than it would be if she were clad in

Aturian clothing, but he had fetched her belongings as soon as she was comfortably settled just so she would have access to that familiarity. Even though the thick tunic she wore was oddly bulky and the leg coverings thick, he reasoned that they were probably necessary for the colder climate of their winters.

"Yes, I slept very well," she agreed, her face coloring slightly in a way that intrigued him. "And I had my belongings brought to me." She turned a curious glance toward him, the thin line of hair on one of her brows arching. "I suspect that I have you to thank for that?"

His feathers puffed out in instinctive pleasure at her recognition, and he dipped his head. "It was my pleasure to see to your comfort. It is not pleasant to be foisted into an unfamiliar environment, so it was the least I could do."

The color in her cheeks brightened. "You shouldn't have put yourself at risk flying through that storm again just for my belongings, but thank you, Jor'ytal."

He fanned his wings out and he dipped his head lower, his eyes lifting to meet her gaze. "It was no trouble at all. I will be happy to be at service whenever you have need. I only ask that *you* call me Jor'y."

Curiously, she began to fan her face with her hand and glanced toward her human escorts. "Oh, well, then please call me Vanessa." She cleared her throat. "Who's hungry? I'm not sure if it's all this fresh mountain air or not, but I'm starved."

Jor'y's head shot up in alarm. "You are feeling the effects of starvation? Why did you not say so immediately?" he thundered, making his female jump as her eyes flew to him in surprise. "When did you last eat?"

"Calm down, man," another male, one who had identified himself as Michael Tackert, murmured from where he stood just a short distance from Jor'y's side, his dark brown eyes dancing with amusement. The male brushed a hand over his short dark curls. "She's just saying that she's hungry—a sentiment I can agree with. I can't remember the last time I've had such an appetite." He turned his head toward the others and gave a cheerful bellow that both irritated Jor'y's sensitive ears and repulsed him as he caught the translation. "Let's get our grub on, guys!"

Carthy nodded, casting another curious glance in Jor'y's direction, the tension easing out of his expression as Jor'y folded his wings politely against his back. The male extended his arm, stopping just within reaching distance before thinking better of it and waving Vanessa forward with an encouraging smile.

"Tackert's right. Let's eat. We've prepared a plate for you and kept it under the warming dome."

Jor'y lips twisted with distaste. He had seen exactly what the humans had selected for his female and themselves. Plain meal cakes, without any of the preserved berries or puffed cream to flavor them, and fresh cooked eggs without any seasonings or toppings that his people enjoyed. The hens, crossbred and modified for Aturia, were the one stock animal originating from Earth that his people enjoyed. It was convenient that the humans would also eat them, but the blandness of their meal made his wings want to shrivel with distaste. The way that Tackert grimaced down at his own plate as he took his seat behind it at least assured him that not all humans were completely without taste.

When the warming dome was lifted off her own plate by Carthy before he took his own seat at her side, Jor'y nearly laughed at the way her nose wrinkled so expressively, her brown eyes squinting down at the food before casting a longing look toward the numerous dishes that filled the table. Her little pink tongue darted out to stroke over her bottom lip before she pushed to her feet and grabbed the nearest ladle sunk into a bowl of preserves. Stephens made a sound of protest as she poured a healthy amount of the berries over her cakes and proceeded to make her way down the table, putting dabs and dollops of nearly everything in sight onto her plate.

Her dainty thumb swiped over the sauce that she placed a tiny amount of at the corner of her plate, and her eyes widened in delight before pouring it over the salted meats with a sound of pleasure in the back of her throat that shot straight down to his groin.

"Miss Williams, that is against regulations. Earth Gov requires that we…"

"As far as this is concerned, they can stuff it," she responded cheerfully, cutting the male off with a piercing look and another arch of her brow. "I'm not going to just not eat because they say so. If I get sick, I'll take full responsibility."

Jor'y stiffened in his chair. "You will not become sick from any of this. I would never put something in front of my guests that they cannot eat. So that you know, our food tests high in compatibility for the human diet. The only exception is some rare delicacies that would not be offered to you."

Vanessa's blunt white teeth flashed in a smile directed at him that made his skin prickle and his body warm all over. He returned her smile, pleased that she did not shrink this time from the sight of his prominent fangs.

"Well then, this is perfect," she exclaimed with a happy sigh as she sank back into her seat, setting her plate in front of her with a small hum of excitement.

Tackert stared at her for a moment, his jaw moving as he wrestled with some internal decision, before he also stood, his chair scraping back from the momentum.

Stephens to the left of him, glanced up in surprise. "Tackert, you aren't going to do it, are you?"

"No offense meant to whoever cooked this, but it looks and

smells about as appetizing as sawdust," the male grumbled. "Miss Williams is right. We're stranded here for gods know how long. I'm with her on this. I would rather have a filling and nutritionally complete meal than subsist on whatever approved bland foods we're told we can have. If our host is certain that it's safe, then I'm willing to take a chance." He gave Jor'y a direct look. "I have no reason not to believe him."

Jor'y inclined his head, the corners of his mouth quirking as the male began to pile his plate with food. In short order, he was joined by the other males. Carthy was the only holdout, his jaw clenched as he stoically shoveled food into his mouth until the low, delighted moans of the others enjoying the morning meal finally broke his resolve. Although Carthy's nearly black eyes were hard with reluctance, he too began to place food on his plate, though in considerably smaller portions as if he still could not quite trust it.

Jor'y sat back comfortably in his chair, his gaze returning to his a'talyna. Just watching her enjoyment triggered a happiness he had not felt in some time that was only fed further by the contentment of the other humans around them. He was aware that humans had unflattering terms for the manner in which Aturians fed from the pleasure energies roused in other beings. They always failed to understand that the Aturian need to feed in this manner was not only harmless but benefited both parties involved. Since he had refused to join during Hashavnal, and did not have a mate to share with, he had subsisted for years off of the smallest exchanges of pleasure, such as this. But with the presence of his a'talyna, it was magnified by a hundredfold, and he shivered from the wave of hot need that washed over him in response.

His heated gaze focused on her, his entire being zeroing in on his small female as she ate. Her eyes rose, and she met his gaze.

He swore he saw an answering desire there before her cheeks darkened once again and she dropped her gaze back to her plate.

This wooing would take time, but he was nothing if not a patient male. With Hashavnal approaching, he wanted nothing more than for her to be receptive to him, and only him, when the Aturian mating season ignited his blood.

He prayed to the gods that she would be.

CHAPTER 8

Vanessa felt entirely too awkward around their host. It was as if he was privy to every forbidden fantasy. Although she understood that those thoughts likely came from her writer's overactive imagination, she couldn't shake that his gaze was knowing as he met her eyes. Even hours later as she sat alone in the impressive study, her datapad set up in front of her and holo keyboard activated with her fingers resting over the keys, she still felt it.

She gave Sa'tari a questioning look as she took a seat at a polished table. "Are you sure it's okay I work in here? I mean, I could work in my quarters just as easily if it's an inconvenience."

"Jor'y was pleased that you enjoyed this room when I inquired of it, so think nothing of it," Sa'tari replied confidently without looking up from her work.

The female sat on a nearby chair, engrossed in some delicate textile work with her claws as she kept Vanessa company. Although her parents employed servants, they tended to move silently from one task to another. She had never had anyone just sit with her in case she might need anything. That level of attentiveness, as if Vanessa were practically royalty, was unnerving.

"And you're sure I'm not keeping you from anything? I don't mind if you have other things that demand your attention, especially with the storm outside," she reminded her companion quietly.

The Aturian shook her head. "No, this is exactly where I'm to be. I don't have any younglings requiring looking after, and my mate has his own duties until this evening. Since we, like much of the staff, elect to have lodgings within the estate, our life is comfortable enough. When we complete our assigned tasks, we take our leisure until we are needed. Nor do we have to worry about the storm, outside of observing basic precautions here, like keeping the windows latched," she said as she deftly looped another tiny stitch with her claw tips.

Vanessa grimaced. *Live-in servants? How antiquated.* She didn't give voice to these thoughts, only peered at the other female curiously.

"And this arrangement satisfies you—to live here at someone's beck and call when you spend all of your time in service?"

She had a hard time imagining that sort of life being preferable to living in the lovely town she only caught glimpses of extending down into the valley just under the shadow of the castle. It brought to mind the unpleasantly crowded quarters of servants in Tudor period households and she shuddered.

Sa'tari blinked at her and lowered her weaving. "Why not? The family quarters are certainly as comfortable and as spacious, if not more so, as having a household in the valetik."

Vanessa shook her head in confusion, her fingers distractedly dropping away from the keyboard. "I don't understand how that's even possible. It would require a massive amount of room to house everyone employed here."

Her companion grinned and shrugged her wings. "Not everyone chooses to live here, though there is enough room that the entire valetik could dwell here without issue. The entire southern wing alone is reserved for staff who wish to stay on and care for the valmek who protects us." Vanessa was certain that her friend noticed her lip curl because the female laughed. "It is not what you think. It is an exchange of power, and we are treated well and given every consideration for our caretaking. Whether we are here or down within the valetik, we are all of the same valetik and are one."

Vanessa caught herself gaping impolitely and shook her head once more in effort to force clarity to her thoughts. "I'm sorry, but what is a valetik exactly? It seems that you use the term for the people here, but you also use it to refer to your homes?"

Sa'tari chuckled, her wings fluffing out lightly behind her. "It is a little of both. As a people, we are a valetik because we share bloodline that makes us one. We are all related to each other to some degree along the line of our fathers. Our homes are the physical extension of our families and community. They would be nothing without us inhabiting their walls, and so we call them after ourselves. A valetik is both our familial identity and our community identity because it is the physical expression of our extended family into a community model. Only the valmek are set apart because of the service they were born to provide, but in the end, they too are part of the valetik, as is this estate."

Vanessa's brow wrinkled. "So you're telling me that this place both belongs to Jor'y but also is considered community property? I'm afraid I'm still not clear how that works out... Is this part of the power exchange you mentioned?"

The Aturian nodded, smoothing out her weaving against her lap. "Yes, we have every right to dwell here to make it easier to care for the valmek line. They could never refuse those who wish to live here, nor would they want to," she added. "Aturians are social by nature, and the valmek line feels those needs just as strongly as the rest of us." She pursed her lips. "Perhaps stronger. We are companions as well as extended family... and for those not related by blood sometimes able to provide more intimate relief." She grinned suggestively. "Not that our valmek has shown interest in such a thing in many revolutions."

"And working here doesn't intrude on your ability to have a personal life?" Vanessa leaned forward in fascination.

Sa'tari gave her curious look. "There is no reason for it to do so any more than any other adult in the valetik. Everyone has duties that they attend to during the day, so this is no different. In fact, we have more leisure time than most, I suspect. We are typically only on-call until late afternoon, with final rounds later in the evening if we have guests. The kitchen staff is off by the evening meal, with long breaks between the meal periods. There is more than enough personal time." She laughed. "Sometimes so much that I am uncertain what to do with myself."

She held up her weaving for Vanessa's inspection. "I have only just begun to pick this up since having all of my duties assigned to your care. The moment that I realized you were a quiet sort, I knew I would need something to occupy my time when you did not need me." She chuckled.

A flush climbed Vanessa's neck. "It's really not necessary for you to sit with me if there's something else you would rather be doing. I can always comm you if I need anything."

"Of course you could," the Aturian agreed mildly. "But I happen to enjoy being assigned to your company and find all of this quite relaxing." She fanned the tip of one wing toward Vanessa's setup, making her smile. "A short day spent tidying your room while you enjoyed your morning meal hardly seems like enough work to compensate for how pleasant this is."

Vanessa's lips quirked. She had to admit that it was nice having company rather than sitting alone in the silent study.

"You're sure?"

"Of course. Think nothing more of it," Sa'tari hummed

happily. "Do not let me distract you from your work. That is what you wished to accomplish here, yes?"

Looking down at her datapad, Vanessa nodded. "Yes, this part of the ca—uh, estate seems to be set up the most comfortably for working."

Her companion nodded silently, clearly feeling no need to respond to that observation as Vanessa stared down at the blank document in front of her. She worried her bottom lip with her teeth. Her editor would be expecting the first chapter within the next couple of days, but for the first time she had no idea what to write. Her mind drifted yet again to the stoic valmek with his mysterious gold eyes and imagined him brooding at the study's large window, perhaps staring down at the town stretching down the mountainside. There was a certain majesty and a tangible loneliness of spirit conjured up with this image, and seemingly with a will of their own her fingers began typing.

Her mind fell into a world where a winged alien prince stared out at the world, his loneliness eating away at him until a woman was stranded at his doorstep. She would have blushed with embarrassment if there was any chance of anyone familiar with her current situation reading it, since the resemblance to reality was unmistakable.

Thank the gods that her readers were mostly women on Earth and in the more populated colonies along the trade routes. While it was possible that there were a few readers on the Aturian southern continent, she was certain that her secret would be safe. She had no illusions that what she was writing would be considered scandalous under Earth Gov regulations—a doomed and forbidden romance between an alien prince and a human. She could tempt them and incite their fantasies as long as no one knew the truth of the matter. Though it would likely be banned eventually on Earth, there was a good chance that it might even make her a colony-wide bestseller where such things were less stringently enforced for the discreet.

A new giddiness filled her as she worked as the story unfurled within her imagination. The proud nobility of the alien, his wings fanning wide as he bowed over the hand of the heroine. Her eyes wide as she stared up at his far greater height with awe and an undeniable pull of attraction that defied all reasoning. If Vanessa put her own struggles with her desire into the experiences now enjoyed by her heroine, Lainey, that too would be her little secret.

Heat climbed higher into her cheeks as the pair, encountering each other alone in a hall, were unable to pass by without touching. Their hands grazed, and his longer fingers caught hers and entwined, drawing her up short so he could gently pull her close to him. He leaned down, his breath brushing her ear.

"To what force in the heavens shall I thank and give praise that you were dropped at my gate?" he whispered.

The heroine leaned into him, drawing in his scent, her senses leaving her.

Wait.

Vanessa's imagination screeched to a halt as she dragged in a deep breath of the familiar spicy-sweet scent, and she saved and dismissed the file as she heard the scrape of claws with Jor'y's approaching footsteps.

She imagined she was nearly scarlet as she turned in her chair to face the imposing figure of the valmek, his gold eyes shining down at her. His gaze slanted toward her datapad with a note of curiosity.

"My apologies, did I interrupt your work?" he murmured in his rich, rumbly voice. "The storm has provided the perfect opportunity for me to catch up on a few things and I hoped you would not mind the company."

Gods, that voice could melt her panties off at twelve yards.

She shivered at the tingly warmth it sent driving through her and shook her head. She only barely had the presence of mind to smile and discreetly check the time on her comm. She was surprised to see that she had been caught up for over three hours in her fantasy.

He smiled before making his way over to the large private desk that dominated the room. After seeing the proprietorial way that he had sat at it the night before as he doled out orders, she had wisely avoided sitting there, electing to sit at one of the tables. Watching him out of the corner of her eyes as she returned to her work, Vanessa was grateful that he didn't attempt to make small talk, nor did he look disgruntled at sharing the space with her. Instead, he lowered himself gracefully into his chair and initiated the startup sequence on his desk's data system. Within minutes, his attention was bent toward whatever work he was doing.

Outside, she could hear the strength of the storm picking up, the wind howling as it buffeted the walls. Every now and then, there was the smallest moan from the building that hinted at the ferocity of the weather and Vanessa shivered, grateful to be safely indoors.

Well, safe enough.

She snuck a look at the imposing Aturian from beneath her lashes. In profile he was especially gorgeous, long pencil-thin white feathers draping down the back of his head and shoulders in a manner that reminded her of an aristocrat of a bygone era. Common sense told her that all the Aturians had such feathering on their heads, although most images she had seen before arriving on Aturia had depicted aliens with feathers cropped short just below the ear line. None of those had wings or feathers anywhere else on their bodies from what she had been able to tell.

Were there genetic variations among Aturians that left some without wings and body feathers? She hadn't been successful finding any information about it and worried that it would be rude to ask. Pondering the matter silently, she scrolled back through her work and read over the previously written chapter. A scuff of movement outside of the study door alerted her to the fact that one of her team had planted himself there. From her peripheral vision, she watched Jor'y's feathers puff up as he slanted a hard gaze toward the door before relaxing once more as he completely dismissed the man's presence.

She decided that she would follow suit. As much of a distraction as Jor'y was, his spicy scent filling the very air she breathed, she could ignore it. Just as she could ignore the annoying squeaks of whichever of her guards was pacing in the hall. The scent of peppermint hit her nose and it wrinkled. Stephens. He had to have given up carci sticks lately because the man seemed to have a limitless supply of strong mints that he constantly sucked on. Apparently, he was her assigned babysitter. Well, he could wear a tread in front of the door if he wanted to—she had work to do. Her readers expected it.

Although she didn't have the social responsibilities and career demands of her parents, and she had little doubt that her chosen vocation was a disappointment for them since it had zero actual affluence attached to it, Vanessa refused to disappoint her fans. She didn't have to be a huge celebrity to feel that commitment, and since she was born into the luxuries that came with her class thanks to her parents, it just made it feel all the more important to her to work hard. If she wasn't turning out chapters regularly enough for her readers it was all too easy for her to feel less and less worthy of her privileges that were attached to her name simply because of her birth.

If she had to work herself to the bone, then so be it. That was what this trip was for. It wasn't a leisurely vacation. She couldn't even remember the last time she took one. No, this was solely for focusing on her work without her mother being able to insist that she attend one function after another. That she missed the familiar

Yule celebrations that were the only highlight of the year for her was worth being able to actually work in peace.

Intent on ignoring Stephens, Vanessa breathed deep, focusing on the wonderfully spicy smell of the male in the room with her. It took little time for her to sink back into her world, her senses full of that enticing aroma as she took it with her and wove it into her world.

She was only distantly aware of Sa'tari occasionally moving around the room, sometimes leaving for small amounts of time to return with some drink or snack that were set at Vanessa's side. Each of which were met with polite, distracted mumbles to which the female never seemed to take offense. Jor'y, she was always aware of, however, and over the course of the hours they quietly worked, she couldn't fail to notice that her hero had taken on more and more of the valmek's qualities.

Her cheeks heated as she finished the chapter, grateful that Jor'y would never realize just how much he had inspired her.

CHAPTER 9

By the sixth day of snow and winds that not only howled but seemed determined to scream ill omens like a banshee, Vanessa was beginning to think that the storm was never going to ease. Not that any of the Aturians seemed concerned. Other than the occasional restless twitch of his wings or tail, Jor'y seemed to ignore it even better than he did the humans underfoot. The morning meals were pleasant enough, but she could see the way his temper seemed to fray over the course of the day.

Since the guards were around to keep an eye on her, Vanessa naturally felt guilty about it. It was because of her presence that his peace was being disrupted. She knew better than most just how important that was. She had even attempted, after one especially loud hiss on the third day, to confine herself to working in her rooms. Although it had been pretty miserable, and she had discovered that she found it hard to work when she missed the weight of his presence in the atmosphere of the room or his scent filling her senses, her plan had worked up until the point that he had commed Sa'tari, insisting to know why they were absent.

That had put an end to working in her quarters. Every day

afterward, Sa'tari escorted her—on orders—to the study where Jor'y was always waiting, already busy at work. Yet he always looked up from his work at her arrival and greeted her with a warm smile. She always did her best work during those first few hours they were together. Eventually, though, he would get up and leave to see to business elsewhere in the estate, often with a displeased snarl at whatever human was there on shift by the door, and she would find herself missing him and the way he would lift his head and chuckle at some amusing commentary passing between her and Sa'tari.

Vanessa scowled at her datapad as another violent shriek of wind battered the window. The storm seemed to fray her nerves even worse when he wasn't around too, as if his mere presence made her feel safer despite the blizzard outside.

Leaning back in her chair, she turned an exasperated look to her companion. Over the last few days, she had become surprisingly close to Sa'tari, finding comfort in the female's simple enjoyment of life, quick mind, and even quicker humor. Spending her breaks hearing about the female's family, especially her mate, made her feel a little jealous too. Sometimes, she would give anything to have the sort of uncomplicated happily ever after that her heroines enjoyed, where being in love and living life to the fullest was all that was needed without all the mess that came with her position as a Williams.

As a kid, enchanted with old stories of adventures of children far from home, she had toyed with running away. As an adult, she wanted to run away for a similar and yet quite different reason. She rubbed a hand over her face.

"Okay, tell me please that this is normal, and you're not having an ice-pocalypse, because that wind is seriously starting to worry me."

Sa'tari looked up and grinned, drawing her attention away from the intricate blanket piled in her lap. "It always feels that way. Every winter, the storms come, and it feels as if this will be the last storm to end this world like in our beginning stories."

Vanessa raised an eyebrow. "Oh?"

The female nodded and smiled, her voice dropping to a whisper though they were the only ones in the room. Jor'y's absence always seemed to take her guard too, which meant there was no one to overhear outside the door either, as far as she knew... if the story was all that much of a secret to begin with. The timely presence of the guard and their disappearance was no coincidence, although she still wasn't sure if their presence was more for Vanessa's benefit or if the men were trying to gather info on the valmek. One never knew when it came to those employed by Darvel or Earth Gov.

"In the old stories, Aturia was a tempest. Storms raged and the winds and snow cut, destroying everything. The world was said to be inhabited by giant ek'thanak, great fur-covered beasts who thrived in the brutal climate, eating the lifeforms born beneath the surface where the great mother bore all living things." She smoothed her work and began to pick up the stitches once more. "They dug into the earth with their long, terrible claws, pulling the creatures up to devour them, or would wait to see if any curious beings would leave the safety of the warm caverns and meet their grisly fates."

Vanessa wrinkled her nose and laughed. "That's quite a charming visual."

Sa'tari grinned. "Not so charming for the poor beings being eaten, but I am certain the ek'thanak would agree with you. Of course, the gods became angered with all of this. The beings were all very miserable, and none less than the first of the Aturians. Our wings gave us the ability to move through the deep caverns easily enough, but rumor had come down of vast, limitless skies. We thirsted to fly far and experience everything, even with the brutal cold that the ek'thanak breathed would threaten to kill us as surely as their claws."

Propping her chin on her fists, Vanessa regarded her friend with fascination. "So, what happened?"

"They sent a hero, the First Mother of the Aturians. She had already reached a distinguished age and was an elder, but she also had considerable wisdom that the gods knew she would need to defeat the creatures. They gave her a potion that restored her physical youth and vitality and armed her with weapons crafted by their own forges." Sa'tari's eyes sparkled with relish. "They sent her into the above world, and she saw the great skies and mountains and claimed them all as her own. When the ek'thanak came, she killed them, one after the other, and stretched their guts between the mountains, making the first fertile valleys. But it was still too cold for our kind to survive long, so she tracked the last ek'thanak, Vor'don, to the furthest corner of the world. He was so large that he blotted out the sun, but our First Mother would not relent."

"And did she kill him?"

Sa'tari shook her head. "She took the great chains that leashed the hunting vel'par of the mountain god, Osh'kunval, and the spear of Ka'damanali, the great queen below. She drove the spear into Vor'don's hide, pinning him to the tallest mountain, and with him wounded, she took the chains and leashed him there. Then, the darkest night ended, the snows ceased and the sun appeared. Our people took to the skies, and we celebrate Hashavnal in honor of her, Ha'shana, for she brought joy to her people. She took a mate from among the gods and bore the rest of our race, and we were made plenty and strong. And so we honor her every year even when Vor'don rages from his chains. The gods allow him only to hunt during the winter, when they loosen his chains, but they never allow him free and the spirit of Ha'shana always chases him back beyond the mountains."

"Wow," Vanessa murmured. "And is that why some of you are winged and some aren't?"

Sa'tari startled, her facing paling.

"No," Jor'y's deep voice rumbled. "Some of us do not have wings because our species has been brainwashed by colonizers into believing that this is what is best for us," he growled.

Vanessa jerked upright, her mouth dropping open.

"What? People are doing that to themselves?"

"More commonly to their young," he clarified as he approached. "It is an unfortunate political situation that we will battle with as long as many of us are convinced this is our way of being accepted." His eyes skimmed over her, warming. "But enough of that dreary topic. It should not follow after our story of hasha, our joy. I hope I am not interrupting," he added, glancing toward her datapad before lifting his eyes to stare at her with such intensity that her breath momentarily left her body.

"Of course not. As it happens, I was just taking a break," she said cheerfully, ignoring Sa'tari's amusement as the female watched their exchange from where she sat, her blanket once more lowered into her lap.

Jor'y's head cocked in a quick bird-like motion as he regarded her, but he nodded, his lips curving with a devastating effect on her libido. She swore that someone had cranked up the heat, evidenced by the slick now coating her upper thighs. Surely it couldn't all be for him. But gods, if it was, then he was far too aware of it as he dragged the scent in with every deep draw of his breath.

"It seems that my timing is fortuitous then. I had thought to see if you would be interested in a private tour of the estate." He hesitated with an uncertainty that she found impossibly charming. "Although we cannot go outdoors and see it in its best setting, I was under the impression that you enjoyed such sights of historical significance."

If the invitation had come just days earlier, she would have likely fled with embarrassment from his company, despite being intrigued by his offer. Their days of quiet companionship had since made her comfortable with his presence and more than a little interested in some privacy. A private tour sounded like the perfect opportunity. The fact that it could possibly give her imagination additional fodder for her story also did its part selling her on it—or so she told herself.

She nodded and stood, dismissing her holo keyboard as she scooped up her datapad and paused. She slid a questioning gaze to Sa'tari, feeling guilty for leaving the female there when she had come with the intention of keeping Vanessa company. The female, however, beamed and brushed off her long tunic as she stood and gathered up her weaving.

"I think I will go greet my mate before I go set up a warm drink in your quarters for when you return. Some parts of the estate can get drafty this time of the year, and I am sure you will have a need for it. I certainly will," she added with a chuckle before departing, leaving Vanessa alone in Jor'y's company.

"It seems that you are all mine, then," he purred, the sound shooting straight down to her clit.

It promptly responded with a throbbing desire.

Gods, this was ridiculous. He was perfectly charming, which made him all the harder to resist. If he had been sleazily hitting on her it would have been easy to dismiss him. She wasn't sure that he altogether understood what he was doing to her. They were different species, after all. It wasn't his fault that her hormones were raging like a teenager's.

Gah! She was determined to enjoy this outing.

"It seems so," she replied with a feigned confident smile. How was it that this male of all beings had the ability to shake her confidence? She didn't understand how he wielded so much power over her. No, it didn't bear thinking about. "I really want to thank you. It is very kind of you to take time out of your busy day to show me your home. From what little I've seen, your estate is so beautiful."

He grinned down at her, displaying many of his sharp teeth, and yet the smile itself was crooked and had such a heated intensity that she wanted to squirm. Her breath caught, when, as if taking a page out of her book, he clasped her hand in his, but rather than bend over it, he flattened her hand against his chest.

"For you, it would be nothing less than a delight."

His words were spoken so solemnly that she might have thought he was jesting if not for the sincerity in his eyes as his beautiful white wings fanned out wide, one curving around as he stepped up to her side. Though there was something protective about the gesture, as if he were drawing her beneath his wing entirely, there was an erotic nature to the brush of his feathers against her skin. Softer than the finest silk, that light touch made her skin prickle even as it was followed by the slightest of shivers.

She thought his smile widened for the briefest moment, but she wasn't given any opportunity to look closer or examine his reaction before he clasped her to his side, his body thoroughly warming hers.

"So that you do not get cold," he observed before drawing her from the cozy study, nestled against his side.

His warmth surrounding her, Vanessa nearly melted right there in the corridor. For a moment she wondered what it would feel like if she were in her heroine Lainey's position, and the warm press of his body was due to the imminent kiss that they would share. Jor'y leaned down, his nose brushing the top of her head, and she felt her pulse race in eager expectation until he drew away.

"Come, we will go this way first," he murmured, steering her to the left. "The halls this way leading to the northwestern turret are spectacular."

Biting back a curse, Vanessa smiled up at him, hoping that he didn't see the heat of sexual frustration in her eyes.

"Sounds perfect," she agreed, and followed it with a silent reprimand to her libido to behave as Jor'y led her down the hall, his massive dark amethyst frame pressed firmly at her side.

The sacrifices authors make for inspiration... Yeah, not even she was buying that one as she was unable to resist leaning into his warm side with a quiet sigh. He was going to be the doom of her yet.

CHAPTER 10

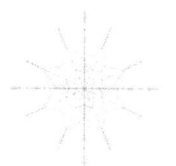

*J*or'y knew just from the taste of the air that her body was priming for his, just as his own was rapidly doing for his mate. Her response fueled his own, making his cock, swollen heavily in its sheath, uncomfortably hard... and yet she made no invitation. He tried not to stare down at her in his bewilderment as they walked along the corridor. She was unmated, he was certain. How was it that she was able to resist the a'talynal?

She certainly had not sought him out. If not for the time that they had spent together in the o'dari, he would not have had any time with her at all. Every day he had left, and every day he had waited patiently for her to do so and declare her interest.

Had he not made himself attractive enough to garner her attention that morning? He had even seen to it that the o'dari, his private library and meeting room, be made available for her to work so that she would be pleased with his home. He had done everything he could think of to indicate his interest. He had even gone as far as warning the rival males in his territory. And yet, despite her obvious interest, she had not sought him out.

What was he doing wrong?

His impromptu decision to take her on a tour of the estate was yet another pitiful effort to impress upon her the comforts of his home. He was at a loss and would have been tempted to seek advice from one of the human males who seemed to be intent on being in his path if he felt any of them would genuinely assist him. He was not entirely ignorant of human laws. He wasn't well versed in them, but upon his mate's arrival, he made it his business to learn what he could of the mating laws among humans. He had been shocked to discover that, despite some of the vids that circulated, mating, breeding, and even casual sexual contact between humans and other species, was illegal.

Was that what kept her away?

That the natural course of things was being interfered with by human laws frustrated him immensely. It also inspired a strong hostility within him against those who would deny her the care and devotion that would be found from her a'talyna. If she did not wish it, then she could indicate as much and he would leave the matter alone. But everything about her was receptive: the pleasure and desire in her scent, the smiles she gifted him, even the intriguing coloring in her cheeks when she was in his presence. All that was left was for her to give her consent by issuing invitation.

Aturian culture did not allow any interference within a mating without incurring considerable shame. No law, no kin, and no individual had any say in how one mated or who they took pleasure with. Thankfully, because of this, like the case with the vids, the Darvel colony on the southern continent could not enforce their laws outside of their colonial jurisdiction.

He knew now that there would be consequences if she mated him, but the part of him that had yearned for rotation after rotation held out hope for his mate. Especially when she was as close to him as she was now, tucked beneath the curve of his wing.

Despite how small she was, the top of her head only just barely brushing his chest, her lush body still so delicate compared to his own, he hungered to join with her and no one else, and experience the a'talynal coming to life between them. The fact that he was already beginning to enjoy her adventurous spirit, intelligence, and her strength of will in the face of opposition just made the draw to her all the richer.

The wing cupped around her shivered, the white feathers trembling delicately, and he swallowed back a groan.

"Your home really is incredible. I don't think I've seen such a perfect blend of history and modern conveniences before. Even on Earth, people are only willing to go so far with updating historical structures," his a'talyna observed. "This is remarkably unparalleled."

He dipped his head, leaning forward so that he was a little closer to eye-level with her, his feathers fluffing with pleasure. Her voicing her approval was a balm for his anxiety, soothing some of the worry assailing him.

"It delights me to know that you are enjoying my home. I hope that the o'dari has been to your liking?"

Her brows drew together. "O'dari?"

He inclined his head. "It is what we call the room where you have chosen to work. It is my private library and workspace, and where I hold important meetings when they are necessary."

"Oh, the study!" The color in her cheeks rose again as she strode more determinedly down the hall, her steps clipped with her distress. She glanced at him from the corner of her eye. "I'm so embarrassed. I didn't realize that I was intruding on anyone's personal work area when I asked Sa'tari if I could write in there. I mean, I knew that you worked in there too, obviously, but I thought it was a public room." She gave him a chagrined smile. "The atmosphere there is so pleasant, but I didn't mean to barge in like some sort of demanding guest."

"Your presence there is hardly an intrusion," he protested, reaching out so that his knuckles could brush the side of her arm. "And you are not what I would consider demanding. On the contrary, I find your presence very pleasing," he admitted, uncomfortable with giving further voice to his interest when speaking as such would have been considered highly impolite and pushing. He swallowed thickly when she did not protest the familiarity and continued, "When Sa'tari told me of your desire to work there, I was more than happy to open it up for you."

Vanessa drew to a stop, her head tipping up as she stared at him in surprise. Soft, plump human lips parted as her wide brown eyes rose to meet his gaze. He wondered if he had pushed too far, as her lips pressed together once more in an unrecognizable expression. He stared back at her warily, his heart hammering with dread when suddenly the most beautiful smile he'd ever seen tugged at her lips, her eyes warming.

His own smile that had begun to curve the corners of his mouth grew in response. "Truthfully, it is a joy to have you in every place I call mine, knowing that some small portion of your presence remains with me even when you are no longer in the room. I would gladly have you take up the entire estate if it were possible," he said, and was met with husky feminine laughter that shot through him like the sweetest elixir.

"In case you haven't noticed... I talk to myself when I work. I can't imagine that you'd be able to get anything done at all, or your staff for that matter, if I somehow managed to take up every bit of available space here," she answered, her eyes dancing.

"Perhaps then to keep it restrained to my own personal space then, where I will gain the most maximum enjoyment of it."

She arched a delicate brow. "Don't you think that would make it difficult for you to get your own work done?"

He stepped in closer, his wing folding around her a little more.

"Such a distraction would be well worth it," he admitted. "I have certainly enjoyed every minute of it so far."

Her eyebrows flew up at that statement, shock once again coloring her expression, and he quickly retreated, going so far as to take a step back again. By the gods, he was no good at this courtship thing. He felt completely out of his depth. He was far better at managing the estate and seeing to the welfare of his valetik than indulging in emotional needs that he had begun to doubt he even possessed until now.

"Besides, with the storm raging, I have been provided a pleasant reprieve from my work. Feel free to enjoy the space. It would give me great pleasure to know that I can provide this."

At his words, her expression grew thoughtful, making him shift uneasily in place, his wings twitching slightly. He had no clue of what was going on in her mind. Not even her dark eyes betrayed her thoughts. Then her lips quirked once again, magically settling his anxiety with nothing more than just a hint of her smile. The back and forth between intense pleasure and anxiety reminded him of his first time flying, and even though his heartbeat in his chest just as heavily as when he was a youngling on his first flight, he was also caught up in the exhilaration of it.

This one moment with his a'talyna was more precious than any other experience he had ever treasured. And one that, he hoped, would become a beautiful memory of how he had found and claimed the joy of his heart.

"I guess if you're enjoying it as much as I am, then I might as well just wallow in the luxury of having all of that at my disposal," she replied after a moment, her lip curving slyly as she gave him a playful nudge with her shoulder.

A rumble of adoration instinctively made its way up his throat as he stalked after her. His tail stiffening behind him, feathers spreading, he caught up in less than two steps and cupped his wing around her once more. The movement catching her attention, Vanessa's head turned toward his wing, her eyes sliding over his feathers. Jor'y held his breath, waiting for her to be repulsed, but instead, her smile widened with a distinct expression of admiration as she lifted her hand to trail a finger along one long feather that ran along the length of her opposite arm.

It was magical.

His entire body hummed as if he had been struck by lightning. A tremor ran through his muscles, and his feathers vibrated subtly, but not so faintly that she wouldn't feel it beneath her exploring fingertips. He groaned, a protest on his lips, when she jerked her hand back, dropping it once more to her side as she turned an embarrassed look up at him only before facing forward once more.

"I'm so sorry," she choked out, hastening her step. "That wasn't appropriate."

He allowed her the space to walk ahead of him as he followed at a leisurely pace behind her, shortening his own strides. His head canted to the side as he regarded her.

"There is no reason to be sorry," he murmured softly. "I am not."

Caught off-guard more than he had expected her to be, she stumbled, and he rushed forward, his wings sweeping around her at the same moment he encased her in his arms' embrace. He held her so close that he felt the rush of air expanding her lungs. Her head tipped back, and she gazed up at him, her dark eyes drawing him in.

He dropped his head slightly, bringing his lips closer to hers. How would she taste? Was her skin as soft as he imagined?

Her lips parted in a silent question, her back arching slightly as she went on her toes, her mouth drawing closer to his.

His breath caught. This was the moment. *Finally!*

Nearby, the viewscreen flashed with a warning, an alarm

going off just loud enough that Vanessa dropped flat on her feet, her head turning toward the accursed thing.

Her eyes were wide as they skimmed past the art that had absorbed so much of her attention straight to the viewscreen. Up until that moment, it had been displaying serene images of Aturian landscapes, interrupted by datastreams. An alert now filled the screen in red letters, warning Aturians in the midcontinental belt to stay indoors due to extreme weather hazards. In the corner, the vid stream of the valetik showed the secure households, each locked up against the elements. Everyone was certain to be keeping an eye on the daily alerts on their own screens, but he knew also that they would be comforted by the fact that they had the warning early enough that not one of their kin had risked being caught in the weather.

Vanessa stared, captivated by the blaring alert for a moment before her eyes drifted to the window opened up on the screen showing the valetik and the current condition outside. She blanched.

"That... really is one hell of a storm," she observed quietly.

He inclined his head, both in agreement and out of an innate desire to comfort her. "It is, but you are completely safe here. The estate has backup systems that will keep us comfortably warm, but even in the off chance of those going offline, there are plenty of old hearths in the rooms and emergency fuel stored in the cellars below."

She blew out a long breath and nodded. She didn't look entirely convinced, and the smile she turned on him once more was weaker than it had been, but her effort to battle back her fear was admirable.

"So, shall we continue with our tour then?" she asked, the strain in her voice barely audible as the snow billowed with the howling wind on the screen.

He glanced at the corridor ahead and grimaced. The common

wing was coming to an end. Soon it would split off, going separate directions for the wings housing unmated females and unmated males. Even with his position, he could not enter the unmated females' wing, and while a female may freely enter the male wing on his invitation, everything in Jor'y protested taking her anywhere near there. He acknowledged that his distaste was likely due to the fact that he did not occupy that wing since he was *the* valmek. Even if the rest of the valmek line hadn't died out, he still would not have been housed there, and no more inclined to take his a'talyna there. That it was currently only occupied by his human guests did not make it any more appealing.

He fluffed out his wings uncomfortably as he grasped at the first thing that came to mind. "Perhaps the great armory?" he suggested, and inwardly hissed at himself.

That was hardly romantic.

To his surprise, Vanessa's eyes lit up with interest. "Do you keep antique weapons down there as well?"

"Actually, yes." His reply was slow, unable to believe his good fortune that she was actually agreeable to his impromptu suggestion. "Do you have an interest in weapons?"

A small, wicked sound of amusement escaped her that thrilled every quill of his feathers. "I can't say I know many women who aren't a bit dazzled by old weapons. Especially blades, like swords."

"We have something like that," he said quickly, latching on to the direction of her thoughts. If he could dazzle his mate with his skill at the ki'thwan, then he would gladly perform for her for hours at her pleasure. "We will need to return to the o'dari and proceed left and down the staircase from there."

His entire body froze with wonder as his female stepped in close, leaning into him as she wrapped her much smaller arm around his.

"All right. Lead the way," she whispered, her voice so near a purr that it set him into motion.

He was nearly rushing her back down the hall, her laughter further warming him as he too laughed and slowed his pace to more manageable strides.

CHAPTER 11

Vanessa didn't know what she had expected, but not something that practically looked like a museum. Granted, there was a large set of wrought iron doors that led to the locker storing the actual combat weapons, but the rest of the armory itself was gorgeous, weapons displayed against vibrant materials that felt similar to velvets dyed to crimson and burgundy hues.

As luxurious as it was, however, it was nothing compared to being held tenderly against his side, one enormous wing curved around her. His body heat alone warmed her thoroughly, and what that didn't do, her own rising arousal was more than taking care of. She was disappointed when he released her to step away, his wings gracefully folding against his back so he could properly show her the armory.

Her eyes tracked him as he walked over to a stand that had an enormous curved blade. It almost looked something like a sword, except the blade was broader than anything she'd seen before and had a long hilt with a wickedly spiked end. The muscles of his arm flexed, the tendons of his forearm standing out as he effortlessly picked it up with one hand, swinging it in a wide arc. His expression, normally appearing more stoic to her with his face's more limited range of movement, lifted into one of pleasure as a fanged smile spread across his face. Gold eyes gleaming, they narrowed as he went through a range of movements, twirling the blade in graceful strike patterns, his wings alternately stretching defensively around him or flattening against his back as needed. Even his tail moved in patterns where the feathers were either flared or snapped shut in a whipping strike.

This was a side to the Aturians that she never would have guessed existed.

Finishing the set, he turned and strode over to her with smooth, even steps, holding the weapon out between his hands for her inspection.

"This is the ki'thwan. It is a traditional weapon often favored among valmeks. I was trained to wield it in my youth and still make a point to go through exercises with my own personal ki'thwan." His eyes sparkled warmly. "One that is a bit less ornamental or possessing priceless historical value," he added. "This one belonged to my ancestor, who was awarded it by Emperor Av'herekthinal for slaying a great beast that ravaged the continent. His own ki'thwan broke in the beast's skull. It is still displayed at the palace, the broken blade caught for all time in the bone."

"It's beautiful," she murmured, her eyes traveling its length in awe.

To her surprise, he smiled and held it out to her, inviting her appreciation. She eyed the blade, marveling at its historical value before reaching out to skim a finger along the length of the blade's flat side. Despite its age, it held a razor-sharp edge. Ornamental or not, it was no less a weapon for its beauty.

Jor'y turned and placed the ki'thwan back on its stand after giving her a moment to admire it. "But that was long ago, long before outsiders came from the stars, and changed the course for our people."

She licked her lips. "There were some good things from that, I hope."

He glanced up at her, his eyes sharpening. "Few," he growled. "We gained advances in our technology, but nothing that we would not have achieved ourselves with a bit more time. We were already advancing by leaps without them. It was never worth the price that was paid. Nothing was. Not even the little pleasures that we enjoy due to the arrival of humanity. You are the one species that seems to have a passion for joys and pleasures almost equal to our own. It is no wonder so many of my people take to yours," he admitted with a quirk of his lips. He hesitated then, his eyes softening as they traveled over her. A wing stretched toward her, fanning down her back in a soft glide of feathers. "The only gratitude I have experienced for the presence of humans is entirely recent… and it is because it is what brought you here."

She blushed, once again taken off-guard by his honest admiration. There was nothing coy or flirtatious about it. No need to decipher cues. He was so direct and honest that it was as refreshing as it was disarming. He had no reason to enjoy the presence of humans based off the little bit of information he had shared earlier, and yet he was thankful for her.

Flustered, she nodded to the ki'thwan. "I'm really surprised that you have such incredible weaponry. I've always been told that the Aturians are a peaceful species, inclined to pacifism. I can't get over the difference that I've seen since arriving here."

His answering smile was sharp with an edge of menace. Knowing that the aggression was not directed at her, she couldn't help the small intake of breath and thrilling rush of desire in the look given her.

"We are," he said with the slightest trill, his wings and tail fanning as he circled her. "My first desire is to share joy and pleasure. It is rooted in our culture and in our natural drive as a species. If you had been taken in by any of those within my valetik, that would have been much of what you experienced. But I am also a valmek, which means I'm of a line of warriors in my valetik which comes with... sharper... needs and desires."

His eyes hooded, the gleam of gold somehow all the more luminous and intense. His gaze slid over her appreciatively, and he took a reluctant step back as his expression slipped once more into a stoic regard.

Jor'y was holding back. For all the desire she'd caught glimpses of, she knew it was hot enough to incinerate all of her defenses. If he directed the full weight of it on her—hell, even a little of it for more than a few minutes—she would be nothing but goo. He was giving her space, leaving the ball entirely in her court. Respectful, honorable, a warrior... Gods, it was the sort of material that melted the pages off every historical romance ever penned.

Whatever this was between them, there was no chance of it having a happy ending, but gods did she ever want to see where it could possibly lead. This was the sort of thing that filled her dreams all of her adult life being offered to her on a silver platter. It was the fantasy that was fueling her newest writing endeavor, all of it focused on this inexplicable draw she had toward him.

Was it worth the risk?

His lips tipped in a quiet smile, and he politely extended a hand. She placed her hand in his and allowed her to draw her to the next display. The moment had passed, and while there was a possibility of recapturing it, the small, frightened part of her was grateful for the opportunity to give it more consideration now that he had made his interest abundantly clear.

She bit her lip as they approached an impressive heavily ridged breastplate with curving spikes along the shoulder plating. It was as if she thought she was expected to give some sort of forever commitment. Jor'y didn't ask for that, and for all she knew, he didn't have anything of the sort in mind. Ever since she arrived, their tendency to seek out others for sexual pleasure—especially around Hashavnal—had been impressed upon her. Why not just sit back and enjoy it? It is not like anyone would actually know. Every touch, every encounter, could be something cherished and enjoyed without guilt.

A warmth settled in her belly as her imagination immediately produced the most graphic examples of just how he might touch her. His long, curved claws scraping gently over her skin. The erotic sweep of his feathers intimately against her.

Holy shit.

She produced a smile and nodded with an appropriate amount of enthusiastic awe as he lifted one weapon after the other, demonstrating their uses as she desperately tried to pull her mind out of the gutter into which it had plunged. The vivid nature of her imagination was usually a good thing—but it normally struck at more opportune moments, where she was privately working and could indulge in such fantasies through her characters. This moment was not it.

Oh, sure, she could jump him in the armory. In fact, she almost went for it until just how public they were was driven home when she heard the sound of booted feet approaching. Glancing in the direction of the footsteps from under her lashes, she inwardly groaned with a silent curse.

Carthy.

He didn't so much as look their way, his attention presumably absorbed by the weapons on display, but she wasn't a fool. Nor was Jor'y. His eyes tracked the other male, his feathers along his neck and collar ruffling. When it appeared that Carthy wasn't going to make any move but nor did he seem interested in moving on, Jor'y sighed and bent a frustrated look at her to which she responded with an apologetic shrug. It seemed that she was stuck with a chaperone for the time being whether she liked it or not.

If she wanted to explore this thing with him, she was going to have to be sneakier and evade her well-meaning guards. It wasn't like she could invite Jor'y to her quarters. Not only was that too obvious, but she had gotten the impression that males in the unmated females wing wasn't a thing among the Aturians. She could invite herself to his room—and she wasn't sure exactly how she would go about that without coming off as way too forward. *Damn.*

Jor'y fidgeted with the small satchel in his hand before setting the explosive powder down on the table next to a very large war hammer. He had just finished showing her the dark grains. Although they had seemed harmless enough, the slow, thoughtful way he set them down reminded her that they fueled the weapon propped on the floor beside the table—something she could only describe as some sort of harness cannon for what she assumed to be aerial combat.

His hand now empty, he extended it toward her, and she threaded her fingers with his, drawing his warm regard back to her, cutting through his chilly focus on Carthy.

"I believe it is almost time for the evening meal," he murmured. "Shall we make our way to the dining area?"

"Sounds good. Are you coming, Carthy?" she called out with a feigned sweetness that had the man snapping his head up with a faintly guilty expression at being caught eavesdropping.

"I could eat," he agreed. He gave one last glance around the armory before fixing Jor'y with a polite smile. "This place is really amazing. You have a lot of history preserved here. Some of this must be worth a fortune."

The Aturian beside her inclined his head. "Our people do have a very long and colorful history," he agreed, offering no further commentary.

Carthy returned the smile a bit stiffly. "I'll see you in the dining room then," he said as he eased past them.

With the way he had lingered moments ago, Vanessa was surprised how eager he seemed to part with them as quickly as possible. Curious, she stared after him until Jor'y stepped forward, tugging on her hand. He tilted his head at her, his hand tightening on hers in the smallest squeeze. She returned the squeeze with a slight press of her fingers to silently communicate that all was well and stepped forward to his side.

As they left the armory behind them, her mind turned again toward the seemingly impossible task of finding some privacy.

CHAPTER 12

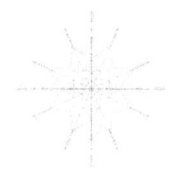

Jor'y scowled at the snow. The storm was a twist to his tail. After several days of foul weather, he missed the comforting glow of the valetik from most places in the estate. Today, like every day for the past nine days, there was nothing but a sheet of white outside as the snow came down so fast that it blotted out everything else. His wings shuddered as a distinct feeling of claustrophobia crawled over him. It was ridiculous, of course. The estate was larger than any other home in the valetik, but he usually spent at least a few hours flying over the valetik and nearest mountains every day. Being shut indoors without any escape was distinctly unpleasant for him every time the winter storms descended.

His one consolation was the fact that he wasn't alone. Having a number of his distant kin living in his abode, even if he seldom saw them, was one comfort, though he wished he had been able to convince Vi'ryk to take quarters in one of the wings. He understood the male's reasoning was to provide a more public face for Jor'y among the rest of the valetik—and there was the fact that his mate wished to live in the valetik near her family. He understood it, and fully supported Vi'ryk's decision... most of the time.

He grimaced. He hated to admit it, but he was more than a little dependent on his cousin's cool head and quick advice. Although Jor'y was unaccustomed to going more than a day or two without Vi'ryk's presence for at least a few hours—which was aggravating enough—he especially felt the lack of it now to remind him that it was necessary to be nice to his human guests. Guests who were sorely testing his patience by their increasing persistence in making a nuisance of themselves.

Ever since Carthy had interrupted his attempt to court Vanessa while touring the armory, Jor'y had struggled to find time alone with her outside of their usual supervised time together in the o'dari. He was certain that men were orchestrating a "guard" appearing whenever he tried to find a private moment with her, and it did not encourage hospitable feelings toward them. In fact, his feelings toward his guests were becoming less and less in line with Aturian customs regarding proper hosting. He needed Vi'ryk in his ear to remind him of that when his patience was tested the most.

Dragging a hand down his face, Jor'y hissed to himself, his ear tipping back when the sound of claws scuffing against stone drew his attention.

"You asked for me?" Sa'tari murmured from a respectful distance behind him.

Turning from the window, he smiled and inclined his head. "Yes, thank you, Sa'tari." Walking across the room toward his desk, he tipped his head curiously. "I have been meaning to talk to you. How are you enjoying your new position? I trust that everything is well."

She nodded, her face lighting up. "Very much so. Vanessa is getting a bit restless, being stuck indoors as we are, but she is very pleasant to assist and pass the day with." Her expression turned sly. "I think having such privileged access to your o'dari helps. It is very generous of you. Do you, perhaps, intend for her to stay?"

He peered back at her, his eyes narrowing. "That is a bold question."

Sa'tari's laughter filled the space between them. "I may not be as close a relation as Vi'ryk, but I would think that I know my valmek well enough to know that you are behaving in an uncommon manner around her. Well, uncommon for you," she amended with a grin.

His crown feathers fluffed with disconcertment. He had not believed himself to be so obvious. Especially not when he had to work so hard to get his a'talyna to notice his attentions. Unfortunately, that made it all the more obvious to the males with her, which was the chief source of his frustration to add to the mounting sexual frustration and his need to link with his mate. Of course his people would pick up on such cues quickly.

He reached back and smoothed his feathers with his hand. "Perhaps I have been behaving a bit out of the norm," he admitted.

She gave him a knowing look. "A bit? You have been peacefully and quite happily sharing your private o'dari with her. When not together, you have been prowling around the estate aggressively searching for her for the last two days." Sa'tari took a step forward. "If I may ask… what is it that you are looking for? Vanessa is easy enough to seek out if you wish to court her, since you already spend a good portion of the day in the same room with her. I am assuming that is your wish," she added carefully.

"Of course I wish it. She is my a'talyna! My blood burns ceaselessly for her," he admitted, noting the pleased gasp that left the female. No doubt it would soon be news among every Aturian in his valetik residing within his walls. "But the ease of locating her in the estate… that is part of the problem," he growled, jerking his head to the left to direct his glare harmlessly at his desk. He would not emotionally wound his kin, even unintentionally, by forcing her to be the recipient of his ire. "She is too easy to seek out. Any time I desire to court her, it is rendered impossible by those... males."

He watched Sa'tari's lips purse with displeasure. For as close as he was to committing a grave trespass against his hosting responsibilities, the interference in his courtship would be viewed by his kin as an equal, if not more serious, breach of etiquette. Although he had been aware of that point, seeing the fury crossing his kin's face brought distinct clarity at just how displeased they would be. He had underestimated it.

"This is not right!" she hissed, her long crown feathers shooting up like a white aura around her head. Her wings snapped, the feathers vibrating from the rapid action as her tail whipped unhappily behind her. "It is the highest of cruelty to interfere in joining... especially of an a'talynal pair!"

He lifted a clawed hand helplessly. "But what am I to do? They are my guests. I cannot dismiss them nor confine them to their rooms, not without violating our hosting customs."

Sa'tari's tail lowered as her expression turned pensive. "This is true. Short of them attempting to harm her, your household, you, there is little else that would be seen as reasonable for taking such actions. Not without risking reprisals from the magistrate assigned to our region." She rubbed a hand thoughtfully against the scruff of fine feathers at her throat. "Perhaps what you need is a secret meeting."

Standing behind his desk, he faced her and planted his hands on its surface and leaned forward. "That is exactly what I have been attempting... unsuccessfully." He tilted his head thoughtfully. "Do you have any suggestions for where this might be arranged? Somewhere that would be pleasing to her... and worthy of courting my a'talyna," he added.

Although he doubted that Sa'tari would recommend some

dark pit of a room, he wanted to court his mate properly, which required more refinement than that.

She nodded slowly. "I think I have an idea. Permit me to speak of it to my a'talyna tonight, and I will see to it that everything is arranged."

With a dip of her head, she turned to leave but drew to a stop after a few moments to look back at him abashedly as if just realizing that he did not give her leave to depart. He was surprised, therefore, when words began to spill from her.

"Jor'y, there is one other thing. I forgot to mention that my brother is returning to the valetik to take a position Vi'ryk offered him at the estate. I only mention it because he returns with his human mate in time for the Hashavnal. Perhaps the presence of another mated human female will be something that can assist in your courting?"

Jor'y frowned, searching his memory. "Your brother is Da'yel, is this correct? I seem to remember that male being a headache with his mischievous nature before he left."

Her lips twitched with an amusement she failed to hide as she inclined her head in agreement. "That would be him, although you would be relieved to know that he has mellowed some with a mate to care for."

No doubt from experiencing the harsh realities of life away from the protection of the valetik as well.

"If Vi'ryk considers him suitable for his position, I trust his judgement," he murmured, his attention distracted by a missive on the datapad on his desk. He scowled at the list of trade representatives due to arrive for the festivities. He hoped that Da'yel had matured sufficiently if he was being employed by the household. He did not need an ill-timed disaster, especially not when he was courting. He looked up at Sa'tari. "What position was he hired for?"

She fidgeted in place and coughed. "He is, uh... to be a

member of the guard here."

He dropped down into his chair, his wings folding back behind him as he settled into it. "I trust he has been informed of the importance of this upcoming delegation?"

Sa'tari quickly nodded. "He has. And I will be sure to inform him of the delicate situation with Vanessa. His mate had relocated to Aturia with no intention of returning to Earth. Abandoning her citizenship rights was of little consequence for her. I will impress upon him the delicacy of this matter."

"Good," he rumbled, a long sigh hissing between his teeth. "You may return to your duties. And, Sa'tari," he called as the female gave a bob of her head and turned to go, drawing her up short once more. "Thank you," he said quietly, the words spoken with heartfelt genuineness.

She smiled and disappeared through the door, leaving him to hope that everything went as well as she planned. His eyes reluctantly returned to the storm raging outside. How different and easier things might have been if he had met Vanessa in the spring. His plumage would be in its customary brilliant hue, and he could have walked with her in the vast gardens or taken her flying for a moment of privacy. He would not have been stuck within the confines of his estate with nosy, interfering men. With his options so limited, he could only pray that Sa'tari was successful.

And that Da'yel and his human mate would be a more a boon than a hindrance to what was to come.

CHAPTER 13

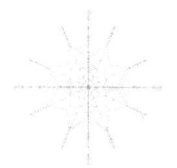

*V*anessa worried her bottom lip with her teeth for a moment as she stared at the unopened comm from her marketer. It was just beneath the opened message from her mother, demanding that she make a visual comm call to verify her identity. It was absurd when they couldn't even get a vid comm successfully across Aturia to speak to someone in charge at Dahlia colony. Carthy had likewise been forced to send a brief message letting them know that they were waiting out the storm safely and would comm when the lines cleared.

Not that she could even let her mother know as much since the comms had come in scant minutes before long-range communications system failed days ago. Her mother's tirade over her being a possible imposter trying to deceive her had been easy enough to deal with, but the one from her marketer, Katherine, she had been sitting on, anxious to look at the reader feedback forwarded to her.

Thank the gods for Katherine. The woman was a godsend, taking on every aspect of organizing Vanessa's professional life the moment the editor approved the initial few chapters and sent them back to Vanessa for revisions. The moment she uploaded them to the server, Katherine took over and sent daily reports. The comm could contain very good news—or extraordinarily bad news that could force her to come up with something entirely different if reader receptivity wasn't there.

Every day, she had opened her comm systems to look at that downloaded message, and not once had she had the courage to open it. In a way, she was torturing herself, but she also knew that she couldn't put it off forever. As soon as the storm cleared to allow a good interplanetary signal, she would be sending a large batch of chapters out to Katherine. If it turned out to be bad, it would mean days of writing would have been wasted and she would have to spend even more hours making up for lost time.

Please don't be bad news.

"Thank the gods for blunt human teeth or your poor lip would be in tatters," Sa'tari teased, making Vanessa release her lip with a wry grin.

"Thankfully," she agreed, lowering the datapad to her lap. "Though even flat teeth take enough of a toll on it, which I remind myself every time I chew it ragged. It's a terrible habit I've never managed to break myself of. One that my mother is forever scolding me over," Vanessa added sheepishly.

The Aturian chuckled as she strode into the room with a tray effortlessly balanced in her hands. Her neck craned as she set the tray of tea and exotic baked goods made with dried local fruits that Vanessa found incredibly addicting and squinted at the screen. "What are you looking so hard at?"

"A comm that came in earlier. It's from my marketer... It's about the chapters I put up. Or more accurately, reader feedback that's come in."

Sa'tari glanced at her, tipping her head in a manner that somehow managed to convey the same inquisitiveness as an arched eyebrow. "So why not open it? No doubt you must be eager to see how your readers are enjoying it."

Vanessa grimaced. That was the crux of the problem. She was eager but also scared shitless. "Yes and no," she said at length. "It's possible that everyone, or even a majority of them, just hates it. Everything is coming together so well with my writing that I think it would kill me if they hated it."

The female chuckled again and poured some tea into a tulip-shaped cup designed to be held beneath the lip by Aturian claws and pushed it toward her. "Exaggerating some, are you not?"

Vanessa laughed weakly and carefully picked up the cup beneath that same lip where it also happened to be the coolest to touch. "Maybe a little," she admitted. "Call it author anxiety with a good dose of imposter syndrome."

The Aturian tipped her head again, her eyes narrowing this time speculatively. "You have readers do you not?"

"Well, sure…"

"Then you are a writer, not an imposter, and that is all that matters. If they do not love it, then you will find out and find the right people who burn to read more of the story."

Vanessa's mouth twitched. "You make it sound pretty damn easy."

"Because it is easy. Your worrying is just making it a hundred times harder than it needs to be," she said sweetly as she took a seat across from her and began to stir a thick sweetener into her tea with a narrow paddle-shaped utensil made of silver. When she finished, Sa'tari lifted it from the cup and waved it in Vanessa's direction with an authoritative flair. "It is romance—love, pleasure, and things of the heart, worthy subjects to any Aturian. Since I am Aturian and your assistant, that makes me the best advisor here, and I say to listen to what your heart says. If you love it, that is most important. You will figure out the exact way to tell your story that makes hearts yearn for more. But the only way to get there is to open your comm and find out. If you had feathers, I swear they would be piling on the floor around you," she tsked, clicking her tongue against the back of her sharp teeth.

Vanessa grinned at the female and picked up her datapad again. Unlike other "friends" she had over the years, the Aturian had zero interest or care to understand where Vanessa came from socially or what privileges she had access to. None of the Aturians she had met seemed to know or care to know about who her family was. Even Jor'y. She never would have guessed just how much just being herself, away from the social politics on Earth, would actually mean to her. Especially when it came to enjoying developing new relationships.

That the Aturians were surprisingly forthright in their views and feelings took some getting accustomed to, but it was refreshing. She liked knowing Jor'y's need for her instead of playing games. And as for Sa'tari, her friend was forthright with her opinion, but it was always offered out of a place of affection.

Besides, Vanessa couldn't say that she was wrong in this case. She let her finger hover over the message for a moment and took a deep breath.

Squeezing her eyes shut, Vanessa pressed down, hearing the audible chime of the datapad as the message projected. Slowly opening one eye and then the other, her mouth gaped open as she saw the headlines of praise, each conveying short message of enthusiasm, not only pouring in from colonies but also from Earth too, thanks to a discreet server that Katherine discovered. Sure, there were a few disgruntled readers who found the attraction of the human heroine toward an alien male to be revolting, but it was so outweighed by the support and messages conveying eagerness to read more that she felt her eyes tear up with gratitude.

Sa'tari gave her a worried look. "It is bad?"

Vanessa shook her head. "No. Not at all." She swiped a hand over her eyes and laughed. "I mean, yeah, a couple of readers made some pretty rude comments, but this… they love it. They all want to know what happens next."

The female grinned. "See. What did I tell you?" She leaned forward. "So, what *does* happen next?"

Vanessa's mouth fell open, her mind going blank. She didn't know. She had been filling pages, several chapters worth, with brief, half-illicit encounters, more fueled by dreams than anything else, and some sweet moments inspired by just being near Jor'y, but she had no idea how to get them together, not when her heroine was constantly blocked by an overprotective brother.

Shit.

"I guess… get them together," she answered. "Somehow."

Sa'tari's expression turned sly, her smile widening. "It seems that your heroine suffers the same dilemma that you do."

Vanessa gave her a startled look, closing the comm. She could feel her cheeks filling with unbidden heat. "What do you mean? I don't have a dilemma."

"Certainly. A female arriving at the doorstep of an alien male who takes her and her brother in from the storm. No similarities to you at all," Sa'tari replied, her eyes squinting in a calculating manner that made Vanessa fidget in place despite her best attempts not to. The female shrugged. "Very well. Perhaps then you will just indulge me in a game to get the inspiration moving. I will need to plan few things, but we can have a little adventure exploring the estate that might give you some more inspiration."

Vanessa blinked at her. "That is… unexpected," she said slowly. "But not a bad idea. Maybe seeing something new around here might fuel my imagination a bit more." Gods only knew that a few of those corridors had fueled her dreams enough to inspire a couple chapters alone. Seeing more of the castle couldn't hurt. "Are you sure that it won't be a problem? I don't want you to get into any trouble taking me to places I can't go."

Her friend smiled happily and sipped from her cup. "Do not worry. It will be fine. Leave it all to me."

"Okay." Slanting the Aturian a curious glance, Vanessa settled back into her chair and lifted her own cup once more, her eyes drifting to the white view on the other side of a nearby window. "An adventure it will be. If nothing else, it should at least be a nice distraction from all this weather."

"A very fine distraction," Sa'tari agreed happily.

The suspicious part of Vanessa that was accustomed to looking for hidden motivations among her companions had her squinting at her friend, but she shook her head and dismissed it. The Aturians were generally of a happier disposition than most species, and Sa'tari was no exception. It wasn't fair to suspect anything else than what her friend suggested.

It was a shame. Some mischief could be amusing.

If she were honest with herself, she really just hoped that, somehow, she would end up running into Jor'y somewhere. It was unlikely, though, since she got the impression that he didn't spend a lot of time in much of the castle, his duties keeping him occupied through the later part of the midday after leaving the o'dari… but she could dream. If nothing else, it could feed her imagination more.

Smiling, she took a large sip of her tea and opened her datapad and set it up, initiating the holo keyboard in the process. She had a most delicious scene come to mind of the heroine getting separated from her friend and encountering the hero in some dark corridor in the depths of the castle. Aware of Sa'tari's amused gaze on her, she allowed the world around her to fade away as she got lost once again in her world filled with stolen moments of hot kisses and roaming hands.

Perhaps this time her heroine's brother would not interrupt. Vanessa couldn't wait to see what further inspiration the next day would bring.

CHAPTER 14

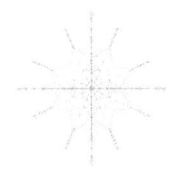

The lower halls of the castle weren't the dark, dreary, or ghostly corridors that Vanessa had imagined. Modernization had reached even there, much to the disappointment of her artistic soul. In fact, the decor verged on cheerful. Over the last few days, with the Aturian winter holidays approaching, the castle had been filled with twisted chains of colorful vines in varying hues of red, each interwoven with berries of different colors and sizes—small purple cones, squat, almost flat pink discs, and perfect little gold spheres. Tall spires formed from woven red, green, and white branches were set out in tall pots at either side of every door.

While the lower floors weren't as lushly decorated and lacked the glass baubles hanging from the ceiling, she couldn't help but marvel at the fact that some of it had managed to creep down there. It didn't look quite like being caught in the midst of a candy cane forest like it did in the main foyer and corridors, but it still jarred her from the mood and setting she had formed in her mind.

Damn.

A grimace pulled at her lips. That was unfortunate. She shrugged off the feeling. Okay, it wasn't as dramatic as she had painted it in the first half of the chapter. That was what she had an imagination for. The brightly lit stone walls could easily become damped and coated with years of grime, lit up with only a few far-spaced torches.

It wasn't that she had anything against the insane, over-the-top cheerfulness of the holiday decor. Quite the contrary, she loved it with the sort of childlike fervor of one who grew up with only pristine order in the holidays rather than a gleeful chaos of colors that others always seemed to have, and she had always lacked in her own home. No, every day she looked forward to and marveled at each new addition added, and even made a point to stroll through every corridor on the main floor to see what was new. She had included plenty of that in her book to add a touch of holiday whimsy that her readers had gushed about in the comm she'd received.

But right now, she wanted darkness and mystery.

"Just a little farther," Sa'tari said cheerfully. "You are going to love this!"

Vanessa felt her lips twist reluctantly in amusement at her friend's enthusiasm. "I don't suppose there's a chance that it might be dark and magical, would it?"

The Aturian glanced over at her in surprise. "Is that what you want? Why did you not say so? This is the optimum level of light for human eyes, but I can set it to the pleasure and privacy lighting if you prefer… Just take hold of my arm so I can steer you. I don't think you will see well enough to keep from running into anything."

Grinning with excitement, Vanessa grabbed ahold of her arm, her eyes widening when, at Sa'tari's command, the hall was plunged into darkness only to reveal a magical sparkle of lights that seemed to cascade through the air. Too dim to really see well by—Sa'tari had been correct there—Vanessa felt like she had been plunged into an entirely different world. It wasn't the same as what she wrote, but it added something more to it, a magical element. While the cascades of light were natural here, she immediately improvised the setting in her head to have a sort of bioluminescent slime that glimmered from where it grew in delicate patterns on the walls.

With her hold light on her friend's arm and her steps a bit slower due to the necessary caution that the low lighting required, Vanessa indulged in what had to be the perfect atmosphere for a romantic encounter. She turned to say as much when Sa'tari's arm slipped out from beneath her hand, leaving her grasping nothing but air.

"Sa'tari?" she called out, her eyes searching the dark. "Where are you?"

She heard a scrape of claws to her left where her friend had been seconds before and nearly sighed in relief until a larger body suddenly pressed up against her, muscular arms caging around her. She choked as a scream rose in her throat, and she felt the male freeze. Glowing gold eyes narrowed down at her, and a deep voice barked out a sharp command that brightened the room just enough that her overwrought imagination was able to clearly see who held her captive. His familiar scent finally seeped through, and she collapsed against him with a shudder.

"Oh my gods. Oh, fuck," she wheezed against his chest. "Jor'y! Are you trying to kill me? Where the hell is Sa'tari?"

He peered down at her, his head tipping the side, his expression completely baffled. "She did not tell you?" She heard his wings flutter anxiously behind him. "I did not know that she had orchestrated this without your knowledge," he murmured, drawing back. "Forgive my assumption, I was just eager… No, there is no excuse. My apologies, Vanessa," he said with quiet formality.

She gaped at him, her mind catching up to what was going on. Sa'tari had arranged for her to meet with Jor'y alone.

That sneaky... Words failed her.

Jor'y made to leave, and Vanessa immediately reacted as she quickly grabbed at him, tangling her fingers with his own, his claws raking lightly against her hand in the process. He stared down at her hand in dismay at the red scratches that they had left in their passing, but she didn't relinquish his hand. She couldn't—not when she finally had exactly what she wanted in her grasp.

"No, it's okay," she stammered.

Had she spoiled the moment already? Her cheeks reddened as he returned her regard from his impressive height. An uncomfortable silence stretched between them as he eyed her. She was beginning to wonder if she needed to say something or make a move when he stepped close to her and pulled her into his arms once more, his chest rumbling with a deep purring trill of pleasure that made her heart jackhammer.

Just like that, her body flooded with desire. All it took was a look, the addictive spicy scent of him, and the muscled length of his body pressed against her own to short circuit her brain and allow need to roar forth. His massive chest rose as he dragged in a deep breath. A low growl filled the hall, and she shivered in reaction, knowing exactly what he scented. It wasn't fair, the sort of effect he had on her, but at least she knew that it wasn't one-sided. She may not have the sense he had, but she could feel the prod of his cock against her belly, sending her own lust soaring higher. There was no doubt in her mind that she drew a similar reaction from him.

Finally, yes.

Everything that about that moment was perfect. She wanted to take a covert glance around just to make sure that no one was going to try to walk on them this time. It couldn't happen... not right now when she was so close to combusting.

"Carthy...?" she began quietly.

"Occupied elsewhere trying to track down where we are

hiding," Jor'y chuckled, his breath warming her ear as he bent down from his great height to nuzzle her neck. "He has all of his men assigned to search different wings. Or at least so one of my guards overheard and reported to me."

Pulling back enough so that she could meet his eye, Vanessa frowned. "Too bad that the storm couldn't take out the personal comms in here too."

He chuckled. "That would make carrying out my duties decidedly more difficult. It is merely inconvenient that Carthy is making use of it in his attempt to find us, but this is a restricted floor," he whispered against her skin as his lips trailed beneath her ear. "Sa'tari selected well. It has been a long time since I had even thought about this part of the estate."

She shivered at the touch, panting. "And where, exactly, is this?"

"The hatchery," he breathed.

Vanessa froze, her fingers curling against his arm. "The... what?" she squeaked. "As in eggs?"

She must have sounded a little horrified because he chuckled and leaned down to nuzzle his nose against hers.

"Do not be concerned. The term is not literal. We do not hatch from eggs... or at least not anymore," he amended. "It has been countless generations since we have due to an evolutionary change within our species. It is only a matter of tradition that we kept the term for the area where younglings are tended to and educated."

She relaxed against him once more, her breath coming out in a shaky laugh. "Fuck. A nursery. We're meeting up for a bit of privacy in a children's nursery and school." Her brow furrowed. "Why is it closed? What about the families living here who have children?"

Jor'y straightened and shook his head, his expression sad. "They have taken to utilizing a different room closer to their wing. The valmek line is dying out in our valetik. For that reason, we no longer fill the estate with young to require a floor to occupy and entertain them, so this space is closed off most of the time, only accessed by the cleaning bots." He glanced around. "It seems that Sa'tari was determined to at least make it presentable."

Vanessa glanced around covertly, looking for any sign of possible entry. Aside from one tightly sealed door to the left of them, there was nothing except a larger door at the end of the hall that likewise looked like it was locked down.

"I guess this means we won't be interrupted by anyone."

"Correct. They would not even know how to access this level. Since this location was where our younglings were protected, it has the highest security."

"Perfect," she whispered as she reached up and grabbed two handfuls of the long white feathers trailing over his shoulders, dragging his mouth down to hers.

His head dropped without protest, his lips grazing her for a moment as a deep rumble rolled through his chest. Without warning, he yanked her up off her feet, his head angling to capture her mouth with his.

Need ignited at the touch of their lips, their kiss rocking through her with a savagery that made her grip him even tighter to her. An erotic graze of feathers brushed her hips, the feeling dulled by clothing and yet still leaving a hot trail in its wake. The sides of his tongue had tiny ridges framing it that made her shiver with every brush against hers. Vanessa had no idea what functional purpose they served, nor the stiff tri-ridged tip of his tongue, but she was certainly enjoying the benefits. Every slide had her squirming against him until he reluctantly withdrew, his lips brushing hers once more in a feather-soft touch before drifting from her lips to her chin.

Trailing tiny kisses across her skin, Jor'y made his way along her jawbone and eventually down her neck. He lingered over her pulse, placing a small stinging nip there that had her jerking up against him, her breasts flattening against his chest, teasing the stiff buds of her nipples beneath her sweater and bra. His deep growl filled her ears before he descended further, his kisses becoming more feverish as his tongue began to stroke over her collarbone, tasting her. The heat of his wings pressed closer around her, one set of these large clawed digits slid supportively under her ass as another set gripped her shoulders, holding her tightly against him.

She might have wondered about it until she felt his arms release her, his hands slowly dragging down her body as if to memorize its every contour. When they came to her belly, his fingers gathered up the hem of her sweater and dipped beneath so that his claws scraped erotically against the sensitive flesh there. She shivered, hot heat pooling between her thighs.

His hands smoothed against her belly, and he suddenly growled, his fingers grasping her hips when she dared to undulate against him, moving her cloth-covered mons against the rigid length of his sex hidden beneath his own clothing. He closed his mouth around her shoulder, his teeth pressing lightly against her sweater, and groaned. His large frame shuddered all around her, his wings flexing closer around before relaxing at the same moment his teeth released her. He brushed his nose against the base of her neck, moving upward until he pressed his forehead against hers, the light pressure of his hornbase completely alien and yet somehow right.

"You cannot touch me like that. I will have no restraint if you do. Tonight, I mean only to court you, my Vanessa," he rasped, his voice strained as he pleaded. "Nothing more. Please do not test my honor in this. I fear I am far too weak when it comes to you, and I refuse to take my a'talyna in the corridor."

She swallowed back her disappointment, embarrassment rapidly rising to stain her cheeks. Fuck, how had she misinterpreted his signals? She knew that Aturians were sexually liberal compared to humans, but she hadn't cared enough to read about their customs regarding sex. Who knew what sort of rules or rituals she was violating? In attempt to save face, she shifted her head just enough against his to approximate a nod. "You're right. This is probably moving a little fast."

He chuckled and drew back, gold eyes gleaming down at her. "Not entirely fast enough for me, but Aturians are not as reserved as humans. If I had my way, you would be accompanying me to my quarters... if I could be certain of a way to get you there without being accosted by a human male. And if I was certain that you would accept my invitation to join?"

The latter he posed as a question as his head tipped inquisitively, and Vanessa stilled in surprise. Was he expecting her to make the first move? Well, she almost had with the way she had initiated their kiss, but what if he was waiting for an outright invitation? Oh, gods, why had she never bothered to do further research? She knew the answer to that. It was because she had expected to be in the human colony on the southern continent, far from any Aturians except for those who might be employed by the Darvel Corporation.

She wasn't shy about her sexuality, but she wasn't entirely sure if she was ready to take the bull by the horns, so to speak, and be the one to initiate it. Not when she was accustomed to the man being the aggressor and initiator, taking much of the decision out of her hands so that she was just able to happily go along with it.

Jor'y smiled and lowered her to feet, gently depositing her. A wing smoothed against the back of her head as he caressed the side of her face with one hand. "Do not worry, my Vanessa. You do not have to make a decision at this moment. There is never any pressure. Males are taught patience in courting our females. If you will allow me freedom to do so, I would be happy to prove myself worthy."

She gaped at him a little. He was practically a prince, and he was asking for permission to prove himself... worthy? She was starting to feel like she had slipped into a completely different reality. The more time she spent in it, the less she wanted to return to the one she had left. Speechless, she nodded in agreement and was rewarded with a flash of sharp teeth as he grinned down at her.

Looping her arm in his, he was suddenly as gallant as any of the gentlemen her mother had introduced her to as he escorted her toward the doorway at the end of the hall. They stopped in front of it for only a moment as he pressed his hand against the keypad. A burst of stale air hit her the moment the door slid open. It smelled faintly like some sort of chalk, aged paper, and cloth, and a hint of limestone that mingled with the distinct scent of the festive berries that Sa'tari had clearly hung in there earlier.

She had no idea what awaited her inside, but she gasped in pleasure as the lights came on the moment that they stepped inside. The room was round and spacious, with a small podium at the furthest point. Several storage latches on one wall held numerous tables and benches pinned up against its surface, keeping them out of the way until they were needed. All except for one long, wide bench set up in the middle of the room, laden with plush pillows and heavy fabric.

At her side, Jor'y trilled deeply and let out a single soft-spoken command. "Night observatory setting initiate."

She gasped as the lights dimmed, all except for a soft violet light at the foot of the bench. The rest of the light was provided from above as countless bright stars shone down on them.

"What is this?"

He nudged her toward the bench with a satisfied smile. "Just a setting for astronomical education... and utilized in more intimate places for restfulness and seduction," he admitted.

Vanessa raised an eyebrow at him. "I thought that there wasn't going to be hanky-panky going on?"

He chuckled, his eyes sparkling with amusement. "I do not know what that is, but if you are referring to joining... no, there will be none of that, but you have given me permission to prove myself."

"I don't follow what you're talking about," she admitted as she allowed him to pull her toward the bench.

With infinite gentleness and care, he dragged her down onto the soft surface with him, his wings closing around her, cocooning her against him as he lay back against the pillow. It put her in the perfect position to see the stars above her as his hand began to stroke along her shoulder. The claws at the joint of his wing gently scraped her shoulder and she smiled, settling more comfortably against him as soft music piped in around them. He whispered to her in a soft voice, telling her stories of his ancestors, and stories of his own childhood in his valetik's mountain.

His deep voice was soft and melodious, leaving her hungering for more, clinging to his whispered words. With every soothing touch and the gentle roll of his voice, she felt closer to him than she had ever felt with anyone. Even more so when he coaxed her own stories from her and listened with eager anticipation as she spoke about her family and life on Earth, their voices blending into soft murmurs to accompany the melody.

As the hour grew later, Vanessa smiled and cuddled against him. If this was what courtship entailed, she enjoyed it a lot more than she would have imagined. She was accustomed to getting to know her prospective partners on a series of dates with meaningless chatter over meals and equally meaningless activities. If someone had suggested this as a date, she probably would have thought them crazy, but here she was, surprisingly content. She was so relaxed and comfortable that she was just shy of being draped bonelessly against him.

Just when she had decided that this was all there was to it, his hand swept low again with a low tone in melody. Hooking his claws on the hem of her sweater, he dragged it up, exposing her belly and bra. Her breath stilled in surprise, and he nuzzled his cheek against hers.

"Permit me?" he whispered huskily.

She nodded and gasped with pleasure when a claw flicked a nipple encased in the silky cloth of her bra, and she moaned, straining toward his touch. He kept every brush of his fingers and claws light as he explored her. He cupped a breast, and she nearly begged for him to do more before his hand was moving again even as her panties began to dampen. She contorted to meet his touches, her breath coming out in soft, strangled pants as she raced toward pleasure. She was so absorbed in his touch that she almost missed it when his body slid to the side, his wing still circled around her, its claws gripping her as he swung around to crouch over her.

Gold eyes rivaled the holographic stars above them as he stared down at her. With a flick of his claw, the fabric of her bra parted and fell to the sides, baring her breasts. His tongue stroked over his lips, the tiny ridges on its sides somehow catching the light with the saliva that appeared to cling to them. She stared back up at him and swallowed. Cupping her breasts in her hands, she offered them and was surprised at the speed at which his head descended to capture a nipple within his hot mouth.

A strangled moan escaped her as his tongue curled and stroked over the nipple, the ridges lightly scraping it as his mouth tugged at it. With the tri-ridged tip flicking at the tip, he nearly had her coming apart, whimpers escaping her as she gripped handfuls of long feathers trailing from his head. She was distantly aware of him removing her pants and panties, but didn't care with the tantalizing pull of his mouth on her breasts, switching from one to the other. On a particularly hard tug on the feathers that made him growl, she was immediately filled with chagrin and released them as if burned.

He released her nipple to peer down at her, his eyes almost liquid in the heat of their intensity.

"Do not stop. My crown feathers are not so delicate… and trust me when I tell you that I enjoy it." His eyes narrowed with a predatory satisfaction. "You will need to hold on for this next part as it is."

"Oh, okay," she stammered. "But what…? Oh, fuck!" she wheezed when he suddenly dropped, his mouth latching onto her sex.

Her hips lifted instinctively, and he took full advantage of it, his hands cupping her ass to draw her closer to his mouth even as his wing claws locked on her, holding her upper body in place. His tongue undulated and twisted, the ridges hitting in strange patterns as he moved the agile muscle, caressing the outer petals before plunging deep inside her cunt to flex and twist as if attempting to taste every inch of that hidden place.

And the depths that his tongue hit! Her eyes nearly crossed as an orgasm caught her by surprise. The second one rose on its heels with the rhythmic thrust of his tongue, its twisting action grazing her clit with every pass as he withdrew and plunged in deep again. Stronger than the last, she felt her entire body quiver with the crescendo of pleasure. Transferring one hand from his crown feathers to one of his horns, she held him in place, her hips moving against his mouth as she chased her climax. The vibration of his growl against her sex sent another wave of pleasure surging through her that broke when his tongue disappeared and his lips wrapped around her clit, sucking hard as he flicked it with the peculiar tip of his tongue.

The scream that left her was primal and probably loud enough to bring in a team to investigate to ensure that she hadn't been murdered if any had heard her. But she reveled in the hot burst of ecstasy flooding through her even as her own orgasm projected outward from her in an explosion. She didn't know the source of the loop feeding back into her, but at that moment she couldn't think clearly enough to analyze it. All she could do was ride the wave of pleasure until it finally quieted, and she was shifted once more into Jor'y's embrace, his arms and wings closing around her in an intimate and loving hold.

Turning her head, she looked back up at him. "What about you?"

He nuzzled her nose with his. "I received everything I longed for from it. Anything more than that is yours tonight."

What was left unsaid was the promise that other nights would have even greater pleasure if she wanted them—mutual pleasure that went far beyond the taste he had given her.

She didn't know how the hell she was going to survive that, but she was game to find out.

CHAPTER 15

Jor'y grinned unrepentantly at the red-faced human standing before him. The male, barely coming up to his shoulder, glared back with an indignant expression as he slammed his hands down on the table between them.

"This is unacceptable! I understand that this is your home, and we're here at your invitation, but protecting Vanessa Williams is *my team's* assignment. One that we take very seriously. And we can't do that when we don't know where she is!" Carthy swiped a hand through his short black hair. "It's bad enough that we have to deal with the fact that you are always lurking around her. Do you have any idea how dangerous what you're doing is?"

Jor'y allowed his wings to partially expand, spreading out from his sides in an expression of innocence. He would play this game for now before bringing home the fact that Aturia was not their Earth nor beholden to their regulation.

"Dangerous? Unless your females are equipped with something that I have not read of that makes mating lethal, I do not see how."

Carthy's hands curled into fists on the wooden surface. His weight shifted onto them as he leaned forward. "Don't play with me, Jor'ytal. Our civilizations have been allies long enough for you to know that, in accordance with United Earth's laws, any of this cross-species mating that you jest so casually about is illegal. Even rumors of Miss Williams fraternizing with you privately could bring her under suspicion. That alone would have the power to damage her reputation and career."

"Then it is a good thing that there is no one within my estate to spread rumors," Jor'y replied coldly. "No Aturian on this mountain would communicate such information to humans, not when we consider such matters very private and sacred, and any interference with them—including speculation over it, an enormous transgression. I trust that *your team* will not actively seek to harm her."

The latter was said in a dangerously soft voice, but the human, to his credit, grimaced as if the idea were personally repugnant to him and nodded. There was a weighty silence between them before Carthy dropped back into his chair with a sigh. Propping an elbow on the arm of his chair, he flicked a couple fingers dismissively.

"You don't have to worry about that from our quarter," he grumbled in a resigned voice. "I am certain that not one of my men would do anything to harm Miss Williams, and they are under orders from me to keep quiet about our time here except in a direct need-to-know basis. As far as our superiors will be aware, she was within our custody the entire time we were here. But we are still going to have a problem."

Jor'y tilted his head. "I do not see how. If she agrees to the mating, then she remains here with me as is right." He held up a silencing hand before the human could protest. That his a'talyna would remain with him was not a point he was willing to argue. It would simply be the natural order of things for a mated pair. "However, if she does not, she returns to the southern continent with you. What is the human expression... no harm, no foul?"

The other male's lips twisted in a rueful smile. "That would be the phrase. Unfortunately, there's one thing you haven't considered."

He could not think of a detail he had not considered. The storm would clear within the next few days, but they would have comms back in no more than three days spans, during which time the crew would be capable of alerting the human colony of their situation, a fact that he had already communicated to his guests. Lowering himself back into his seat, he regarded the male patiently. "Which is?"

Sighing, Carthy rubbed the bridge of his nose. "You haven't calculated how cheap Corp is. We may be hired out from United Earth's military branches, but we work directly for Darvel. They aren't going to discreetly pull us out when they already have a shuttle arriving with a diplomatic party for your holiday festivities. On the contrary, those of us not guarding Miss Williams will be convenient extra bodies on hand. They aren't going to waste the opportunity or an extra shuttle." He lifted his eyes grimly. "They won't ignore your close association with Miss Williams. Everything we see, they will see. And no amount of festivities is going to distract them from that."

The male sat back and rolled his shoulders. "Let me be direct. If she accepts you—and that's a big if—then I'm sure it will be no problem. Aturians have sovereignty that Corp and Earth Gov can't contest. But what if she doesn't? If they even so much as suspect that anything went on between you, they can demand her immediate arrest. Hell, even if she does accept and it's not made official before they get wind of it, they still have grounds to arrest her. You're facing a potentially very tricky situation."

Jor'y frowned, his wings twitching with a ruffle of feathers. "I will not cease my courtship unless my Vanessa demands it. I cannot, but... I would be open to suggestions and assistance so that the issue of our mating is resolved before they arrive."

Carthy's brow dropped low in a fascinating visual display of annoyance. "Are you fucking serious? You can't seriously be asking me to go against everything to help you break the law and mate with her."

Jor'y met his eyes with his own hard, flat stare.

"Why not? Is the human mind really so narrow that it would demand to reinforce constructed barriers between hearts based on misguided notions of species purity?" He curled his lip. "You should be aware that most civilized sectors consider United Earth's legal policies in this to be morally reprehensible." At the surprise on the male's face, his sneer broadened into a hard smile. "Oh, yes, even out here in my mountains with my *primitive appearance* and customs, I had no problem making myself informed on these matters. Now, allow me to be equally direct with you."

Jor'y pushed to his feet, his wings widening even as his crown feathers rose aggressively. "Vanessa is my a'talyna, my heartsong —a rare female of unequal compatibility to me in particular. You cannot understand what that means. As long as she is in agreement, I will do everything I can to prove my worth as a mate to her. While I understand the sacrifice that she would make to remain with me and will respect her decision to go should she choose to leave, I want to make her happy. So yes, I am asking for your assistance because I do not understand your culture."

Dark, piercing eyes regarded him for several heartbeats before Carthy let out another loud sigh. He rubbed his face with both hands, and then they dropped away to reveal a faint crooked smile. "I certainly can't argue against that. I've actually become pretty familiar over the course of my career with what several species have to say about those laws, and the fact that we still hold onto them hasn't really set right with me. And... well, I guess I'm something of a romantic at heart. Some of the other guys are probably going to shit bricks over this, but okay. For what it's worth, I will try to give you some cover. Just do me a favor and try not to be too obvious when the delegates arrive. As for wooing," his expression turned apologetic, "I'm afraid you're going to have to be as clueless about the mysteries of a woman's heart like any other man. The best I can offer is listen, show that you care and appreciate her. My momma always said to be myself, but so far that hasn't worked too well for me, so take that however you like."

"That is not all that helpful," Jor'y grumbled.

Carthy snorted as he stood. "I'm sure it's not, but there you have it. Now anything specific to customs on United Earth just ask me or one of the guys and we can give it our best shot in answering any questions you have. Otherwise, good luck." He lifted a hand in parting as he strode away but suddenly stopped and turned with a snap of his fingers. "Oh! Here's a tip. Get a tree. Women love all the over-the-top holiday traditions."

"A tree."

"Yup, a tree." He chuckled, resuming his quick pace to the door. "I have to admit, if this doesn't all blow up in your face, then it's bound to be interesting."

Those words did not rouse confidence in Jor'y and left even more questions than it had answered. Maybe Sa'tari had some insights with all the time she had spent with Vanessa. No doubt she had heard his a'talyna speak of the traditions she was missing from her homeworld.

With a flick of his claw, he activated his comm. "Sa'tari, please meet me in the o'dari."

If a special traditional tree would make his mate happy, then he would discover just what he needed to do to accomplish it.

CHAPTER 16

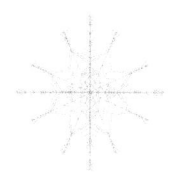

He bent his love back, staring boldly into her eyes. He wanted her and no one else, and he wanted her to know this. That though their love was forbidden, that he couldn't deny the yearning that existed between them...

"Vanessa."

Oh, he knew that it was doomed, just as she did, but they were pulled toward each other by some mysterious force more powerful than that which opposed them...

"Vanessa..."

He claimed her mouth with his, their breaths mingling as if their very souls were joining then. His hand slid up her thigh, parting her skirt. He needed to touch more of her, to claim her fully, and...

"Vanessa!"

At the exasperated shout, Vanessa jerked back, eyes wide, her chair snapping back so suddenly that she was nearly thrown out of it. Blinking owlishly, she stared up at her smirking friend.

"There you are!" Sa'tari laughed. "You must be at a good part to be so engrossed." Her smile widened as a telltale blush swept over Vanessa's cheeks. "Or perhaps I interrupted too soon."

That settled it. There had to be something about the Aturians in particular that made Vanessa blush like a naughty child caught with her hand in the cookie jar. It was actually pretty refreshing to not feel so jaded in her day-to-day life. The aliens were unapologetically open about their natures, direct in their mannerisms to the point of being constantly surprising. Even their courtship habits, while baffling at first, were not coy. This also meant that rejections on practically any matter would be taken to heart and honored. This was something she was still trying to wrap her head around when communicating with Aturians, something she was earnestly attempting to portray in her book. It was moments like these that fed her writing as much as her interactions with Jor'y.

Snorting at the direction of her thoughts, she closed her program before crossing her arms and slouching in her chair. She raised a polite eyebrow at her friend.

"So, what is it that you were trying to…" Her words trailed off as her drifting attention caught on the tall figure standing at the door.

"That you have company," Sa'tari purred in delight.

"So I see."

The words fell quietly from her lips, but she had no doubt that her friend heard them based on Sa'tari's soft chuckle. Even Jor'y's eyes brightened to a gleam of molten gold as he gave her an inviting smile and held out his hand.

Though his fingers were tipped with lethal black claws, there was something so refined about the gesture that it seemed more natural on him than with anyone who had ever likewise attempted it. She didn't even have to think about it to push to her feet and walk over to him, the satisfaction in his slitting eyes warming her over.

"Forgive my intrusion," he said. "I know that this is typically still within your work hour, but I had hoped that I might draw you away for a short time. There is something I would like you to see."

"Oh, are you finally going to allow me to see it?" she teased breathlessly.

His eyes brightened with humor, and he leaned forward, his long crown feathers teasing the sides of her face as he brushed his nose against hers.

"To see that, you only have to ask, and I will arrange for you to arrive at my rooms," he replied, his voice thick with desire, its low rumble hitting her in all the right ways.

Gods, it was tempting, but part of her wanted to extend the pleasure of anticipation just a little longer. There was something more to all of this than the simple pleasures of a one-night stand, and she wanted to see where the courtship might go next rather than terminate it prematurely to satisfy her desire.

His expression sweetened with a playful flick of his primary feathers against her right hip as he straightened once more. "But first, I would enjoy showing you something special that can only be appreciated under the right circumstances."

She raised both of her eyebrows. "Something special?"

He inclined his head. "Indeed. And I would be remiss to not share such a moment with the one being who is so greatly treasured by me. If you would permit."

"That sounds like something special all right," she whispered. "I'd be delighted."

Gold eyes softening with warmth, he tucked her under his wing as pale feathers curved around her. He seemed reluctant to tear his gaze from hers for even the moment it took for him to turn his head and address Sa'tari.

"I will return Vanessa to you shortly."

"No rush," Sa'tari assured them brightly. "I have plenty to keep me occupied right here. Enjoy yourselves."

His arm encircled Vanessa. "I will make certain of it."

Vanessa's breath stilled in her chest when he tipped his head to look down at her, his lips curving just enough to show a hint of fang. The hint of danger and compelling gaze contrasted so starkly against his gentleness and elegance that it sent a thrill up her spine. She could almost imagine that she was the heroine in some sort of old vampire romance—if vampires were built with the sleek lines and incredible musculature like the winged predators that the Aturians clearly were.

As his eyes glowed down at her, his horns casting a shadow over her, she revised her opinion. No, not vampires. The Aturians were still too inhuman for that. Demons... demons of lust and desire, perhaps.

She licked her lips in nervous anticipation as Jor'y led her from the study. The hall he led her down was a familiar one, until he stopped in a place between two heavy portraits on the wall. There between them was a large doorway that she had only noted in passing before. He ran his hand over a point in front of him, and suddenly the walls split in a burst of nearly blinding light.

"What...?"

His hand clasped her hip firmly, holding her snug against his body. "The luminous ice gardens can be a bit bright. I apologize. Give it a moment and your eyes will adjust."

Vanessa blinked her eyes a few times, tears blurring them until mercifully her vision began to clear. Her mouth dropped open. All around her were curved walls of what she assumed was glass creating a sort of tunnel. One wide enough that it comfortably held the handful of individuals who were currently enjoying it while giving plenty of room to everyone. As impressive as the architecture and engineering might have been, that wasn't what had her gaping. No, it was the crystalline white space and the hidden midday sun that turned the world around them into a dancing prism of colors that spun and spiraled everywhere she looked.

"It's beautiful," she whispered as she leaned into him with the weight of his wing closing around in her a warm hug. "I've never seen anything like it, except maybe a few images of the Aurora Borealis on Earth, but never like this with these colors."

His chest vibrated with a deep, thoughtful trill behind her shoulder. "This only happens a few times during a revolution. While this tunnel is lovely for overlooking the garden below us any time of the year, it is only during the height of the winter storms that one may enjoy this display for which it was built." His neck craned, eyes traveling along the walls of the tunnel for a moment before focusing attentively down on her, his lips curving once again in a smile that she could feel even when she returned to watching the beautiful dance of ice and light. "It takes the perfect combination of high-wind snowstorms, solar storms, and these special tunnels to create the luminous ice garden. They are entirely unpredictable but always a much-loved experience for my people and seen as good omens by some."

She glanced up at him curiously. "Omens?"

"A blessing of sorts," he clarified, "that we gain a moment of beauty in the worst of conditions. It was built specifically for the Hashavnal because our worst storms always seem to arrive just before then."

He fell silent for a moment as pinks and purples streaked together to merge with reds and blues. Every now and then, a burst of yellow or green would appear out of nowhere like a falling star, quick to appear and quick to burn out and vanish. Vanessa was aware of others moving around them, but there was little conversation. The sound of wind and ice and the surface was a strangely hypnotic sound in itself that had threatened to drown out Jor'y more than once during his explanation.

The wind whistled and sang like so many bells tinkling, or the long, hollow notes of an ancient set of windchimes that had hung on an ancient tree at her grandmother's home. The entire time,

Jor'y's hand remained on her hip, his wing tucked around her left side, pinning her close to him. Every now and then, she thought she could make out the shadow of the mountain, adding depth to the magical illusions created.

They might have stood there an hour, maybe two or perhaps three strolling leisurely. It didn't take her long to notice that constructed within the tunnel were a number of statues made of similar material depicting Aturians, native beasts, exotic flowers, and various symbolic shapes that were beyond her understanding, each one a miniature pinnacle of dancing light that gave the illusion of being touchable rather than just a trick of the light. She didn't think that it could get any better until the male beside her opened his mouth and began to sing.

Jor'y's deep voice resonated among the statues, making them vibrate and somehow pulse their radiant splash of colors in response to the vibrations of his wordless song. A few Aturians paused to listen as they funneled in and out of the tunnel, but never for more than a minute. It was as if there was some unspoken understanding that this gift was for her, and Vanessa felt her chest swell with emotion. So much so that she didn't know how she could even begin to contain it all. It was like something was feeding directly into her, amplifying every experience and every joy, making her want to laugh and shout with a giddiness that she couldn't remember last feeling. Any happiness she had in the past since becoming an adult felt like nothing more than pale imitations and shadows compared to what she was feeling now. It was as if the pure unbridled happiness of childhood innocence was handed back to her.

Distantly, she thought she heard other songs rising, adding to the depth of Jor'y's song, but they were too far away to truly be in concert with him. Perhaps other males were performing for their females. She liked that idea, that their moment was somehow connected to a larger magical whole. A mystery of mating among them that she was included in, even as she felt as if she and Jor'y somehow were also contained within their own little world there.

With the last fading notes of his song, he seized her against him and lifted her until their mouths crashed together. Light swelled behind her eyelids as she returned his kiss, sinking into the current that seemed to come alive between them. A give and take of energy and passion that had her feeding off him as much as he seemed determined to draw every bit of essence from her lips.

She didn't want it to stop, not when she could feel his own desperation, awe, and need echoing through her. She knew it would end, though. The moment his lips left hers, she knew she needed to do something to make the moment continue even though the light around them was gradually fading, the colors whiting out once more. She wasn't ready for that to happen yet to whatever this was between them.

Tangling her fingers in the fine feathers falling down his back and over his shoulders, she held fast, refusing to allow him to fully retreat as she met his burning liquid gaze.

"Your room," she whispered.

He paused. "You are certain?"

At her nod, his arms banded tightly around her, caging her to his chest even as white wings completely enclosed her, their hooked talons clasping around her in an intimate hold. A hissing sound escaped him, and she could see several long feathers down the center of his back that blended in with his crown feathers lifting and lowering in succession as he carried her through the hall, his fanned tail raised high behind him.

The display of snow-white feathers was beautiful, but from the way Aturians smiled and scampered out of their way, Vanessa knew it was far more than just that. It was a mating display of a predator warning off rivals as he prepared to take a female to his nest. His kin, rather than be threatened or intimidated, hooted and trilled in celebration as they yielded to his signals.

Vanessa's blush deepened when she spotted Sa'tari among them, her body pressed close to her mate as she craned her neck back to release a loud trill. There were no promises being made by either of them, but still she was fully aware that this moment had forged something very real between them. What it was, only time would tell. Until then, she reveled in it as Jor'y strode into a low-lit room and took her mouth with all the ferocity of his display and all the need he possessed. Her need echoed his, and she raised to his claim, exerting her own in return with every exchange of their breath.

CHAPTER 17

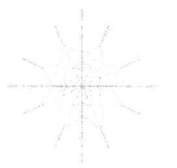

*L*arge hands set Vanessa down only for as long as it took to reverently strip her before laying her out on an enormous soft surface. The bed was far larger than anything she had slept in, the bed in her quarters being closer to in size to what she was accustomed to, and even that was considered luxurious on United Earth. Jor'y lay her in the center where she was far from being able to touch a single edge, luxuriating in a sea of ultra-soft bedding as his large body crawled over her.

Staring up at his chest, her mouth went dry.

Holy hell, there was nothing but miles of muscle as far as she could see.

In the midst of her admiration, the wall of muscles bunched, and a clawed hand gently gripped her chin, angling her head up to meet his heated gaze. He smiled and stroked her cheek with one finger, sending a shiver through her. At her reaction, his smile widened, and he rumbled a string of words in which, though they were spoken too softly for her to make out, the longing in his voice came across clearly . It made her heart leap in her chest and her pulse quicken.

Every nerve felt raw and exposed to his sensual onslaught, and she couldn't find a word to protest even if she wanted to. Her eyes rolled back with pleasure as his long tongue snaked out to lick a path down her neck, her breath catching in small pants in her lungs.

How was he doing this to her? Never had she reacted so strongly to an infatuation. She enjoyed sex, but this wasn't it. It wasn't just the physical touch, though gods knew that his touch packed a punch. No, it was more that every part of her seemed synced to him and responsive, wanting and needing more, not just of his touches but of his attention and affection too. She greedily wanted all of his smiles and soft words. She wanted to be kept under his wing, held lovingly against him as they passed time together. This need was both startling and overwhelming, so much so that she instinctively clung to him, her fingers gripping feathers and smooth expanses of muscle.

Somehow Jor'y understood her need and pressed closer to her, his body pinning hers beneath him as his hands trailed down her thighs, opening them. The sweat on her skin was cooled by the slight breeze stirred by his wings, which seemed to flap in gentle restless movements that he appeared either unaware of or unable to control.

"Wait," she whispered, forcing her fingers to loosen their death grip on him. She flattened her hands against his chest and pushed gently. "I want to see you—all of you—first."

Gold eyes met hers once more, accessing, reluctance evident in the thinning of his lips. His eyes narrowed and, finally, he nodded. With a pained expression tightening his mouth further, he lifted his body away from hers. Vanessa was surprised that she had to battle her own instinct to stop herself from grabbing ahold of him once more. It was like dragging two strong magnets apart, the wrongness of it assaulting her mind.

She focused on his massive body as he pushed himself into a crouched position between her knees, exposing his entire body to her inspection. Folding her legs under her, she pushed up to her knees, putting her at eye level with the rippling muscle and elegant spray of feathers that erupted along his shoulders and sides from where his wings met flesh. She explored them with her fingers, worshiping every indention and swell of muscle, every thatch of fine feathers. The moment her fingers skimmed his feathers, she felt his muscles stiffen, his hands suddenly coming up to grip her shoulders as if surprised by the move, before relaxing under her admiring touch. Though a number of scars formed a fine webbing in random places over his body, not one of them detracted from his perfection but told a story of his strength.

To her delight, she noticed that tiny downy feathers resumed on his lower belly to frame a genital slit from which a vivid fuchsia cock protruded. Long and thick, at first glance it looked almost like a human cock as it jutted out from the folds of his protective slit. She noticed, however, that the corona was thicker, and possessed a firm double-peak at the tip, each with a small slit indenting it, and a taller third peak between them that seemed to be of an even firmer texture pushing forward like a hard nub. From there, the shaft had two lines of bumps that ran on either side from the root to the bright scarlet tip. Between the two rows, there were numerous fine silvery threads of tissue that vibrated, lashing the air as they quivered.

She stared at those vibrating tendrils and hesitantly stretched a finger out toward them. They immediately slicked around her finger, cushioning and massaging it as she slowly wrapped her hand around his cock and get it a gentle squeeze that had him groaning, his wings jerking in tiny spasms behind him. The fanned feathers on his long tails snapped against the bed. Vanessa grinned and took him a little firmer in hand, slowly stroking up the length. The tiny tendrils tickled her palm and to her surprise she encountered a slick, sweet-smelling substance. She stared down at his cock in surprise as she dragged her hand up toward the head and released him, her mouth rounding when she noted that the two side peaks at the tip were excreting a natural lube.

Curious, she brought her fingers to her lips, fully aware of Jor'y's hot gaze following the movement. His breath sharpened at her wet finger touched her tongue. A sweet citrus flavor bloomed over her tastebuds and a hint of rich musk that reminded her of the chocolate oranges she loved to buy every year when the holidays came around. They were an old tradition as far as seasonal sweets went. Moaning, she dropped down to take him into her mouth.

The irony that she was getting a taste of the holidays from his cock didn't escape her, but she couldn't care less.

A most happy Yule to me!

Wings slapped at her back before their claws latched onto her shoulders and arms, and Jor'y barked out a moan that devolved into a long growl as he began to helplessly pump his hips, dragging his cock back and forth through her hand as she sucked down as much as she could with every eager bob of her head. To her relief, the tendrils flattened under the suction of her mouth, snapping against his cock rather than tickling the inside of her mouth. Whatever that did for Jor'y, it made him snarl, his claws digging into the bedding beside her as more of the sweetness was released into her mouth.

Claws tangled in her hair, he pulled her mouth away so quickly that his cock popped free with an audible sound. The brightly colored length bobbed in the air until it was caged between their bodies as he yanked her up against him, flattening her against him so that his mouth could plunder hers once more. The thrust of his textured tongue into her mouth made her suck it in deeper into her mouth, eager for more.

Jor'y pushed her down against the bed, his arms braced, keeping most of his weight off of her. His wing claws held her firmly in place against him as his hips nestled between her thighs. His hands wrapped around her legs, yanking them up around him, and Vanessa felt the hot tip of his sex press against her entrance.

"Jor'y," she gasped against his mouth.

"Open for me, a'talyna," he whispered, his claws biting into her thighs, his wing claws dragging along her shoulders. "Let me drink deep of your sweetness."

She arched against him as his slickened cock pushed forward, burying slowly into her. Her walls stretched to the point of verging on discomfort as he slid home, at the same time something sparked deep within her. He gave her a moment to adjust, words whispered in adoration over her skin in every place that he tenderly brushed his lips. They remained still until the need in her rose to a feverish pitch, demanding that she move. She jerked her hips in silent demand against his, and Jor'y purred against her throat as he began to thrust.

Vanessa's eyes rolled back as each moving thread and bump along his shaft rubbed every erogenous spot within her channel. It drove her lust to greater heights as he rocked against her, and that the strange electric current snapped into place between them once more. Whatever this new feeling was, it rose in response to her hunger, an erotic flame searing through her as it rose in response to every smack of his pelvis against hers. His tail whipped, the feathers fanning her flesh, but it did nothing for the inferno rising with her pleasure. Her fingernails scored his skin as she writhed under him, needing something more. Needing relief.

His answering growl licked across her senses as he pinned her firmer beneath him, his mouth clamping onto her shoulder as his thrusts turned to a primal rut, pressing her down into the bedding and against his wings. The head of his cock kissed her depths thoroughly, somehow touching all the sensitive points around the mouth of her womb. She strained against him to gain more friction, the unfamiliar needs demanding something more as she whimpered and writhed. Her mouth fell open to drag in heaving gasps for air, her body quivering like a bow drawn taut as her pebbled nipples slid against his hard body.

She thrashed her head, her heels pressing into the back of his thighs, the inferno of her rising orgasm consuming her with a delicious ache that demanded satisfaction. Jor'y's hands tightened around her legs, and he angled her hips higher, the feathers of his tail occasionally brushing the backs of her legs as he drove deeper, a snarled trill rattling deep in his chest. His mouth released its grip on her shoulder long enough to turn his head and press his lips against her hair.

"My a'talyna," he chanted in a hoarse, breathless voice, his hips grinding down against hers. "Give it to me."

She shivered, the fire whipping higher through her blood, making her cry out in an ecstasy that paled to the orgasm winding through her. Whatever he wanted or needed was his, if that would be enough to push her over the edge.

"Please," she begged. "More. Gods, you can have anything if you just don't stop!"

He chuckled against her skin. There was a brush of his lips and the prick of his teeth once more as he swiveled his hips. His cock swelled, and she felt something deep within her as the vibrations along the top of his cock increased to the point that the entire shaft felt as if it were quaking, a hot spray of cum jettisoning through her, triggering her own release.

Vanessa shrieked, her fingernails digging into his arms as her pussy spasmed around his sex. Her climax shot through her with such force that it carried that fire along with it as it ripped through her and along that current of energy until she was certain she might have scorched even Jor'y with it. A loud snarl escaped him, and his cock began to jerk repeatedly, each spasm releasing more cum, making her own orgasm roll into another as she felt a golden warmth flow into her, sinking into her bones.

Jor'y held her tighter as they rode out their orgasm, inaudible words snarled against her skin as they clung to each other in a primal grinding dance.

When they eventually stilled, he turned, his wings shifting beneath her to roll them over effortlessly while keeping her body splayed against his. Only gradually did his wing claws release her from their iron grip so that they could waft cool air over her heated skin.

He pressed a kiss against her forehead. "Rest, a'talyna."

She shook her head weakly. "I can't," she mumbled. "I have to return to my room. We don't need to give the guys anything more to have a heart attack about."

"I have resolved their meddling."

She lifted her head and rose an eyebrow. "It did seem that they weren't quite as determined to insert themselves into our private time today... but still," she sighed and dropped her head against his chest, "it would complicate things."

He huffed a discontented sound.

"Rest, even for just a short time. I will rouse you and walk you to your quarters soon."

She pressed a kiss against his chest in thanks, earning another rumble in response that made her smile.

As promised, Jor'y woke her a short time later. She hadn't even realized she had fallen asleep until she felt the glide of a cleansing cloth wiping her body clean. Although the male wasn't thrilled about returning her to her rooms, the look he bent upon her as he attended to her was one full of warmth. His expression had an uncharacteristic softness to it as the corner of his mouth quirked up and his eyes glowed liked hot honey. His eyes met hers and that smile grew, brimming with so much affection that threw her mind into chaos. Even more so when she felt an answering swell of emotion that made her heart tighten as if trying to contain too much.

This couldn't be love—not already—could it?

Her mind rebelled. It was too soon. There was no way she would just fall for someone so soon. It had to have been the sex. It was *that* good. She had never felt closer to someone on an emotional level than she had with Jor'y. That had to explain it.

And Jor'y... well, he was Aturian. They enjoyed sex the way other beings enjoyed a rousing game. Or at least so she understood.

She stared at him with unabashed fascination as he lifted her hand and brushed a kiss along the inside of her wrist.

"I was not too rough, was I? The Havanshal draws close and with it the initiating of the Aturian breeding season. It makes us... enthusiastic," he admitted with a cautious smile.

She laughed, relieved that he hadn't posed a more intimate question. She wasn't ready to analyze her feelings yet. She shook her head.

"Not at all. That was... amazing."

"You are amazing," he breathed, brushing his lips against hers. "Thank you for this gift."

A gift, huh? She blushed a little even as a part of her heart sank. Well, if that was how he thought of it... as an exchange of gifts... she wasn't one to kick a fuss over it. *And hey, at least it's seasonally appropriate.*

"Sure thing, handsome. I will be happy to do another gift exchange in the future if you're willing."

He purred in response, and she returned his kiss with a playful peck of her own before nudging him back so that she had room to climb off the bed. A few more flirtatious kisses later and she was dressed and being escorted back to her room. Even though she insisted on going back, it felt like her heart sank more the closer they got to it.

She was being silly, and yet after a lingering last kiss before she closed her door and settled into the cold emptiness of her bed, she sighed with perhaps longing or regret, or both, before drifting off to sleep.

CHAPTER 18

*A*rm stretched out across the bed, Vanessa's fingers wiggled as if seeking something before slapping down on the comm beside her, silencing the alarm. She groaned, rolling over in the bed. It was early still, and she wanted to cuddle. Why wasn't she wrapped up in strong arms and held against a certain someone's chest anyway? That was where she belonged. She missed the sound of a strong heart beating under her ear.

Wriggling across the bed in search for the warm body that was assuredly somewhere nearby, cool sheets met her hand and cheek. She wrinkled her nose and grumbled, squinting in confusion against the morning faint morning light streaming through her window. Pushing up onto her elbow, she glanced around and sighed, noting where she was.

Oh, yeah. He wouldn't be there. She had returned to her own room.

She debated burrowing back under the blankets, but they hardly seemed quite as inviting now. So much for sleeping in. Vanessa kicked them back and sat up, swinging her legs off the side of the bed. She stared at the beam of sunlight that was stretched across the floor, streaking like a faint arrow on the stones in front of her feet.

Sunlight. It was weak, but it was there. She hadn't seen actual sunlight in days.

Rising from the bed, she hurried over to the window, her feet silent against the cool stone floor. The snow was still coming down hard, but the sky was brighter with the hint of sun behind the clouds, and she could make out the valetik below. Her eyes tracked a winged figure as it rose up from one of the buildings, flying unhampered through the snow on large white wings. Resting her land on the stone ledge below the window, she watched the Aturian's graceful flight as they rose higher up the mountain.

The storm was over. That meant that comms likely were back up. She could send in her chapters and touch base with Katherine. So why was she watching an Aturian fly when she should be jumping straight into work. That was what's most important, wasn't it?

She dug her fingers into the stone ledge, the garland of festively dyed berries and plants digging into her knuckles.

Carthy would be comming for a retrieval team soon, if he hadn't already, to take her to the colony. She frowned. If that happened, she would likely never see Jor'y again. She rubbed the space over her heart, wincing at the twinge there.

No more Jor'y? No more hours working together in silence, strolling through the estate companionably, or stealing private moments. No more seeing the way his eyes heated with desire, or his lips curved in amusement or peeled back in a protective snarl. No more being cocooned in warm feathers and held as if she were treasured. No more of someone looking at her and treating her as if she was the one person who mattered more to them than anything.

How the hell was she going to be able to go back to the emptiness of her life before him?

"I could stay," she whispered, tasting the words as she spoke then aloud as she gauged her own reaction to actually hearing them rather than a thought roaming around in her head as it had been over the last few days.

She could stay. She didn't recoil from it, nor did it bring any feeling of dread or apprehension of the future with it. It felt... right.

Was it love, though?

Her teeth worried at her bottom lip. She felt something, she knew that, and it certainly wasn't just lust. Oh, she felt plenty of lust, it kind of smacked her right in the face, but lust wasn't what had her searching for him first thing in the morning. She just wasn't sure if it was really love or not. She had written of love enough times, she should know, but felt as if she were half blind from her position in the middle of it. Whatever it was, she felt a lot of it. She felt joy just being with him, her heart leaping whenever he so much as entered the same room. She loved to see him happy and knowing that she was a source of that for him as much as he was for her.

But was she in love... a lasting love to span the rest of her life? That was what worried her. Because it would have to.

If she stayed, there would be no going back. Ever. Those who went into exile and tried to return lost everything, including all rights as citizens, if they were allowed to return at all. She had heard rumors of women who attempted to return with half-alien children, often when some tragedy befell their mates, who were sent away from the United Earth consulates stationed on those worlds within the Alliance.

Was their love strong enough to withstand all of that? And what if something happened to him?

Her blood chilled at the possibility, her heart clenching at the thought of Jor'y's light being snuffed from the world, leaving her alone. But was that any worse than returning to Earth, pretending to pick up her life how it had been before, and never knowing what happiness they could have had together?

So many questions. It made her head hurt. And it wasn't like he had asked her to stay. She still was trying to figure out Aturian culture. Their Day of Joy was coming up, and from what she understood preparing for that event, in addition to their instinctual drive to mate this time of the year, wasn't always permanent if they weren't done with a mate. Had he made any indication of wanting to mate with her?

Her teeth sank into her lip deeper.

The truth was, she wasn't entirely sure. She would feel really foolish if she decided to announce that she was staying, and it turned out that what he felt went no further than a spirit of merrymaking. Just instead of hugging or kissing someone with the joy of the season, it was a festive fucking.

Last night, he had only escorted her to the entrance of her wing, leaving her to walk to her room alone. Was that the behavior of a male in love after a night of passion? And if he was in love with her and truly courting her in a lasting sort of way, why would he avoid being seen around her rooms?

She rubbed her temples. She wasn't sure if she was ready for such an uncomfortable conversation, especially if she had to be the one to initiate it, but what choice did she have? Her time was running out. She had days of enjoying his company and giving herself time to see where things led, and she didn't feel significantly closer to knowing what exactly he wanted. It was far too easy for her to get swept up in the magical atmosphere of the season, especially when the Aturians took it beyond what most humans even bothered with.

Even now she could see a pretty good handful of Aturians making their way through the sky, hauling large, heavily canvased loads between them. Their wings flapped almost synchronously in graceful arcs as they made their way to the estate. The weather hadn't even cleared yet and there was already a hustle of bodies, no doubt hurrying to make final preparations for the festival. Vanessa groaned, bringing up her opposite hand to cradle her brow.

How the hell did she get herself into such a situation?

"Vanessa, is all well?"

Spinning around, Vanessa forced a tight smile to her face, murmuring a soft greeting to Sa'tari as her friend entered with their customary pot of steamed o'jar that they now shared every morning. The female tipped her head, her lips pursing with concern.

"I'm fine... I see that the weather has cleared."

"I would think that would have brought you happiness instead of worry. You have been complaining of the storm for days now," the female said, setting the tray on her small table.

Vanessa laughed weakly and sat herself at the table, smiling her thanks at the cup handed to her.

"I admit that seeing some sunlight is welcome. Unfortunately, it means that my time here is running out," she admitted.

Sa'tari glanced at her in surprise. "You are not leaving, are you?"

"I don't think I'm going to have much choice."

Her friend snorted in disbelief.

"There are always choices. Either go or stay. Those are your choices. And going is the wrong choice."

Vanessa met Sa'tari's gaze grimly. "It's not that simple. I'm merely a guest here, one who wasn't even invited for that matter, and my stay solely the consequence of the storm that's now letting up. My travel visa is specifically for a rented cabin on the southern continent. While my presence here can be forgiven because of the storm, I won't be allowed to remain here for the remaining time of my visa, even if I wanted to. Not legally, anyway."

Sa'tari shook her head and set her cup down firmly on the table, her eyes beseeching. "You cannot go. You cannot leave Jor'y!"

Groaning, Vanessa ran a hand through her hair. "I know it's hard for him to find a partner for Hashavnal and how important that is, but it's likely I won't be retrieved until after the festival anyway."

To her surprise, the female's eyes brightened with anger. "What has the Hashavnal to do with this? This is not about the Hashavnal. It is the a'talynal. You have a'talynal and you would leave him all the same?"

Vanessa's brow knitted in confusion. "I've heard him call me a'talyna before, but I don't even know what that is or what you're talking about."

"He did not tell you?" Sa'tari gaped, her feathers fluffing out in an expression of pure shock as the anger faded from her eyes.

Whatever this a'talynal thing was, it clearly was of some importance.

Sa'tari dragged her chair closer. "The a'talynal is the heart-song. It is something that comes up between beings who have compatible energies, which is very treasured because we share joy."

Vanessa shook her head. "I don't know what that means. Do you mean you enjoy sex more with them?"

Her friend grimaced. "Yes and no. Yes, we do enjoy sex more, but not for the reason that you think. It is not just the act." Her feathers fluffed out a little again, her wings flicking with embarrassment. "This conversation is usually between mother and offspring. This feels very strange to have with an adult." She leaned in. "It is an exchange of energies during the act. We draw in and consume each other's joy."

Vanessa's eyes widened. "Like demons! Like a succubus!"

Sa'tari snapped back, her wings unfolding with fury. "No," she spat. "Not demons. Not a succubus. These are words we hear from humans as if our ways are filth! Like Aturians are evil parasites."

Guilt overwhelmed Vanessa, followed quickly by remorse. She had spoken reflexively because she had toyed with the thought before but only with an artistic humor, not because she felt that they were evil. Now that the words were spoken aloud, she understood exactly how bad that sounded. She hadn't even realized that those were insults that had been hurled at Aturians before, her own exposure to aliens up to now being limited to what she had read in the media. Like most species, there was very little public knowledge about them.

"I'm sorry, Sa'tari. I wasn't thinking. I didn't know that they actually called you that. I certainly didn't mean anything cruel by it. I'm afraid it was just the writer in me that's been on flights of fantasy, and I just said the first thing that popped into my mind. I don't think you're evil, or parasites. Actually, that you share that kind of intimacy with someone is pretty incredible," she admitted.

The tension slowly eased from the other female, her eyes narrowing as she lowered herself back into her seat. "You speak truthfully?"

Vanessa nodded earnestly. "The Aturians I've met have been some of the kindest people I've known. I couldn't think such a thing about you." She paused, her lips tightening. "I don't want to bring up a painful subject, but is this how…" she swallowed, "how they have convinced your people remove to your beautiful wings?"

A bleak expression descended over Sa'tari's face. "Some, yes. It is easy for colonizers to come and point out that we are primitive and dangerous. To show us a mirror and make us ashamed of ourselves because we resemble something they dislike. Then they say that our wings and feathers are also dirty and carry parasites which can sicken us. I think that calling us monsters was the first thing that broke our minds and spirits, or else we would not have listened to the rest. Perhaps that is why Hashavnal means so much to us. It gives us pride and hope when there is little for us to have, and we have to fight for what we enjoy. It may seem silly and unimportant to you, but it means very much to us, even more so when it is celebrated with a'taynal."

Vanessa nodded, her lips thinning. She had made a mistake in her assumptions. She allowed her eyes to trail over her friend's wings with open admiration.

"First, I think your wings are beautiful and have no doubt that a lot of the response has been fueled by envy and fear. Your people are very strong and resilient, even in this weather."

Sa'tari reached across the table to grasp Vanessa's hand. "I am glad you can see the truth of this and do not see us as others have. You worried me," she scolded before smiling beautifully, "but I am glad to see that the a'talynal was not misplaced. I would hate to kill you."

"Wait, what?" Vanessa gaped at her.

Another shrug of wings and her friend patted her hand. "Nothing to worry about now, but I would have protected my valmek from a destructive pairing. I do not have the spirit for killing like a valmek, but I would have done it to see to it that his grief was cut short rather than hear poison from you that would break his soul."

A shiver ran through Vanessa as she saw the honesty in the other female's eyes, and she once again reminded herself that the Aturians weren't human. From Sa'tari's point of view, it was a reasonable response considering that there were things at play that her species took very seriously. Time to get the conversation back on track.

She licked her lips. "So, this a'talyna thing, it's a sexual and energy compatibility."

"Yes, precisely," Sa'tari agreed with a pleased nod of her head.

"What about love?"

Once again, Vanessa was treated to a befuddled head tilt. "What of it?"

"An a'talynal doesn't mean love. It's not like being fated to fall in love and be together forever, is it?"

Understanding lit the female's eyes. "Oh." Her expression grew sad. "No. It does not. Although the a'talynal is treasured and unpredictable, which makes us embrace it eagerly, it doesn't mean love. You have to make your own love."

Vanessa swallowed back her pain. She hadn't wanted for her suspicions to be confirmed, but there it was. The interactions between her and Jor'y, even with this magical a'talynal thing between them, didn't mean that he loved her. Even if he wanted her because of the a'talynal, without love he could leave her once he met another female that he felt that with whom he did love. Once again, she was presented with a very real possibility of just being a convenient body at a convenient time.

"Do you have a'talynal with your mate?" she whispered.

Sa'tari's eyes brightened, and she nodded. "Yes. Gal'ythron is from a nearby valetik. We met when our valetiks gathered for the spring trading season. I had met with two other a'talynal males before him at my parents' arrangements. Despite the a'talynal I had with them, neither were good matches, so I was not entirely convinced that I would have much luck for a third try." Her expression grew fond. "But that did not stop my Gal'ythron. He courted me through the entire trading season, and he worked hard to prove that he was a good choice as a mate. He was so sweet and caring, and somehow, amid all of that, I had not been able help but to fall in love with him."

Vanessa sucked her lips in anxiously. "If it's motivated by something so powerful as this a'talynal bond… how do you know if it's love? How did you know when he loves you?"

Sa'tari reached forward and brushed a stray strand of mussed hair from Vanessa's face, her smile tender. "I know because he told me. Because a'talynal is wonderful and gives you great heights of desire that you never feel a hunger from its absence. It makes for great sex. But that is all it is. It does not soften our hearts or make us want to pass the rest of our lives together just because we cannot imagine not having that person in our lives."

"Does anyone choose a mate for the a'talynal without love being present?"

Her friend fell silent for a moment, her eyes revealing nothing. "Sometimes," she admitted. "Sometimes there are those who feel desperate when it has been a long time with no sign of an a'talynal that they will choose the first partner they see and go through the motions of courting just to win the other's agreement. This does not always work though, because the other may wish to wait for someone that they feel love for. But I will not lie and say that it has not happened before."

She wanted to ask if Jor'y was just going through the motions of courting. The words were on the tip of her tongue when her comm pinged. Biting back the question for the time being, she lifted her comm and accepted the transmission.

"Miss Williams," Carthy greeted her. "Good morning. I'm sorry if I'm disturbing you."

Vanessa let out a breath and forced a smile to her lips. "Not at all. What can I do for you?"

"We have a transmission coming in from the southern continent, and I think you should be here when we receive it. Can you please meet us in the systems room?"

The southern continent. It was happening then already. *Too fucking soon.* She swallowed back her panic and nodded.

"Not a problem. I will get dressed and meet you there shortly."

"Thank you, Miss Williams." Carthy paused, his expression contrite. "I just wanted to tell you that I support whatever decisions you make from here on out and will do whatever I can do to help make sure that they are honored."

Vanessa blinked. That was surprising.

"Thank you, Lieutenant."

He nodded briskly and terminated the transmission, the holoscreen winking out. Vanessa stared down at her comm for a moment longer before rousing herself into motion. She downed her o'jar and smiled at her friend.

"I guess I better get down there before someone from the colony has a fit. Thank you, Sa'tari, for discussing all of this with me."

The female harrumphed. "The one you should discuss it with is your a'talyna. He will have the answers you really want."

"I will," Vanessa promised. "I swear that I won't make any decisions without talking with him about it first."

Sa'tari eyed her. "Good enough." She flapped a wing at her as she turned to gather their cups back up onto the tray. "Hurry and dress, and then I will take you to the systems room. Terribly uncomfortable place, not like the o'dari, but naturally they would not be there."

Vanessa wanted to ask why not, but there was no time to get into another lengthy conversation so she mentally tabled it and hurried to the storage unit. She dug out her best slacks and blouse, for once grateful for her mother's interference. She had a feeling she was going to need her best armor for what was to come.

CHAPTER 19

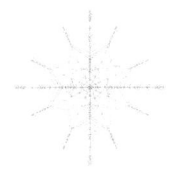

Sa'tari hadn't been joking when she said that the systems room wasn't comfortable. All the festive decor halted just outside the room, leaving the inside colorless and bleary with its plain gray walls. The fact that the female didn't enter with her just made the space feel even more barren as the four men turned to look at her grimly.

Carthy nodded a polite greeting from where he stood in front of the comm system, while at his left Fowler seemed intent on chewing his bottom lip ragged as he stared worriedly at the large comm screen he sat in front of. Stephens barely glanced her way, but when he did it was with a gruff greeting. Tackert was the only one who seemed more at ease from where he sat in the chair that he had commandeered from whatever Aturian had occupied that spot earlier. She murmured a hello and returned Tackert's friendly smile. Of all the men there, Tackert had been the one to make less of a nuisance of himself and seemed to even be on somewhat friendly terms with Jor'y.

"Okay, Fowler, we are all present. Go ahead and accept transmission," Carthy ordered.

"Yes, sir." His freckled pale hands slid over the controls. "Accepting now."

The holoscreen opened over the large supporting surface. Whatever interruptions the winds might still have been doing, it seemed that they weren't enough to interfere with the comm signal because Vanessa found herself facing a man packed with lean muscle and possessing a strong jaw and square chin. He had the appearance her mother would have romantically called formidable, enhanced by the distinctive salt and pepper of his neatly trimmed hair. With his hands behind his back and his piercing gaze, Vanessa might have pegged him as military personnel if not for his suit with the Darvel logo emblazoned on a pin tacked onto one lapel.

His eyes cut to Carthy before zeroing in on her.

"Miss Williams, I am pleased to see that you are well and accounted for. When we received word that your shuttle had gone down over these coordinates, we had hoped that the locals would find and take you in. I'm glad to see that our faith was not misplaced."

"Thank you, Mister... ahhh..."

His lips twisted in a faint smile. "Bradshaw. Darrel Bradshaw. I am the governor and Darvel representative of Dahlia Colony."

She smiled in return. "My apologies, I thought colonies were usually under a governor sent by United Earth. I've never heard of a representative also being the governor."

He frowned, disapproval showing in every line of his face. "Normally it is not the case, but Dahlia is a rare exception. Our colony is small and our relationship with the locals is peaceful, so that does not require strong military leadership. Since I am ex-military, I was selected for the position with Earth Gov's blessings."

"Thank you for clarifying that matter. I'm relieved to hear that the southern colony enjoys a good relationship with the people here. They've been very considerate hosts and have cared for us when we could have easily died. I hope that will be taken into consideration with any trade negotiations," she said diplomatically.

"I had not realized that you were aware of our upcoming negotiations." He squinted at her as his lips thinned. "Be assured that we have nothing but the best intentions toward our northern allies. Whatever trade agreements are made will be beneficial for both sides."

"I'm sure," she murmured in polite assent.

A tight smile tugged at his lips. "This incident has moved up our intended visit. The local festival our meeting was scheduled for is in three days, but due to your presence there without less than adequate protections for what's considered a rather heathenistic season of debauchery among these aliens, our estimated time of arrival has been moved up to fourteen hundred today."

"Sir, I assure you that my team has observed the conditions here and found the local populace to not be of concern. Even so, we have had no problems protecting Miss Williams on our own," Carthy objected.

Bradshaw directed a bored look down his nose at the lieutenant. "You are not from around here, are you… Carthy, is it?"

"No, sir. My team and I are assigned to the *Anointed*, as you are aware." Carthy's jaw clenched.

Bradshaw chuckled, a small, condescending smile curving his lips. "My point exactly. I was just wondering if perhaps somehow you were unaware of the fact that you possess limited knowledge of the species. Forgive me for pointing out that you have no idea what sort of rut these creatures will get into as it gets closer to their breeding time. That is what this festival is for them, a holy day that ties into their breeding cycle in honor of some mythical mother of their race. They are not bad creatures, but try as they might to be civilized, they are still victims of their animalistic nature."

Vanessa gaped at the crude description falling so effortlessly from the governor's lips. Was this what Darvel's colonists really thought of the people with whom they shared this world? The disdain for the Aturians' sacred winter festival was strange, given humanity's own love for their spiritual and secular winter celebrations. If nothing else, that should have been some common ground between their species. Why else meet on that day?

"I see that I have offended you, Miss Williams." Bradshaw lifted a brow as he regarded her with amusement.

She ground her teeth. "I would say so. Our shared reverence for the season should bring us together and encourage our fellowship."

He snorted and shook his head. "Admirable sentimentality, but then you are a novelist from what I understand. The reality is not always as pretty of a picture as you would like to imagine it, and I think your parents would prefer not to have your standing tarnished if you had one of these Aturian brutes fall on you in a desire to rut. But it is of no consequence. We will be there to save you from yourself if needed." His eyes slid to Carthy once more. "Make sure that this Jor'ytal is notified, and that our rooms are made ready."

"Yes, sir," Carthy gritted.

"And Carthy, there will be other dignitaries from Earth. I expect you to understand that their safety will also be considered your top priority while we are there. Earth Gov was foolish to send a woman among those who are leading the trade agreements. Make sure that your charge is moved to an isolated spot where both women can be protected from the males roaming around."

"I believe that won't be a problem," Carthy replied stiffly.

Vanessa just barely constrained her laughter. Bradshaw would be shitting himself if he knew that she was already in such a place where males of any species weren't allowed.

"Very good. I will see you all at fourteen hundred."

"Sir." Carthy gave one last final nod before the holoscreen snapped shut, terminating the connection.

"What a fucking prick," Tackert observed.

Carthy cut him a sharp look. "Mind yourself, soldier."

"Right. Sorry. What a fucking prick, sir."

The lieutenant's lips twitched, and he looked over the other men at his side. "Okay, boys, it looks like time is no longer on our side. Let's get rolling. We need to inform Jor'ytal and start notating everything—and I mean everything. If the governor is going to try to use any moment of our presence here as an excuse to swing things in his favor, I want a formal notation ready for our host and to file with our superior officer on *Anointed*." He turned to look at Vanessa. "Darvel is playing fast and loose with the regulations here. If they slid ex-military personnel in as a representative without full knowledge of the government, there could be hell to pay. Earth Gov's direct supervision of Darvel is the only thing that allows them to have a colony presence in Alliance space."

Fowler paled. "Sir, you are suggesting possibly going against Darvel."

"Not just suggesting it," Carthy replied. "There's some serious bad shit going down with this planet. Aturians are nothing like we've been led to believe, especially those in the outer rim. Have you not noticed that they're healthier and stronger than any Aturian we've met on previous trips to the colony? Why do you suppose that is? Everything on this planet stinks of being buried past our knees in illegal shit. I'm not sitting with that on my conscience. Are any of you?"

Fowler shook his head. "No, sir."

"Hell no, sir," Tackert agreed.

There was a moment of silence, and Stephens sighed and shook his head. "No, sir."

"Good. Tackert, you are with Miss Williams and me. Fowler, Stephens, I want you two to get on comms. Contact the Anointed and let the general know exactly what is going on, and then get on making those reports."

"Yes sir," the men replied, Stephens sliding into Tackert's spot, pulling the chair up beside Fowler in front of the comms.

Tackert strolled up to Vanessa's side, grinning.

"Looks like we're going to be making merry with the locals, in a fashion. Are you ready?"

Vanessa raised an eyebrow. "Still going to hover over me?"

He chuckled. "Nah. Jor'ytal will bust my ass down into the stone floor if I tried to, I imagine. But are you ready for all the madness that's coming your way? Seems to me there are decisions to be made."

At her surprised look, he grinned. "Just because I keep my nose out of what is going on as much as I can doesn't mean I'm blind. But I say, good for you. We all need somebody in our lives, and we don't always have control over where we find them. But this isn't going to be easy. But we can always hope for a Christmas Miracle."

"Difficult does not even begin to describe it," Carthy grumbled just ahead of them as they exited the Systems Room. He glanced back at her from the corner of his eye. "And I wouldn't hold my breath for any miracles. You're going to be up against one hell of a fight."

Vanessa didn't say anything. At her side, Tackert nudged her with his arm, drawing her attention back to him.

"Don't mind Scrooge there. I have faith. I think a lot of people around this place do and will be pulling for you."

"I really haven't made a decision," she admitted. "I'm scared and feel like I don't know the rules with what Jor'y wants or expects."

He nodded sympathetically. "My cousin fell for an alien. It's tough, especially when you have to be slick getting comms to your family. I still hear from him every year around this time. The family misses him, but he did what was right for him, and in the end we all had to pull for him. There are enough hiccups in life, especially in marriages, even without adding complications of alien cultures to the mix. We should support those who are adventurous to take that step. That shit there is for you and him to work out," he added with a wink.

"So I've been told." Vanessa smiled over at him. "You know something, Tackert, I like you."

He grinned and tipped his head toward her. "I'll be sure to let my wife know that she educated me well on the ways of marriage. She takes credit for it anyway, and not wrongly."

"Wise man to recognize," she teased.

They walked down the hall for a while, following Carthy's lead before he spoke again.

"I liked what you said about coming together in the spirit of the season. That resonated with me. My family always did put a lot of heart into Christmas, and I admit I've been feeling down being on this rotation off Earth, but that reminder helps." He glanced over at her. "Just don't forget that whatever misunderstandings you have with your alien, there are things that we have in common at the very heart of it. All of this here, the merriment of a promise of hope, life, and happiness. That's a big part of it."

She drew in a breath, considering. Damned if he wasn't right. Their cultures were different but not so different in the ways that mattered most. Whatever his reason for courting her, it was done in the spirit of hope for the future. She just needed to talk with him and to figure out where to go from there.

CHAPTER 20

"Are you certain this is correct?" Vi'ryk asked.

Jor'y stared up at the tree as he flapped his wings, shaking loose the snow from his feathers. "It does seem strange, but the human leader Carthy suggested it. It is a holiday tradition among many humans. He advised that human females took great joy in such things. I would not have expected something like this from a species that tends to be more reserved, but it seemed unwise to ignore advice."

The storm had let up enough that flying was no longer impossible. It still was not recommended for any but the strongest flyers, but he had not been the only one eager to embrace the challenge of a hunt. A number of males from the valetik had welcomed the opportunity to stretch their wings once the estate had been able to re-establish comms. They had brought down a number of large ga'thal for the upcoming feast that were currently being prepped for storage in the kitchens, but not least among their prey they sought to collect was the tree standing erect in the great hall in front of him.

And erect was an accurate description in more than one way.

He cleared his throat and glanced over at the female staring up at the tree with an expression of admiration. Sensing his gaze on her, Sa'tari turned and shrugged her wings.

"I know. That thought occurred to me as well, but Vanessa assured me that it is not phallic. I just cannot conceive of how it would not be considered such. It seems almost remiss to celebrate that aspect," she observed, gesturing toward the tree to emphasize her point.

Jor'y could not disagree.

The long dark violet trunk was an impressive spire proudly jutting up toward the ceiling. The leaf capsule at the top was devoid of the feathery silver branches that sprouted from it during the spring. There were several minor capsules that rose like small ridges along the sides in various points, remnants of old capsules that still sprouted growth, covering the tree in silver during the growing seasons, but they were barely visible from a distance. The unfortunate side-effect was that the tree looked like a giant male member. With the numerous nodes running up its stark length and the leaf capsule, as well as its deep color, it mirrored a part of his own anatomy all too well with the exception of the missing v'lica that ran along the top of his cock.

It was a peculiar human custom, but he was eager to please his mate. After last night, he felt closer to solidifying his bond with her. The courtship was going very well. It was only fortunate that the weather allowed them to hunt out the tree. He could not wait for her to see it.

As strange as it was, it was conveniently also one that rather worked for an Aturian festival. He could see surprise and excitement on the faces of his kin as they worked to string lights in the human way up its length, as others painted symbols of fertility, good luck, and prosperity on the exposed areas of its length in mimicry of what was painted on their own bodies during the Hashavnal. The assumption as to what the tree represented was obviously shared among those of the valetik within the estate, but it struck a discordant note with what he had learned about humans.

Still, if it made his female and his valetik happy, he did not see any harm in including it in their customs. Not when it obviously fit in so well. Truthfully, it was surprising that it had not occurred to his people to do this before.

"It definitely draws the eye," he observed optimistically in attempt to drown his doubts. "But not in a bad way. It looks as if it belongs with our traditional decor. Perhaps it would also serve to make the human delegation feel more welcome."

Vi'ryk made a doubtful noise, but Sa'tari beamed, her feathers fluffing out in a way that drew an indulgent smile from her mate at his position by the door. "That is an excellent idea! The delegate wishes to see a traditional Hashavnal, but I think incorporating elements of the human celebrations that complement our own will be a great way to welcome them."

Jor'y was not entirely confident that it would do anything of the sort. Although his human guests had become easier to bear over the last couple of days thanks to Carthy, his experience with humans had formed strong impressions of their volatile, xenophobic, and often brash tendencies. That things had improved with his human guests gave him some hope for a future relationship between their peoples. As had his a'talyna, but he also believed that she was unique and one of a kind, so he avoided measuring the other humans against her. As far as he was concerned, she was close to perfect... perfect for him, anyway.

His comm went off.

"Jor'ytal, sir," the human spoke uncertainly. It amused him that these human males never quite understood exactly how to address him. "Jeremy Fowler here."

"Speak."

"Sir, we've received a strange transmission here in the systems room."

Jor'y frowned. "Strange how?"

The male cleared his throat. "A small, unknown flyer is approaching from the east, occupants two lifeforms. They are requesting to land. Identifying as Da'yel."

That was surprising. He had not expected the male to attempt transport with his mate while weather was still not yet satisfactorily safe for travel in a shuttle.

Sa'tari's eyes lit up as she spun toward Jor'y, her wings flapping with excitement. "Da'yel is here already? I assumed he would wait until the snows cleared a little more," she said, echoing of his own thoughts. "This is wonderful timing!"

"Yes, the perfect time," Ri'vyk murmured drolly, his eyes glittering with resigned humor. "Arriving just in time to cause chaos as we try to finish preparing for Hashavnal. I certainly hope assigning him to the guard was not one of my worst ideas."

Jor'y bit back a growl, his own anxiety over the male surfacing. His last memories of Da'yel were of an undisciplined and reckless male. It would be disastrous timing if he ended up being cause of some misfortune so close to the arrival of the dignitaries. Not only were the trade agreements important for his valetik, but Jor'y also would be very displeased if anything upset his ongoing courting. Da'yel was an unpredictable variable.

"Sir?"

He groaned. Fowler was still waiting for a response.

"Instruct him to land on the west-front landing. It should be the most stable location we currently have. He will still need to exercise care with his human mate as the conditions are still inhospitable for a human female to be exposed overly long to it."

"Understood, sir. Transmitting your instructions now. Fowler out."

That dealt with, Jor'y returned his attention to the tree. Ribbons and garlands twined up its length where the holy symbols were not painted, as were the lights that dressed much of their own decor around the estate. Brilliant little baubles were attached carefully to the small leaf capsules dotting up its trunk, emphasizing the round protrusions, making them appear even more like an Aturian cock.

"There should be some decor at the very top," Sa'tari said. "Vanessa mentioned that it was common that a star might be set up there, though the reason could differ depending on the tradition celebrated. She said her family put a star at the top to represent their sun. The tree looks incomplete without it."

Jor'y was at a loss. He protected his people and oversaw their valetik's financial interests. Coming up with creative designs was not something he had great experience with. Glancing around helplessly, his eyes fell on a long, discarded rope of lights. Striding over, he bent and retrieved them, drawing them up close for his inspection. As a youngling, he had entertained himself for hours tying knots. Perhaps he could make a simple spray of light to resemble a star?

"What if we did this?" he suggested. In one hand he gathered the light string into a bundle, wrapping and knotting it until it appeared to spray out light radiating from the center where he gripped it. "We can bind it here and anchor it at the top of the leaf capsule."

Vi'ryk tilted his head curiously, his mouth opening, but Sa'tari interrupted, pushing forward, her wings flapping wildly once more. "How clever. That is perfect!"

He grinned and turned it over to his eager cousin even as Vi'ryk sighed and her mate, Gal'ythron, chuckled from his post at the door over her enthusiasm. Hurrying over to the workstation beside the tree, Sa'tari bound it and grabbed a metal hook before rising quickly into the air with a rapid beat of her wings. Those on the ground held the trunk steady as she drove the hook into the capsule, twisting it around the spray of light and anchoring the other end of the metal hook back into the hard bark. No sooner had she finished than Jor'y grimaced.

That... had not helped.

For many long minutes, he could do nothing but stare as a hush fell over his kin. Their faces conveyed mixed emotions between amusement and delight. All because the spray of lights looked less like a starburst and entirely like something else bursting out.

"Oh. My gods. Why is there is a massive dick shooting off in the middle of the room?" a human female asked in awe.

Jor'y spun toward the source, his wings flaring wide in surprise. He distraction with the tree had been great enough that he had not even heard her enter, nor the large Aturian male standing beside her.

Da'yel gaped up at the tree at her side, his expression slowly shifting to a wide grin. His female, a small, curvy human with a short shock of bright yellow hair peered at the male beside her curiously, her brow knitted in confusion.

"Is this some Aturian sex celebratory thing that I'm not going to understand?" she asked drily.

The male coughed out a laugh and shook his head. "This is not any custom I know of." His vivid green eyes tracked over the room until they found Jor'y, and his grin widened. "Cousin, perhaps you can further... ah, illuminate us as to what we are seeing here? Because my a'talyna is right. Why, with that slight curve at the top, it bears a quite nice resemblance to my..."

His female grabbed a handful of crown feathers and yanked his head down, flattening her hand over his mouth as her pale cheeks turned red.

"I don't think anyone needs that much detail about your equipment, my love," she laughed. "Let's leave some things to the imagination here." She gazed back up at the tree and shook her head. "Good gods."

"Hello. You must be Lucy! Do you like our Yule tree?" Sa'tari hurried over, her eyes bright, eager for the human female's input. "I would love the opinion of another human before we show it to Jor'y's female."

Lucy looked at Sa'tari before her eyes widened further at the tree. "That... that is a Yule tree?" She choked on a sound suspiciously close to a laugh, her hand scrubbing at her eyes. "Oh, man, that somehow has managed to even beat a lit-up palm tree. It's even better because it doesn't need a dark room to look exactly like..." She trailed off, the red in her cheeks changing to a shade that looked almost dangerous to Jor'y.

He groaned inwardly and exchanged a worried look with Vi'ryk. He knew it! This courting gift was going to be a disaster. Judging from the reaction of Da'yel's mate, the tree was both shocking and laughable. Vanessa would think that he was mocking her beloved traditions.

The female squealed suddenly and pulled her hand away from her mate's lips, shooting the male a displeased look as his slowly drew his long tongue back into his mouth. He grinned back at her unrepentantly before striding over to sweep Sa'tari into the embrace of his arms and wings.

"My beautiful one," my male crooned, drawing his mate's attention like a laser.

Her expression turned noticeably rigid in a way that Jor'y found even more alarming than her color. The female looked ready to tear Sa'tari apart. He hissed quietly to himself. While normally that might have been amusing to see, there would be chaos if his cousin killed the female in self-defense. Idiot male!

Da'yel, the clueless male that he was, glanced back at her and happily motioned her forward. "Lucy, please come here, there is someone I want you to meet."

"Oh, I just bet," she muttered, her eyes narrowing as she

folded her arms over her chest. "This trip is turning out to have all kinds of surprises. And who exactly am I meeting?"

Sa'tari glanced at the female, her own eyes widening in awareness as she shoved her brother away to greet her.

"Da'yel, let go! You did not introduce us properly first." Her smile directed at the other female was welcoming. "I am so happy to meet you at last, Lucy. I am his sister, Sa'tari."

Lucy stilled, her mouth parting before her arms dropped down by her sides. A nervous laugh escaped her as she swiped a hand down her face.

"Oh, wow, I swear I'm not a psycho. I should have guessed who you were since he's told me so much about you, but I was just surprised."

Sa'tari chortled with laughter. "It is no fault of yours. My brother should know to use his brain when bringing his mate into a new place with a lot of our people milling around and so much confusion." She gave her brother an annoyed look that Jor'y felt entirely.

Dread swept over him, drawing his attention from the little scene to the tap of human boots approaching from the outer corridor. This time, he did hiss aloud, his entire body stiffening to prepare for the worst as his mate entered the hall. Her eyes did not smile when they met his.

"Jor'y, there is something you need to know…" Her words faded on the last syllable, her eyes caught on the very thing that was likely to be the source of his downfall in his mate's esteem. Her jaw dropped, color filling her cheeks. She coughed and cleared her throat, her eyes cutting to him before returning to the tree. "Jor'y, what is that?"

"It's your Yule tree!" Lucy shouted out around a giggle. "Hi. I'm Lucy, by the way. Da'yel's mate."

Vanessa looked at the other female, and then at the Aturian at her side and back again. "Oh, wow. You're… mates."

Lucy nodded enthusiastically, sliding her arm around her male's elbow. "Yep, he's all mine. We've done the whole courting shebang and are expecting a little one sometime in the late spring," she added, patting the slight curve of her belly.

Jor'y froze, his heart hammering out a loud beat in his blood. Never in his life would he have imagined that, of all of his cousins, he would have envied Da'yel. But knowing that Lucy was carrying the male's offspring, suddenly Jor'y couldn't think of a more fortunate male. He was the first of Jor'y's closest kin to breed, and that made him irrationally jealous. And now, with his blunder, there was a chance he might not get there with the female he loved.

"Sorry if we're crashing your own courting, but that is some gift you've got there," the female continued on, horrifying him further, her smile widening as she unknowingly dug Jor'y's grave even deeper.

Vanessa's eyes trailed from Lucy to him, her eyebrows arching before she dragged her gaze once more to his gift. The silence that filled the room as all of his kin, every member of the valetik who had been able to come and assist with the tree, watched and waited. He wanted to close his eyes so not to see his own shame running up to meet him as she assessed every inch of the tree, lingering on the symbols and spheres, but drawing up to the spray of lights at the top.

Her lips twitched, and she brought a hand over her mouth and held it there for a long moment as she shut her eyes, her shoulders trembling. He felt his anxiety pooling, consolidating in a hard lump in his belly. After several heartbeats, she dropped her hand once more and opened her eyes to look over at him—and she smiled, her eyes bright with a warmth and happiness that stole his breath.

"You really did this all for me?" At his nod, her smile widened further, her hands clasping over her heart. "I can't believe it. You know, I think this is the best Yule tree I've ever seen," she said, her voice trembling with emotion. "You've brought a little bit of home to me when I needed it. Thank you for such a thoughtful gift."

Jor'y recovered his voice and sense enough to reply in turn from his heart. "I will always strive to make my home feel like your home in any and every way that I can."

The warmth in her eyes seemed to brim over, and all for him. He should not dare to believe that all of that in her eyes was for him, but he could not help it. He wanted all of it, and so he was happy to believe that what he saw in her eyes was truly all for him.

Pleased smiles brought out among the valetik, and chatter broke out among his kin. Jor'y ignored them as he strode forward and gathered his female in his arms. As she enclosed him in her embrace, she surrounded him with her sweet perfume. He buried his nose in her neck, ignoring the two human males who seemed unable to pry their eyes away from the tree as they chuckled and wiped tears of humor from their eyes.

Let them laugh. His mate was pleased with his gift. In Jor'y's heart, that was all there was room for.

CHAPTER 21

Jor'y dug his claws into the arm of his chair, the noise of the dining room, busy with the clatter of his clan as first meal was enjoyed, forgotten as he focused on what the human males were telling him.

"The governor and some higher ups from the colony will be arriving in just a few hours with the representatives from Earth. I have no doubt that they fully expect for you to be unable to get everything prepared in time for their arrival," Carthy said soberly.

"Then we will have to disappoint them," Jor'y said, nodding to Vi'ryk. "I will not give them anything they can use against us."

The male met his gaze grimly and strode away, activating his comm as he walked. Jor'y had every faith that he would see to it that their valetik readied all accommodations in time.

Da'yel scowled, drawing his mate closer beneath his wing. "I do not understand. Why not just turn them away? No one representing the interests of Darvel should be trusted."

Releasing the arms of his chair, Jor'y folded his hands on the table in front of him and met his cousin's eyes. "The capital has communicated the necessity of these trade negotiations. Darvel has been insisting that they need to expand north out of the southern continent into more Aturian territory in order to support the needs of their growing colony. The capital's offer to facilitate trade negotiations with the Darvel colony is to prevent United Earth from putting pressure on Aturia to cede more territory through the Alliance. Since our valetik is in the flight routes to the southern continent, they are looking to us to create a line of supply."

He leaned back against his wings, his eyes narrowing. "Make no mistake, it will be profitable for us as well, but Darvel could use our hosting customs to make us look undependable to support their move."

Vanessa gaped over at him from where she was perched on a chair just to his right.

"But that wouldn't be your fault. They are showing up days ahead of schedule!"

Carthy shook his head. "It doesn't matter. They will argue that since Jor'ytal rescued us from the mountain that he should have been preemptively preparing for their arrival." He rolled his eyes. "All on the basis that the colony would need to prioritize our retrieval in order to 'protect' you, Miss Williams. As you heard for yourself, the governor was all too eager to use the situation to his advantage under the guise of safeguarding you. Never mind that a shuttle could have been sent to retrieve us without moving up their timeline." He frowned. "I suspected that Darvel would be too cheap to make separate trips, but I had not been prepared for this. Moving up their visit was a shady move on their part."

Lucy snorted, her small body pressing closer to her mate. "Dahlia is the most corrupt Darvel colony I've been stationed at. Given how Corp likes to play fast and loose with Earth Gov's rules, that's saying something."

"It is interesting that you were released to mate with an

Aturian. What division were you contracted from?" Carthy's tone made the question seem inconsequential, if not for the sharp way he watched the female.

Da'yel's wings folded protectively around his mate, his lip curling in a snarl, but Jor'y held up a hand, silencing his cousin. His own eyes turned toward Lucy.

"I doubt that Carthy asks this without reason. From what I've observed from the male, everything he does and says has purpose. I do not want any more surprises. If there is something I should know, I expect to be informed immediately."

Lucy, suddenly very pale, fidgeted and pushed down her mate's wing.

"I'm protected by Aturian law," she blurted out. "There is nothing that Darvel or United Earth can do about my mated status."

Carthy's lips pressed together before blowing out a breath with a loud sigh. "That's what I was afraid of. A non-gratas. The governor is going to shit when he catches you here."

Jor'y scowled. "There will be no human excrement outside of the waste receptacles. What he does there is his business."

Vanessa leaned forward, stroking back his crown feathers with one hand. "It's an expression meaning that Governor Bradshaw is going to be extremely displeased and confrontational about it." Her eyes shifted up to Lucy. "Non-gratas are humans without citizenship rights and protections, who effectively belong to Earth Gov. They can be leased out to the colony, but they are not permitted to marry or reproduce without documented permission and license from Earth. To mate with an Aturian meant she ran away from her assigned position on the colony, an offense which would have been aggressively punished if she had been caught. That she mated an alien just compounds her crimes in the eyes of Darvel and United Earth."

Jor'y's wings shook with fury as he leaned forward out from beneath his mate's hand, piercing Carthy with a venomous look. "Your people allow this? Our historical and legal regards show that Aturians were assured that humanity did not deal in slaves. It was guaranteed long before the first buildings were erected on Dahlia Colony."

Carthy sighed. "The non-gratas status isn't legally considered slavery on Earth but rather a social station. They aren't technically owned by anyone, just have fewer freedoms as non-citizens. Miss Williams exaggerates a little by wording the matter as a theft of Earth property. Legally, it would be considered kidnapping protected humans. In our lawbooks, United Earth and Darvel are held responsible for the welfare of all non-gratas as a parent would of a minor. Therefore, they have movement and social restrictions that keep them safe and reasonably cared for."

"Reasonably cared for?" Da'yel snarled, his wings closing tighter around his mate as if seeking to shield her. "I have seen the scars on my mate's flesh that showed exactly how they cared for her!"

"I didn't say it was right," Carthy growled back, "nor that I agreed with it, but that's the legal classification of non-gratas on Earth. Darvel's position would suggest that, in this situation, Lucy was kidnapped."

Lucy pressed her cheek against her mate's chest. "But I'm safe. There's nothing that they can do to me. Da'yel is my mate, which means that I'm protected under Aturian law."

Vanessa nodded, her expression worried as her fingers clenched against his wing where her hand fell. "Yes, but..."

"But Darvel could attempt to push a claim against Jor'ytal for harboring a kidnapped human from Dahlia Colony," Carthy interrupted, his brows dipped lower. "I doubt that they could force your return, Lucy, but there is a high possibility that they would use it to bolster any grievances they might have with the valmek. Like saying that they would be wary of trading with a male who might sanction 'kidnapping' non-gratas from the southern continent."

Jor'y's mate shot the male an annoyed look. "That is if they find out she was here."

"Agreed. What are the odds that she'll even be recognized? It's been how long since you escaped Dahlia, Lucy?" Tackert asked, pushing himself upright from the wall he had been casually leaning against.

"Nearly two years now," Lucy replied, her gaze nervously tracking over everyone in the room. "I wasn't assigned anywhere near the governor or any of his people, and I do look different," she added, patting her curves. "Even if I didn't, citizens rarely seemed to notice non-gratas anyways." A hesitant look flashed across her face. "I... I don't mind staying in our quarters though if you think it will help."

Jor'y shook his head. "Aturian laws are clear and are in complete alignment with Alliance law in this matter. You are now a citizen of Aturia, and how you became such is a private affair between you and your mate. If Darvel tries to use your mated status against me and mine, they will not get far using that as a complaint against my valetik. If they even recognize you." He settled back once more against his wings, his sharp gaze focused on the mated pair. "We will carry out our celebrations as if all were normal." His eyes narrowed on his cousin. "But that is also going to require control from you, Da'yel."

To Jor'y's satisfaction, the male nodded stiffly.

"Good. Now that we are all sufficiently updated on the situation, let us turn our attention to more pleasant things."

As discussion turned to the Hashavnal traditions and those of Earth, Jor'y reached over, seeking contact with his mate, needing that physical bond. Her fingers instantly entangled with his, her lips curving as she glanced down at him from beneath her lashes.

He had far more to lose with the arrival of the humans than the contract with Darvel. Of everything on the line, his a'talyna was the most precious. He would tear apart anyone who tried to take her away from him.

CHAPTER 22

*V*anessa stood at Jor'y's side in the docking bay, watching the small contingent exit the transport. Governor Darrel Bradshaw was easy to pick out from the group. Striding silently at the fore of his party, he was clad in a purple calf-length dress robe with burgundy and gold trim, and a pair of loose deep purple pants beneath, gathered tight around his lower leg by polished black boots. There was nothing exceptional about his face, or the mouse brown hair that he had attempted to style in a way that refused to hold, the curls slipping into a loose disarray. Even his neatly trimmed beard and mustache, while waxed almost to an inch of its life, didn't boast any fullness. His bearing was that of a man high on power who barely gave a thought to anyone else traveling with him, so much that he didn't bother sparing a glance for any of them.

Although her stomach churned with nerves as her eyes tracked his movements as well as those of the representatives of Darvel and from Earth, five in total, a lifetime in the public had done much to prepare her for this moment.

Don't show fear.

Vanessa made a conscious effort to relax her jaw, making sure to smile when the party made their way toward them, surrounded by a small number of human guards. Although the transport was large compared to the shuttle she had arrived in, it wasn't big enough to provide extra room for a large body of soldiers to accompany them. Not that arriving with a small force could be seen as anything less than an outright insult, if not a threat.

She had a feeling that Governor Bradshaw wouldn't particularly care how a show of force would come off. Condescension was obvious in every line of his body as his lip curled upon spying some of the decor dressing up the bay entrance just behind them. He wore his disgust openly.

No. This was not a male who cared for the opinion or graciousness of his host. This was a man looking for a fight, someone who came with no other intention than as a means to an end. Until this moment, she had tried to keep an open mind and hope that it wasn't as bad as everyone was assuming it would be. That, yes, there would be risks that they had to be aware of, but some part of her had hoped that the governor was invested in the meeting going well for the good of the people under his care. All of that turned to ash in her mind at the way he sneered at the Aturians and their garlands hung in the docking bay specifically to welcome the representatives to the valetik.

"Governor Bradshaw, I am Jor'ytal. Welcome."

Bradshaw's mouth stretched in a facsimile of a smile that didn't meet his eyes. She wasn't fooled for even a minute as he coolly returned Jor'y's nod.

"It is a pleasure."

He swung his arm to his right, gesturing with his first two fingers at a pair of men in long white and burgundy robes, the vest bearing the insignia of Dahlia and Darvel Corporation. These were representatives of Darvel on behalf of the colony. If she had to guess, both men were well into their fifties with graying beards and collar-length hair braided back, though with the advances in nanotechnology she acknowledged they could be older.

"These are my assistants, Representatives Dwayne Arthur and Stephan Vansago." Each man, bearing bored and vacant expressions, nodded at his introduction. He then gestured to the two men and woman at his left. "And from United Earth we are joined by Representatives Gregory Bartholomew, Ashlan Thomas, and Margaret Avery. They are here to see to it that all of Earth's regulations and stipulations are met during the course of this meeting."

All three representatives wore sharp gray uniform tunics paired with slacks. The younger of the two men, Bartholomew, appeared nearly washed out, fair and beardless in contrast to the dark complexion and long, dark beard of the older man at his side. The woman with them had a riot of frizzing auburn hair barely constrained into an updo that was a few years out of style. That told Vanessa that this was a woman who didn't follow trends and instead stuck with something once she found it suited her, but seeing as it was still fairly recent, she was open to trying new things. That was promising, despite the sharp way the representatives scrutinized everything their eyes fell upon.

Vanessa was grateful she hadn't followed up on her desire at any time to take Jor'y's hand for comfort. While she couldn't say for a certainty how much the Darvel representatives might have had noticed, she had little doubt that Earth's representatives would be quick to notice violations of Earth laws regarding interspecies relations.

Perhaps it was a good thing that he hadn't held her hand for more than a moment, even if she did suddenly want to snatch it back up in an act of defiance.

Jor'y was good to her, perhaps the most caring and noble male she had ever met. The way he put others under his care first was not only admirable but made her want to be there in a more concrete way to help shoulder that burden however she could. He was always alone in his responsibilities, and it was something that weighed on her mind with more frequency. And now that he was determined to protect his cousin's human mate, it roused something within her that made her want to publicly demonstrate that she wasn't ashamed of their relationship.

"It is a pleasure to welcome you to my estate," Jor'y's deep voice rumbled, and he tipped his head in another bow, his dark horns slicing elegantly through the air.

"Thank you, Jor'ytal," Thomas replied, his dark eyes crinkling with genuine pleasure as he glanced around. "Your home is quite festive. It reminds me a little of where I grew up on Vera Colony, right down to the chill in the air and the brilliant seasonal decor."

"It's certainly festive," Avery agreed, almost smiling until she heard Bradshaw's snort of disbelief.

"Shall we proceed then, or did you wish to admire the decor as well?" The governor arched an eyebrow at Bartholomew, who flicked a speck of something from his tunic as he eyed Bradshaw sourly.

The governor nodded impatiently to Jor'y. "It seems we are ready."

Vanessa watched as her lover's lips twisted into a polite smile that was belied only by the narrowing of his eyes.

"This way," he rumbled, his wing extending to lightly sweep behind Vanessa as he turned, silently directing her to remain close by.

Avery's voice floated up to them as they walked through the corridor toward the main hall.

"I'm so pleased to see that you're well, Miss Williams. Your disappearance in the storm made news all over Earth. Have you spoken to your mother? She's been quite vocal over her worry."

Vanessa winced. She hated to admit that she had been putting off that particular conversation. She had no doubt that her mother's worry and flair for the dramatic had combined into quite a media spectacle. She had little doubt that would just be the tip of the iceberg of what she would be treated to. That was going to require a glass of something strong and a considerable amount of uninterrupted time.

"Not yet," she replied. "But I plan to, soon."

But not before she spoke to Jor'y. She needed to get some things figured out before she had that conversation with her mother. If she was staying, she wanted her mother to be the first to know and get that conversation out of the way as quickly and painlessly as possible.

"I trust that our host hasn't been keeping you from communicating with those outside of the estate," Bradshaw interjected.

Gritting her teeth, Vanessa peeked over at Jor'y beneath her lashes. He didn't appear to react at all to the question. The only clue to his feelings was that, as he walked at her side, his tail had a bit more of a distinctive snap to it with each step, the feathers fanning and closing. Schooling her expression, she glanced back over her shoulder at the governor.

"Jor'ytal has generously provided access to everything he has during our stay here, and as you know we've had access to the comm systems the minute the storm cleared, since we spoke to you earlier today. My decision regarding when to comm my mother is based on personal factors and have nothing to do with any non-existent restriction."

His smile made her skin crawl. "I'm very glad to hear it, Miss Williams." He glanced at Jor'y's back. "I hope that our rooms have been ready. I don't know about the other representatives, but I could use a little time to rest before the evening meal after our long journey here from the southern continent."

There was a small murmur of agreement, but it was to be expected.

Jor'y's wings fluffed in agitation. "Your rooms have been prepared. My cousin Sa'tari will be meeting us in the main hall and will escort Representative Avery to the unmated females' wing while I show you to your quarters in the unmated males' wing."

"Your estate is arranged to keep males and females separated from each other? I would not have expected such a level of segregation," Avery commented, drawing Jor'y's gaze.

"Unmated females require a place where they can escape from the attention of males. A male can invite a female to his wing, but males are forbidden to enter the unmated females wing for the safety of any females staying there given our larger size and greater strength. We take such matters seriously. Mated pairs and families have other parts of the estate available to them."

Vanessa just barely refrained from to turning her head and staring at him in surprise.

That certainly explains a few things. Important need to know things that would have been valuable to hear much earlier how strict the rules were, and how much he was bound by them. Her internal grumbling aside, aloud, she kept her commentary as blasé as possible. "Fascinating," she murmured

Jor'y's eyes flicked to her briefly, communicating surprise, before returning to his guests.

"I don't know if I like that," Arthur muttered to the males nearest him, his voice not quite low enough to not be audible to everyone nearby. "How will we protect Miss Williams and Representative Avery if they are kept separate and we are unable to reach them at all?"

Jor'y's golden eyes gleamed cold like polished metal as he stopped and glowered down at the Dahlia representative. "I assure you that they will not require anything of the sort. Sa'tari assists Miss Williams, and I will personally make certain that another female of my valetik is made available to Representative Avery.

We also have security recorders in every corridor of the estate. Security will alert me, or my assistant, should anything suspicious show up. Your presence there is unnecessary for their safety."

The threat was subtle, but it was there. Any man who attempted to enter the wing would be discovered and dealt with harshly.

As promised, Sa'tari stood waiting in the main hall, a welcoming smile on her face as she stood in front of the solstice tree that immediately drew the aghast attention of every human in the party. Someone cursed, and Bradshaw, in true asshole fashion, demanded to know what the meaning of that was. That was expected. What was unexpected was the soft laughter that came from Avery following the quick explanation Vanessa offered.

"I can see that this is going to be an interesting holiday," Bartholomew observed dryly, straightening the cuffs of his tunic, not even bothering to hide the small twitch of his lips.

"I'm still not convinced that this isn't some sort of joke at our expense," Bradshaw growled, glowering at Vanessa's solstice tree.

"Oh, lighten up, Governor," Thomas interjected with a small huff. "I doubt it was intended as anything of the sort, not with all the work that was clearly put into it."

"Certainly not," Vanessa agreed hotly, unable to not speak in defense of her tree. She refused to allow *that man* to speak ill of Jor'y's gift. "It's mine." As several pairs of human eyes turned to her, she smiled and explained. "The valmek arranged it as a gift, knowing that I was feeling homesick with the solstice approaching."

Avery's eyebrows rose. "That was very considerate of him. I admit, this entire visit so far has been full of surprises. It has hardly been what I expected after listening to Bradshaw's comments regarding the difficulties of coming to agreements with Aturians. It seems to not match up at all with what we were led to believe." She glanced appreciatively at Jor'y's wings before trailing over his muscular shoulders and chest, and Vanessa bristled. "Nor are the Aturians anything like what I expected from seeing vids of the capital city."

Jor'y's eyes narrowed, and Vanessa cleared her throat, interceding before anyone commented any further.

"Jor'ytal and his valetik, as well as most valetiks on the outer rim, keep to their species natural appearance. They don't clip their children's wings when they are young nor remove their feathers unlike what has become custom in more urban areas in result of our colonization here and negative experiences with visitors on their world."

"All of those feathers certainly seem unsanitary," Arthur commented in a low voice to Vansago. "I would have fits if any of the Aturians we hired at the colony were getting feathers all over the place."

Vanessa frowned. "I don't think that's for any of us to judge."

The governor sneered and seemed ready to respond when he was interrupted by Sa'tari's quick thinking. The female thankfully stepped forward, inserting herself into the situation as she inclined her head to Representative Avery.

"Everyone must be feeling quite tired. Come with me. It will be my pleasure to show you the room that I had readied for you."

"That would be wonderful, thank you. I do believe I could use some rest," the representative agreed with a tired smile.

Vanessa mouthed her thanks to the Aturian, earning her a small wink from her friend.

"Of course," Sa'tari murmured sympathetically, her wings spreading to usher them forward.

Vanessa craned her neck, hoping to catch Jor'y's eye to communicate her need to speak privately with him. To her frustration, he was engaged in quiet conversation with Thomas as the male admired the festive decor. Tackert cast her a sympathetic look from where he stood guard at Carthy's side. He nodded to her, silently assuring her that he would keep an eye on things in her absence. She smiled at him as she allowed herself to be led away.

Later, she would find a way to speak to Jor'y alone, one way or another.

CHAPTER 23

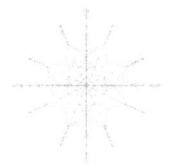

The humans from Dahlia colony were entirely reprehensible. Although those from Earth had their annoying moments, they were almost ignorant enough about his culture for him to forgive their lapses. This was not the case for the Darvel colonists. These males knew exactly what they were doing and went to lengths to make certain to insult him whenever they were given the smallest opportunity. He did not know what he might have done to the governor at the suggestion that he was imprisoning his a'talyna if his mate had not made certain to correct the male's attempt to plant seeds of doubt into the minds of the representatives from Earth overseeing the matter of the trade agreement.

It had continued in the absence of his a'talyna, the males becoming increasingly unpleasant during the short tour through the estate leading toward the unmated males' wing. If not for Tackert and Carthy intercepting and redirecting such shifts in the conversation, he might have lost what little remained of his thread of patience and murdered the governor on the spot. He had been grateful when he had finally been able to escape them. He had wanted to seek out his mate and had been tempted to, except there was work that still required his attention, delaying whatever private interlude they might have until later that night.

He acknowledged that it was perhaps for the best. He had no doubt that his mate also had her own work to see to after spending a significant part of the day helping him to see to organizing for the arrival of the humans. After being accustomed to spending so much time with Vanessa every day, his chest ached from missing her. A sensation that offered no relief until she entered the dining hall with Sa'tari and Representative Avery.

Now, less than an hour into the evening meal, he was reaching that brink again. Not only was Bradshaw appalled as he watched Vanessa sitting just to Jor'y's right, but it made him bristle with indignation and an intense desire to rip the offending organs from their sockets. No one looked at his mate that way!

The male was fortunate that his a'talyna was not upset by him. In fact, Vanessa made a point to ignore the governor as much as possible, devoting most of her attention to the representatives from United Earth. Avery engaged his female and kin in almost friendly conversation with interjections from Thomas as they dined. Bartholomew was largely silent but often smiling as he listened, but he did occasionally prove that he was still very much a part of the conversation when he would break his silence and quietly offer an insight or opinion. What was surprising was that over the course of the meal, Vansago seemed to almost unbend enough to attempt to join the conversation when it turned to favorite seasonal traditions. He spoke fondly of the colony he had grown up on before being silenced by Bradshaw's glower.

The governor was clearly the poisonous head of the worst of what was wrong with the Dahlia colony. The divisiveness he encouraged and seemed to demand was telling.

Even more so was the look of abject disgust he directed at Da'yel and Lucy.

"I am surprised that you allow servants to sit at the table with you. Surely they have their own place?" Bradshaw observed as he stirred the ka'jun stew in the bowl in front of him and took a hesitant bite.

None of representatives had so much as reached for more than the blandest food until they saw Lucy, Vanessa, and her guards fill their plates and bowls with appetizing foods. Those from Dahlia had been the most reluctant but had restrained themselves to little more than the stew and thick portions of lav'y made from root vegetables mashed together and crisped. Jor'y wished he had the power to deny the male even that for the absurdities coming out of his mouth.

"Guards and servants should not be privy to discussions of importance," Bradshaw added with a pointed look at Jor'y's relatives gathered around the table.

Jor'y leaned forward. "The explanation is simpler than you might believe. They are not servants. They are my kin, my valetik. Those who are currently not occupied with a task are dining with us now. Then another shift will dine, just as some of my kin ate earlier. No one is excluded. Those who cooked this meal that you are now enjoying are seated at the table with us. We all have our own duties and responsibilities, but that does not make their position lesser than mine as their valmek."

The governor set down his spoon and folded his hands together on the table in front of him. "I see. And how does a human fit into your social order? What skills does she have to contribute that fits in with your social norms? Humans are accustomed to working for a salary, not sharing resources."

"I did not say that those who labor did not get reimbursed for their work. My cousin and his mate only recently arrived to the valetik. I am sure she will find her place before long."

Bradshaw snorted with ill-concealed amusement. "Ah, so they didn't meet in your charming village. I had a hard time imagining what would draw a human to such an isolated place. This hardly seems like a place where a woman would come willingly. Why, even our Miss Williams had rented a cabin close to one of Dahlia's major cities. She wouldn't have even thought to venture anywhere near here if her shuttle hadn't gone down in your mountains."

Doubt passed through him fleetingly. Would Vanessa have been happier and more content on the southern continent if she had that choice available to her instead of being stuck with him at his estate? Was she secretly eager to leave even now?

He did not think so, but as expressive as human faces were, there were many emotions he was unable to accurately read. Perhaps she agreed with the governor's statement.

To his relief, Vanessa's mouth tightened as she glared at the male. "You speak as if it's some sort of hardship being here, when it's quite the opposite. Being here is far superior to anything I could have expected at the colony. I have no regrets and wish that there were ways that more human tourists had the option to vacation in valetiks. I'm sure there are many who would enjoy the opportunity to experience the quiet life here."

The governor leaned back in his chair casually. "Ah the romanticism of women. You say that now, but the fact of the matter is that most humans visiting Aturia come to spend their time on the southern continent. So, it makes me curious where women such as your kin's mate come from and why they would willingly give up all rights and protections to mate illegally." His lips twisted into a tight smile. "Not that there's anything we can do about it. I'm well aware of Aturia's laws regarding the protected status of mates on this planet."

"I confess I'm curious about that too," Avery added, her eyes bright with curiosity as she leaned forward, leveling her gaze on the mated pair. Unlike Bradshaw, there was no malice in her expression, only genuine curiosity, and Jor'y was grateful to see Da'yel slowly relax. "Interspecies mating is illegal for humans in accordance with our laws, mostly because those laws were put in place to make certain that human space remained solely human. While aliens can visit under temporary visitor visas, there's no danger of being outnumbered in our own colonies. I have never understood why a human man or woman would give up everything they have ever known to mate with an alien. It's a terrible sacrifice and yet one that many people have made." She smiled. "I'm not judging, merely curious. As Governor Bradshaw pointed out, you're perfectly safe here."

Lucy cleared her throat, glancing at her mate questioningly for a moment as something unspoken passed between them, and she nodded before addressing Avery directly.

"No offense meant to you personally, Representative Avery, but you assume that Earth Gov's 'protections,' as you call them, benefits everyone equally. Not everyone even ends up at the colonies because they wish to be there but are sent with little choice in the matter. It is all by the luck of the draw via lottery that many people are selected to perform labor at the whim of colony governments who receive little oversight directly from Earth."

Avery's face paled, her smile falling. "Oh, dear."

A fist thumped on the table loudly, making Lucy jump and earning a sharp scowl from Vanessa even as Da'yel's wing snapped out and encompassed his mate.

"I knew it! I knew that there hadn't been a mistake with our numbers. We *have* been losing non-gratas! In fact, I bet if I pulled up our systems, I would discover that this female is one of the missing ones we assumed was returned to Earth ahead of schedule," Representative Arthur said, exchanging an excited look with his governor.

Lucy ducked closer against her mate, an angry hiss erupting from the male.

"I don't know what you're so excited about," Vanessa

snapped. "Like Representative Avery said, Lucy is completely safe here. You have no power over her anymore now that she's an Aturian citizen."

Bradshaw shot Thomas a hard look. "Did I not tell you earlier that Earth Gov needs to argue against the Alliance's policy to allow aliens to legally mate with non-gratas as protected humans? I hope you will report this to your superiors so we can see some changes. I have lost over two thousand non-gratas over a fifteen-year period. That is unacceptable! It is no wonder that Dahlia colony is practically falling down around our ears. Limited resources and escaped non-gratas have had a detrimental impact on us."

"I've never heard of any colony 'losing' so many non-gratas," Vanessa observed, taking a pointed bite of her food. "It makes me wonder just what's happening in the colony that is making the risk of escaping and the reality of never returning to Earth colony space worth it."

"Indeed," Thomas growled with a deferential nod to Jor'y's mate. "I believe that this is something that our superiors will need to be made aware of, rather than seeking an adjustment to inter-stellar law within the Alliance, which is no easy accomplishment. It's as irregular as having a Darvel representative acting as governor. We were assured that your past career in the military guaranteed loyalty to Earth interests, but this is all very suspicious."

Avery made a small noise that could have been agreement, but Jor'y was certain since she now seemed to busy herself with her food as Bradshaw's face reddened to a shade nearing purple as he stabbed at his own food furiously. Bartholomew took advantage of the sudden opening in the conversation.

"In terms of trade with Dahlia, regardless of who the governor may or may not be in the near future, I am still very curious to know what your valetik has to offer our people. Regardless of whether an investigation occurs or not, we have seen the situation on Dahlia over the last few weeks and it is evident that they need assistance, especially with winter now well underway. Despite the southern continent being milder, the people struggle to stay warm and fed, while you seem to have plenty and the bedding ten times warmer than anything we enjoyed at the colony."

Jor'y nodded, grateful for the change in topic. From the corner of his eye, he noticed his cousin stiffen, his wing curving around Lucy. Even Sa'tari seemed overly anxious as she shifted on her seat beside her mate.

"You are correct. Humans requested to set up a colony on a milder continent that suits your biology and crops well, but compared to the rest of our planet, it is far more limited in resources. The bedding you enjoy is made from yal'tev wool, as is most of our winter and cool weather clothing. They live high on our mountains, shepherded by our valetik. There are risks during the stormy season, but this is their home environment and we rarely lose more than one or two beasts in the worst of the winter storms."

Bartholomew tipped his head, curious. "Would you consider trading some of the livestock directly?"

Jor'y regretfully shook his head. "They wouldn't thrive on the southern continent. They require our colder climate to survive. This is their natural habitat."

"I see," the male murmured, his long, thin fingers rubbing his chin thoughtfully. "And foodstuffs? What of that? It seems that while our grain crops do well enough here, a number of other fruit and vegetables yield little."

"Humans do not trust Aturian food items," Jor'y reminded him.

Rather than turning red and mumbling incoherently, the male met his gaze and nodded. "This is true. However, it seems that you have a good grasp on what we can eat, especially considering that you've kept a number of our people well fed for many days on your fare. Perhaps you can come together with a list of what crops you have and share instructions on how to prepare them to vary the colonists' diets? Unfortunately, Miss… Lucy, was it?" At her nod, he continued, "Miss Lucy is correct in pointing out that the conditions of the non-gratas in Dahlia Colony are deplorable. Citizens receive rations first as priority, but there is no reason to see non-gratas going hungry. I am trained to oversee nutrition and food in human colonies and was assigned to come on behalf of Earth once the government got wind of the conditions being reported by Dahlia in their request for expanding their territory."

He shot an annoyed look at the governor. "This does not mean that I'm in favor of petitioning for the expansion of the colony. Far from it," he gritted out, making the other male redden. "But I acknowledge your need for more resources, Governor Bradshaw, even if that means we need to learn how to maximize the land that we have and to trade for what we cannot. That land does produce wealth, even if it is not in wool and crops."

Jor'y nodded. The southern continent was mineral-rich, and its warmer climate made it hospitable to many of the more exotic fruits of their planet that took more care cultivating in the mountains.

"There are fruits that do very well in that climate, as well as species of edible flowers and important dye plants that can easily be cultivated there. The dye plants alone should add revenue to your trade, as many valetiks would be happy to trade for quality dye. You should be able to find this information in plenty on the Aturian servers."

"Excellent!" Thomas boomed happily. "It seems we've come to an agreeable solution. What do you think, Avery?"

The female smiled and nodded. "It seems very satisfactory to me. Don't you agree, governor?"

Bradshaw muttered something unintelligible that Jor'y's translator could not pick up but jerked his head in a nod.

Jor'y smiled, triumph filling him as he settled back against his wings and listened to the conversation turn once more to happier subjects of celebration and merriment. At his side, his a'talyna caught his eye, the corners of her mouth tilting up as she winked in a shared moment of victory. He knew then that what had been accomplished would set down a foundation that would benefit Aturians and the human colony both.

It was a good feeling, especially knowing that it was accomplished only because of the help of his a'talyna at his side. That day had proven one thing to him with abundant clarity: he could trust the welfare of the valetik within his mate's hands explicitly. Nothing made him happier or prouder to call her his.

If only she would stay.

CHAPTER 24

Vanessa smiled as Jor'y, after given the 'all clear' from Tackert over his private comm line from where the male was stationed at the far end of the corridor, pulled her into the privacy of his rooms. At last, they were finally alone. She wiggled against him as he pulled her against his chest, his feathery wings closing around her.

"I have longed to do that all day," he groaned against her neck.

She laughed at the tickle of his breath against her skin and reached up to stroke the long, silky feathers draping down his back. Gods, she couldn't get enough of touching him.

"I have too," she whispered. "But we really should talk."

He stilled and raised his head, his eyes questioning. "Talk? I have been informed that when human females say this, it is a code for some unpleasant news that is about to be delivered."

Vanessa choked and shook her head, her eyes crinkling with laughter. "What? Who told you that?"

His lips pinched shut, unwilling to betray his source. Vanessa leaned into him and snickered. He was loyal almost to a fault, even if it was entirely inconsequential. Still, she couldn't help but to admire that about him.

Standing on her toes, she pulled his head down and brushed her mouth lightly against his. The contact was sweet, drawing longing from deep within her heart, and all too brief. The moment his arms circled around her and he shifted closer, she dropped back down to the flat of her feet and put space between them before she could become too distracted. Threading her fingers with his, she tugged him toward the bed where she sat on the side of the mattress, drawing him down beside her. Jor'y's wings spread, brushing against her shoulders and back in a soft caress before folding behind him and he met her eyes with the reluctance of one preparing to face execution.

"It's not bad," she whispered. "Trust me, I want you to do all kinds of wonderfully dirty things to and with me, but I just want to talk first."

His gold eyes didn't so much as leave her face long enough to blink as he nodded in agreement.

She licked her suddenly very dry lips. "This thing between us... where do you see it going?" His mouth turned down, his wings twitching with the confusion darkening his eyes. "I mean, what do you want?" She hurried on before her nerve failed her. "Because I really need to know that now, before I do or say something stupid. And before I even begin to seriously consider making a decision."

His head tipped, his eyes narrowing. "You are my a'talyna."

He said that as if that explained anything when it only confirmed her worst fears.

Vanessa shifted uncomfortably, and she dropped her gaze in embarrassment, her heart sinking. "Is that all?"

She should have known. She wasn't Aturian and not his own kind. How could he possibly feel more? She was nothing more than a biological reaction for him. Fine to scratch an itch or two, but something that wouldn't make a lasting relationship for her. She couldn't settle for less than love, not when she felt it so strongly for him.

Gods, she did. She was truly messed up in love with him. She had finally fallen. How ironic it was with someone who couldn't or wouldn't return her feelings.

She attempted to pull her hand free from his, but his fingers tightened, refusing to release her.

"I do not understand," he growled. "Why do you pull away from me?"

She shook her head. "I know that the a'talynal is very important for your species. Sa'tari explained it, but I'm sorry. I need more than that."

Jor'y's nostrils flared. She might have considered his expression angry once before, but she recognized the hurt and confusion in his gaze. His lips parted several times as if he were about to speak, but nothing came out. It was several minutes before he found his voice, but it was rough and gravelly his words came. His wings drew up protectively around his shoulders, betraying the greater depth of his pain.

"You do not wish to be my a'talyna?"

She shook her head and cupped his cheek with one hand, smoothing her fingers over the skin there. "It's not that I don't want to be, because I do. I just can't live with that being only the reason that you want me. I don't want to be so easily replaceable."

His eyes went wide, and he openly gaped at her. "You speak as if a'talynal comes so often that it is so easily replaced."

"But it could be," she whispered. "If that's all there is and I give up everything, I could still be replaced if you found another a'talyna that you could actually..." she choked, a tiny sob working its way from her throat as she turned her eyes away, not wishing to see the truth in his gaze any longer, "...love."

"Love." The word was hissed softly, the syllable drawn out. A pair of large, warm hands cup her face as he forced her to meet his eyes. Golden depths shimmered with warmth and a depth of feeling that gave her pause. "How can you not know that I love you? A'talyna may have drawn me to you and created a bond between us that made me wish to court you, but it is not why I wish for you to stay... or not the only reason. I want you forever, as my mate, because I love you and cannot breathe or know my heart beats in my chest without you at my side."

"You love me... and want to mate me?"

It hardly seemed believable to her. She was afraid that it had to be some conjuration of her imagination, half-terrified that it was a hallucination fed by her deepest yearning.

He nodded and stroked his hand through her hair, his eyes shifting to watch the strands fall between his fingers with obvious admiration. His gaze returned to hers, and his expression softened, a smile playing at his lips.

"How can you doubt it? You are my light... my joy. There would be no Hashavnal without you, nor any sunrise in every morning throughout the year. My days without you would return to the darkness I lived in for so long that I cannot remember when joy last truly brightened them." He drew her hand up and brushed a kiss across her palm, his eyes fastened on her. "You are my miracle and most wondrous gift bestowed on the gods, to return my joy to me. That they chose to do so in time with the Hashavnal, I cannot see as anything less than the miracle it is."

His claws gently brushed back her hair as tears filled her eyes.

"I know that you have a difficult decision, a'talyna. I understand that it can bring you pain and isolate you from everything you know. I understand too that this means you cannot give me a promise now, especially when you did not understand my heart."

Tipping her head back, she smiled up at him. "You have no

idea how much I want to throw caution to the wind and give you that answer."

He pressed his lips against her brow, and for a moment she could feel that energy bond snap into place between them and a feeling of love flow into her. Now that she recognized it, she knew exactly what that sweet, tingling warmth was.

"There is no rush, a'talyna. As much as I crave to know that you will be mine, I want you to give yourself to me without doubts between us. I want you to be certain when you join your life to mine. I will wait for however long that takes."

Vanessa leaned into him and sighed. "You are right. Thank you. You are a good male, and there haven't been too many in my life who weren't just looking out for their own interests. That you care about what's best for me means everything." She let out a happy sigh. "It's no wonder I fell for you."

Jor'y stilled and then his arms wrapped around her, drawing her close against his body, his wings enclosing them together in warmth. In the shelter of his wings, he peered down at her, his golden eyes glowing with happiness.

"I will treasure and protect the gift of your heart for all of my life," he murmured. "Allow me to show you again how much."

She groaned as his claws skated down her body, lightly scraping against her skin on their path over her breasts and down her belly. Even though contact was separated by her thick sweater and leggings, it felt like a trail of fire running over every inch they touched. Her breath caught when his hand suddenly cupped her mons, the heel of his hand pressing against her clit.

"Love me," she whispered.

His lips brushed against hers. "Always."

CHAPTER 25

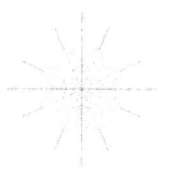

Jor'y worshipped his mate's body. He could do no less than that. He would praise the names of the god at every curve and dip as if they were sanctified altars upon which to lift his adorations if he could. Even still, his whispered words of devotion and thanks were muted against her flesh as he kissed every inch.

Although he knew she had much to consider and there was a certain gravity hanging over their time together, knowing that he held her heart strengthened the a'talynal bond between them to the point that he felt bathed in her love. She might have to settle things still in her mind, but as far as he was concerned, he was now hers for the rest of his life.

"Jor'y," she whispered on a panted breath.

He curled his wings around her as he drew her into his lap, pressed her chest against his, her legs parting to settle on either side of his thighs. His hands slid up from her hips, pushing her sweater up her belly, baring soft, warm skin beneath his palms.

The hot press of her sex through the fabric against his lap sent a frenzy of need climbing through him, his cock already resting stiff between them. He caught her mouth with his once more, delving into its sweetness, unable to resist and incapable of being swept up into its heady power as she responded eagerly. Her body rocked against his as she made small sounds of pleasure.

Every movement of her body brought deep, vibrating vocalizations from him, his wings twitching around her. Growls and rumbling purrs blended into each other, his throat clicking in sharp little singing sounds as a wave of ecstasy rolled through him at her taste and the feel of her body against his. As wondrous as these were, even more potent was the richness of her energy rising to him, infusing him with her essence that made him hunger for nothing other than that. He could feast on his mate for the rest of his life and never feel want for anything.

She was the sum of everything that he wanted and needed. And she was afraid of being replaced? That he would discard her for another a'talynal? Impossible. With the bond strengthening between them, he had drawn in so much of her energy that he was now dependent on her and her alone. Her every reaction sweetened her flavor and brought joy to his own heart knowing that he was satisfying his little mate, proud he had that effect on her. That his mate craved him as much as he craved her. He knew that just from the way she eagerly drew back on his own essence.

It was incredibly erotic. Far more than he had ever experienced before. This was not only the gift of the a'talyna, but the power of the bond reinforced and enriched with love. He was powerless before it and empowered by it. It made him want to draw out their mutual pleasure even as his blood ran hot, demanding to find that pinnacle with her.

In appreciation for the gift of her love, Jor'y made sure to trace his claws over her skin as he worked the material up, knowing how much she enjoyed the erotic tease. Her skin shivered beneath his touch, vulnerable as a tiny winged dol'seshy that he had once owned as a youngling. And like the dol'seshy, entrusting herself entirely to his care as he held her in his lap and, releasing her mouth, pulled her sweater over her head. She gasped as the air hit her flushed skin.

"I have you, a'talyna," he managed to get out when she made another soft sound in the back of her throat.

Between them, the bond snapped and pulsated, feeding him her desire so that his own rose higher. His body shuddered, feeding back his own lust on that line between them so strongly that he felt his mate quiver within his arms as the potency of his rising desire hit her.

Unable to resist tasting her flesh, his lips traced a trail down her neck, the faintly salty taste of her skin filling his senses. She gasped again as his tongue stroked over her collarbone and slipped down over her breast to curl around the bead of her nipple. Delicate fingers gripped his crown feathers tightly as she ground herself against him and, for a moment, he was all too aware of just how fragile his a'talyna was. Her body, held tightly against his, was so easy to break. Reflexively, his wings tightened around them, his wing claws flexing with an instinctive need to protect her.

His eyes crossed when her hips bucked over his cock, his hands snapping down to the covering as his claws flexed with a need to tear them from her.

"Jor'y, stop teasing. I need you."

Her whispered plea tested his control, his claws digging into her cloth-covered legs. At his nudge, she stood, her feet braced around him as he peeled the fabric down, lifting one foot and then the other as he dragged it free from her delectable body. He appreciated how easily the material slid off her body without a tail to encumber it.

Tossing the fabric to the side, he crouched low, his claws pricking at her bottom as he dragged her hips forward. The scent of arousal flooded his nostrils, beckoning his taste. His long tongue slicked over her sex and a hand shot to one of his horns, holding him firmly in place.

He chuckled and drove his tongue deeper, lapping at the sweetness issuing from that most intimate place until she bucked against his mouth, her fingers pulling at his crown feathers until he finally allowed her to tug his head away. Tipping his head back, he smiled up at her, enjoying the answering heat in her own eyes.

His female suddenly dropped into a crouch, her knees hitting the bed, and shimmied her bottom backward. Her pink tongue stroked over her lips as her hand curled around his cock, squeezing it in a way that made his hips push forward. She smiled at his response, her eyes glittering with a secret feminine power. He watched, breathless and entranced as she dropped her head and her tongue lashed against the head of his sex.

Wings snapped out wide, the muscles in his legs went taut as his tail drew up high behind him. The feel of her tongue stroking over him was like a hot brand of ownership, sealing him to her, and when her mouth closed around him, drawing on the essence of his body in tugs that matched the draw on his energy, he nearly came on the spot from the intensity of the pleasure shooting through him. He just barely clamped down on the explosive chain reaction barreling through him to pull his cock free and yank his mate back up his body until she again straddled his lap.

His blazing gaze met hers, determined that she see and know the full depths of his desire. Her eyes, deep pools of love and need drew him in, especially when they widened in wonder, her breath hitching.

"One lifetime is not enough," he whispered, dropping his head against her shoulder as he dragged her bottom forward, aligning the head of his cock with her entrance.

Her small hand cradled the back of his head, caressing his

crown feathers. "Then we will make every moment, every breath, count."

Arching her back, she pushed down, the liquid heat of her sex opening to his penetration, enveloping his cock in its tight sheath. She shivered, and her channel tightened in a pulsing grip as the first small orgasm swept over her until his first seed of this mating released from him. He groaned, his wings fanning behind him for a moment before snapping closed around her, drawing a soft, pleased laugh from her.

Vanessa pressed her back against his wings as she rocked against him, the pace guided by his hands gripping her hips. As the energy sang between them, the mutual feeding tightening between, the pace grew more frantic. A sheen of sweat broke out over their bodies, the wet sound of their rutting filling the air as the need of the breeding season that had been riding him for days bloomed fully. The v'lica on his cock swelled with mating heat as his cock grew larger inside her, engorged in a way that it only could this time of the year. He could tell by her scent that his mate wasn't quite yet in season, and that reassured him that they wouldn't accidentally breed before she made her decision. That didn't stop his mating glands from opening on the knots on his cock. The moment they released their essence, his mate would be marked. It wasn't something he could stop, not knowing that his sex was swollen within her. He could not pull out if he wanted to.

"Vanessa, a'talyna," he groaned. "I am sorry. I am going to mark you."

His blinked up at him through a haze of lust. "What... does that mean?" Each word escaped her in breathy pants.

He shivered, unable to not be pleased by what was happening, even if it removed this aspect of her choice. "Any male with a sensitive nose will smell that you are mine. My mate," he rumbled.

A clarity entered her eyes, and she nodded. Her legs squeezed around him as she bounced down on him, meeting his every thrust. A spark kindled in her eyes, and her lips curved in invitation.

"There's no one else I want," she admitted. "There is a lot to weigh and consider, but the way I feel about you isn't one of those things. It's too late for that. Mark me, my love."

Growling as a shudder of relief passed through him, Jor'y pressed up into her, his hips snapping in a way that elicited a loud moan from her, grinding deep with every thrust. His female's delicate hands suddenly seemed stronger than usual as she grabbed ahold of one horn and another handful of crown feathers. The sting from the pull on the feathers drove him into her harder and faster, his growls becoming urgent snarls as her sounds joined his with whimpers and passionate cries.

It was the sweetest music to his ears.

There was a thrum, the tension along their bond growing tighter, energy passing between them coiling. His claws pressed lightly in her flesh and her small flat teeth dug into the meat of his chest, muffling her cries. His head tipped back, a bellow rushing up his throat as his female screamed as the energy in their bond detonated, the ultimate and highest pleasure slamming into them both. His seed released in heavy jettisons, her channel around him milking every drop as her sweaty body slumped against his, her muscles trembling from the aftershocks.

He held her there, hoisting her a little so that she lay against his heart, her breath fanning his skin as they remained sealed together.

It took some time for his cock to go down, but he relished every moment of it. Even though their time together was limited to avoid getting caught, he indulged himself in every moment to touch his mate and express the great depths of his affection, love and need for her. By the time her body released his, her eyes were nearly shut with a sedate peacefulness. He hated to rouse her and even more he hated leaving her at the hall of the unmated females' wing. She was no longer unmated, and everything within him rebelled against it. He watched her slip away before turning his back on the dark corridor and returning to his empty room.

He would be patient and wait for his mate.

CHAPTER 26

Vanessa tried to keep her footsteps light as she made her way down the dark hall to her room. After so many days living there since her shuttle went down in the storm, she was familiar enough with the route to and from her room that she thankfully didn't require any light that might give her away. Her steps were certain as she walked. The bend in the hallway was coming up, and then she would only be five steps from her room.

Taking care not to rush to keep her footsteps light, she moved as quickly as she dared. As she got closer to the bend, some of the tension in her heart eased. Just a few steps more and she would have made it. Holding her breath, she rounded the corner.

A beam of unexpected light cut through the dark, nearly blinding her and Vanessa squinted against it and stumbled, her arm and side smacking hard against the wall to her right. A curse bubbled up to her lips, but she bit it back, her attention trained instead on the source of the light.

"Miss Williams, are you all right?" Representative Avery's voice was hushed as it cut through the hall and accompanied by a quick rush of footsteps that brought the light bouncing closer. In the next moment, a luminated face was peering over at her with worry. "I am so sorry if I startled you. What in the world are you doing out and about this late?"

"Representative Avery! I'm fine. There's no need to worry. You just took me by surprise." She laughed weakly, uncertain if the woman was going to believe a word she said. "I'm used to walking the halls of this wing when I can't sleep and had forgotten that I wasn't the only one up here. I hope I didn't wake you."

"Please do call me Margaret since I very nearly both ran you over and gave you a heart attack."

"Okay, Margaret. And you must call me Vanessa."

Margaret Avery smiled, her expression relaxing. "Thank you, Vanessa. You know, you're braver than me to be running around here with no light, though I understand a sleepless night. I had the same thing in mind myself. I never could sleep well in a new place," she admitted. "I thought about taking a closer look at a few of the tapestries in this wing. They're incredible."

"That they are," Vanessa chuckled in agreement. "But much better to see in the morning light. Maybe I can show you a few of my favorite ones tomorrow? For now, would you like to come into my quarters and join me for a relaxing cup of o'jar? I keep some powdered root and sweetener in my room to make it instantly for when I get a need late at night. It only takes a minute to heat the water at the heating disc."

"I don't think I've ever heard of o'jar," Margaret murmured. "That would be lovely, though. Maybe something hot to drink will help me get the rest I'm really going to need if I have to put up with that windbag tomorrow."

Vanessa laughed again as she led the other woman to her door and laid her hand on the key-lock panel, opening the door for them. The lights came on as they stepped inside. "I'm assuming you mean Governor Bradshaw."

"The very same. How Darvel talked Earth Gov into letting that man be governor is beyond me. I've never seen a colony more incompetently run, and his personal politics and all his whining... far too many days of all of it. Not that I should be discussing such things with a citizen," she admitted, a dull flush climbing her cheeks.

"I agree with you even after just a few hours in his company. Really, the way he was talking to me over the comm systems was enough to tell me all I needed to know about him. You're free to speak how you like around me. I'm certainly not going to judge you for it, nor do I care to discuss your opinions with anyone else, since they're your own to share as you see fit," Vanessa added as she headed toward the small table and took down a pair of cups from a display shelf.

Setting the kettle on the heating disc, she opened the small pot, the spicy-sweet scent of the ground o'jar root rising up pleasantly to her nose. She took a moment to breathe it in before scooping the root into a pair of filters set over the cups.

Margaret slid into a chair at the table. "That is truly admirable, and quite refreshing. I have become a bit jaded, I suspect. It is hard not to be when everything around me is all political games." She sighed and sat back. "Perhaps I'm due for a change in scenery. I get tired of playing these games between Earth and Darvel's colonies."

Vanessa carried the steaming cups to the table and smiled in sympathy and set them down before taking her own seat.

"I have to admit, being away from Earth has been nice. I don't miss all the little politics and intrigues of my family's social circle. Nor being valued only for my name and my career being considered a waste by my peers, unworthy of my family and the advantages I've had in life."

"Once I would have admired someone in your station, but it took me only a few years working as a representative to cure me of envy for those in the public eye. I don't think I would enjoy your life, if you don't mind me being honest."

"Please do be honest." Vanessa laughed. "I admit though that I miss some of the things about the holidays, but the Aturians are making up for much of that."

Margaret's lips tipped up. "They certainly have made a grand effort, especially Jor'ytal. For him to go through all of that effort to make you more comfortable is incredibly sweet. All of the Aturians here have been incredibly nice, despite Bradshaw's attempts to ruin any good feelings that they might have for our species." She took a delicate sip, and her eyes lit up. "And they certainly aren't subpar when it comes to food and drink. This is fabulous."

Vanessa's eyebrows went up. "If you don't mind me saying, you and the other two representatives from Earth seem less… rigid… when it comes to rules regarding human contact with alien cultures and food."

"I suppose we are," Margaret said after another long sip. "You learn to be a bit more pragmatic about things when you spend a lot of time on other worlds. Although our work often has us dealing with Darvel and Earth's governors in the colonies, we spend even more time in alien courts and cities. If food is judged safe for humans and there is a local human population eating it despite advisories from Earth Gov's Health First Council, then we are likely to eat it. Or at least that is the case with Thomas and I. We have worked together for years. I'm glad to see that Bartholomew is on the same page, even if he is a bit more reserved. My opinion, which is not very popular on Earth, is that there needs to be a sharing of cultures so that we can understand and appreciate each other."

Vanessa swallowed the suddenly bitter o'jar in her mouth and nodded. "I wish more people thought the way you do. Maybe then there wouldn't be Aturians in the cities who believe it's necessary to cripple and disfigure themselves to be accepted. For all that they celebrate this Day of Joy, I get the feeling that many of them don't know joy the way the outer rim Aturians know it. How could they, when they probably live with the pain of having their wings severed in youth and then the regular plucking." Her voice faded, and she shook her head. "And then being demonized for their sexual bonding needs. It's unnecessarily cruel and we perpetuate that as a species with our world's every contact with theirs."

Margaret's lips tightened. She took the last swallow from her cup and set it down. "You're right, Vanessa. That is unacceptable. Thank you for this. You've given me a lot to think about. I think I will write up some comms to be sent within the next day or two for the duration of our visit. There are many observations that I need to share with Earth, regarding not only the colony but Aturia as a whole."

Understanding passed between them at that moment, and Vanessa felt her lips pull up into a smile, hope filling her chest, as she walked Margaret back to the door. The handheld lamp flickered back to life, and the woman stepped out once again in the hall with a nod. Nothing else needed to be said. She couldn't change Earth in a day, and it perhaps wouldn't happen in her lifetime, but knowing that Earth's relationship with Aturia could change for the better gave her hope. Her shuttle crashing in the mountain had put her in the right place for a lot of things to come together.

Perhaps she was truly meant to be there?

She had never been one to believe in fate, but for once something just felt right about everything.

Was that her decision then? Was she ready to stay?

Vanessa glanced at her datapad and licked her lips. Perhaps the easiest way to find some clarity was to finish her story. It would be cathartic to experience the loss through the tragedy of her characters. Feeling that firsthand as she worked out that ending could help put a lot into perspective.

Nodding to herself, she sat down and drew her datapad to her.

The storm had let up, and now it was time to go. They had their time hidden there within his castle. Hidden away by the storm where they had been able to escape their very different lives for a short time. The time for goodbyes had come, and her heart was breaking with every step she took to him, knowing that this would be their last touch and last kiss as the sun rose in the sky, the first light of Solstice morning. It would have to last a lifetime in her memories.

CHAPTER 27

Lucy blinked her eyes rapidly as she lowered the datapad. "Did you really send this out?"

"Late last night. I got the notice this afternoon that it was uploaded for my readers. It's finally done," Vanessa sighed, sitting back in her chair.

"I told her not to, that it was a terrible ending," Sa'tari said from the other side of the room where she fussily straightened Vanessa's belongings. "It is too sad."

Vanessa sighed. "It's supposed to be. A story like this that ended happily would be banned on Earth. A relationship that develops between two star-crossed lovers but concludes with a parting of the couple in a bittersweet ending in which the heroine is changed for life but goes back to her own life and world dances on the line of acceptability but passes the test. It's tragic."

"It is stupid," Sa'tari argued with a defiant snort. "She is the happiest she has ever been, but she will break her own heart because 'it is the right thing to do.' Who says? Who owns her life and happiness that she is beholden to them? No one who I could see. She had no mate she left behind, no youngling. Only responsibilities that other people say that she owes them. So she is just going to offer herself up as a sacrifice for people who care only about their own selfish wants. It is a terrible ending."

Vanessa blinked. As she had written the ending, she had argued back and forth with herself over her own decision. She thought that the final chapters communicated the struggle, and yet her friend had pared down the struggle in such a fashion that it felt almost... trivial. Had she really been agonizing over a decision that was being based solely on what others expected of her?

It wasn't because Earth particularly had a lot to offer her. She didn't agonize at all over what she would be leaving behind in terms of possessions. Sure, there were a few creature comforts from Earth that she would miss, but there was always a good chance of finding something similar in her new home. And those that she could not find, did they really matter that much to have had influence? Or had she been taking a simple matter and blowing it out of proportion all because she was afraid of making a decision?

"Lucy?" She turned to the only other human in the room. If anyone would understand her position, Lucy would.

The woman bit her lip and met her eyes sheepishly. "Sorry, but I have to agree with Sa'tari on this. I mean, the ending is well written, but... it's really sad. I've been reading the chapters as they've come available and have become... well... invested in them as I've watched them come together and fall in love. In some ways, it brought back some really great memories of falling in love with Da'yel. For me, personally, this is not the ending I would have expected or wanted."

"But you understand why it was written this way, right?"

"Well, sure," Lucy hedged. "Her reasons for leaving him are probably ones that citizens on Earth may relate to, and I know that public image and receptivity of your work is very important for you, but the romantic in me wanted to see them defy the odds."

Vanessa glanced down at the datapad and grimaced. Perhaps she should have written both endings and conferred with someone first before sending anything out. Writing the tragic ending had helped her work out a lot in her head, and she was pretty certain of the direction of her decision because of it, but was giving her readers that ending the message that she wanted to leave the world? After all, this would likely spell the end of her career if she took this step.

"Well, crap," she muttered.

Lucy laughed and leaned forward, her arms extending across the table toward her. Sympathy shone in her eyes. "You wrote this for you, didn't you? You think that this is what everyone wants, but the words written here are powerful. I can practically feel the heartache coming off them. As much as I hate it, the writing is very evocative of pain."

At Vanessa's reluctant nod, she gave a wistful smile. "You know, it's a big decision you're facing, but Sa'tari is right. Sometimes the hardest decisions are actually really easy when we set aside what decision would be expected of us. What would be sensible and loyal to all those who care about you? I had to make that decision when I left Dahlia, knowing that I would never be able to see my family again on Earth or the close friends I made in the colony. I felt like I was betraying them. Betraying my parents who cared for me and loved me all my life and betraying my friends who have been by my side, sharing workloads and grief. I made the decision that was best for me. Is what you have there worth what you have here?"

Vanessa frowned. "My mother will be disappointed. She had her heart set on me marrying someone she approved of, even though I never planned to do that, so she would have been disappointed anyway. I do think it will hurt her, though, that I will never return to Earth. It will be like cutting ties with her, except we will still have comms."

"And she could visit," Lucy pointed out. "If she cared so much to see you, nothing would stop her from taking a ship to Aturia. She can certainly afford it more than most."

Vanessa's lips quirked. "That is true. There is the matter of my career dying, but I know that won't stop me from writing even if I have to publish on the interstellar channels like the interspecies porn distributors."

Lucy giggled, her eyes dancing with humor. "I can tell you that it will at the very least continue to be profitable. Don't let the way things appear to be on Earth fool you. A lot of men and women take advantage of the opportunity to get forbidden media. You wouldn't believe the kinds of things a few of my friends had. Your public career might end, but I think you just might discover an entirely new market for your books."

"That could certainly be amusing and far less stressful," Vanessa agreed.

Sa'tari tilted her head and she stepped forward. "You are afraid that you will long too much for your home?"

"Gods, no! Actually, getting away from Earth has been a blessing." She bit her lip. "I am afraid, though."

The Aturian bristled. "You still doubt?"

Vanessa quickly shook her head. "No, not at all. I know that he loves me, and that I love him. That's not what I'm afraid of. I'm just afraid of making the wrong decision. My mother has controlled most aspects of my life, and what she hasn't controlled I have had legal departments and educators to fill that role. I'm afraid of being the one responsible for this decision."

Lucy blew out her breath, letting loose a dry chuckle. "Welcome to the real world, Vanessa Williams. We are all terrified." Her eyes narrowed. "I will tell you one thing: if you love him and want to be with him, and you've worked out how much it will hurt to leave him and you've obviously weighed the pros and cons to death—the only thing in your way is yourself. Love is a leap of faith." A smug smile crossed her face as she sat back again in her chair. "I leaped... probably a bit too recklessly." She chuckled. "Only took me three days to make the leap too, and I never once looked back or regretted it. Trusted my heart and a few other essential parts of my anatomy to do it and it was all on board."

Vanessa choked on her spit, her eyes tearing as she coughed. "That... that would be a way to put it."

"The a'talynal is very satisfying," Sa'tari hummed in agreement, a knowing smile spreading across her face. The female had no doubt that Vanessa was already quite well aware of that fact. That knowledge was probably helped along by the fact that Vanessa's skin was a deep red for the way her cheeks felt like that they were flaming. "Love and a'talynal together with friendship and caring are the most important things for any Aturian. Anything else we need will come."

"And come and come," Lucy teased. "Gods, all the coming alone is worth it."

"Oh, gods, stop," Vanessa pleaded, a helpless giggle escaping her.

The other woman sobered, though her eyes still sparkled with humor. "You are right. Sex and love aren't everything, though they are good places to start. And you both work well together outside of the bedroom instead of just inside, which is important. Having something in common to work towards and do together is great. Da'yel, for instance, loves old Earth sci-fi movies. He finds them quaint. Since I also love them, we spend a lot of time watching ancient reruns of *Star Trek*. Next Generation, not Deep Space Nine if I can avoid it. He likes to torture me with it every now and then, though. Our first Yule, we watched *Generations*, the only movie with a Christmas scene, to give him a taste of the holidays with his sci-fi."

Vanessa's nose wrinkled. "I'm not sure if we have anything we both enjoy in common. Most of our time together is spent working, taking walks through the estate, or sneaking off together."

"That is something," Sa'tari pointed out. "You both enjoy your work but make time for each other. Sounds like a good place to begin. You have all your lives to learn more things to enjoy together. It is always an adventure for me and my a'talyna," she confided.

"Sounds good to me too," Lucy said. "And I'm not saying that out of entirely selfish reasons of wanting another human woman around—not that you aren't great, Sa'tari. No insult meant."

"None taken, sister," the Aturian assured her. "It is natural to desire familiarity." She glanced over at Vanessa. "We may jest with you, and I may point out here that you already smell thoroughly mated, but it is all about what you feel."

It was. Vanessa already knew that, and she could tell that Sa'tari was well aware of that fact and framing the question aloud for her benefit. What she felt had been the pinnacle of her decision making and had allowed her to grow closer to accepting changing her stars to remain on Aturia at Jor'y's side. Excitement took root, working its way through her. She had already made a decision but had been too afraid to trust it and put it into words. But she knew the answer.

"So, what of it? Do you feel like you have made a decision?"

"You know something? I believe I do." Vanessa returned Sa'tari's smile and then Lucy's before she turned forward to face the viewscreen and grimaced. "And I think that I'm going to need some privacy for this next part."

Lucy's eyebrows rose. "Why do you look like you are preparing to face the firing squad? Do you have to make legal arrangements?"

"More like preparing to face something far more difficult—my mother. Then it will be the lawyers to make sure all of my credits are transferred here to me before Earth Gov locks up access to my bank account."

The other woman's nose wrinkled adorably. "Sounds 'fun.' All right. Comm if you need us. Come on, Sa'tari, let's go find something entertaining to occupy our time."

"There is still more preparation for Hashavnal to be done," the female pointed out, and Lucy grinned.

"More phallic decorations?"

Sa'tari shared a conspiratorial smile. "We can always fashion some ourselves."

Lucy wrapped an arm around Sa'tari's. "That's the spirit! I just know that we're going to be the closest sisters. Let's go hunt for dick imagery and leave Vanessa to her unpleasant tasks." She glanced back over her shoulder, shouting back, "And then come see us when you're done! I have a feeling that this is going to be a three-woman—ah, female—effort if we really want to have fun."

"Sounds great. I'll hurry then."

"Be sure that you do!"

Vanessa grinned as they left her quarters, a tiny chuckle still making her body shake slightly. Another point in favor of staying. Her smile slipped, however, when she faced the screen. Clearing her throat, she addressed the estate's AI.

"Please connect me to the comm system. It's time to talk to Mother."

A testament to how cooperative the weather was now, the screen came to life after only a few minutes while the uplink established. On the screen, her mother strode forward, her hand clutched to her chest.

"Vanessa! It's about time you called me. If I hadn't heard from officials confirming that you were alive and well, I would have been a wreck."

"I'm sorry, Mother. I didn't mean to worry you. There was just a lot on my mind that I needed to work out before comming."

Her mother nodded. "Of course, dear, after being stuck inside with aliens for days on end. Naturally, I hope after all of this you are planning to return home. Cary was quite beside himself when you disappeared. I really think you should reconsider."

"Mom, I'm not coming home."

Her mother sighed and folded her arms across her chest. "Okay, stay another month, but then I want you home on the next starship to Earth."

Vanessa drew in a deep breath. "No. Mom, you're not hearing me."

"Don't be ridiculous. I can hear you just fine."

She suspected everyone in the wing, if not the entire estate, heard her mother's shrieked "What?" echo through the halls. At least they were spared the next forty minutes of crying as her mother tried to present argument after argument against the idea.

Vanessa shook her head, finally cutting her mother off. "Mom, no. I love him. I'm staying here with Jor'y."

"The alien?"

"Yes, Mom. The Aturian."

She was certain the responding scream was heard everywhere that time.

CHAPTER 28

*V*anessa wanted to tell Jor'y her decision right away. She hadn't expected that it would be impossible to get him alone over the course of the next several days. Although they still sat together at meals, the governor began insisting to have their conversations in the privacy of the o'dari. Jor'y spent much of his day locked up with them, or showing them the grounds and how the estate made different things. She was able to trail after them during the tours, and found them both interesting and informative, but he could barely so much as glance at her without drawing the attention of the governor.

Jor'y also seemed to recognize that fact as he communicated his frustration through covert glances and the odd twitch of his wings or claws that seemed to instinctively attempt to reach out toward her before he got control of them once again. That was the only thing that reminded her that he loved her during their separation. Those stolen glances kept her heart from breaking when he seemingly ignored her presence beyond the dictates of strict politeness and hospitality.

He even addressed her as if they were strangers. Even though she had understood the reason behind it and not only agreed with it when Carthy brought it up but had also insisted on it when Jor'y had protested hotly against it, as each day passed it was cutting deeper. Of course, at the time, she hadn't considered the fact that they would find themselves unable to escape being watched. Not only did Bradshaw keep Jor'y occupied until late, but the man was *everywhere*.

If it wasn't him, then it was one of his assistants from Dahlia or his guards, lurking around corners. It was bad enough that Jor'y hadn't been able to sneak her into his rooms since that first night, nor could they find even a single moment to escape Bradshaw's notice. And she wasn't the only one being affected. Just a glance at her mate told her that he was running out of patience. The signs were small, like his wings fanning and his tail snapping, but they hinted at the irritation bubbling to the surface despite the polite and almost friendly face he showed his guests.

His restraint was impressive, even for someone who had been raised in the social circles she had. She hoped that she was just as subtle about her feelings. While she had a carefully cultivated social persona and the outward face she showed others in settings such as these, her own mounting stress was slowly tearing it down.

It didn't help that seeing Da'yel and Lucy together made her feel a little jealous of the couple. She wanted what they had, to be held close against Jor'y's side, his wings tucked around her and their fingers entwined. She wanted what they had only been able to enjoy in private so far. She could only imagine the torment that he felt when his eyes rested on the couple for a moment and pain would etch into his features before smoothing out once more into a polite mask for the benefit of the governor.

Not for the first time, she wished that the bond that was initiated during their moments of intimacy was likewise as effective at other times. While she was far more tuned in to him than she likely otherwise would be, she suspected that having that would have done a lot to reassure them and diminish the mounting stress during the times they were forced apart.

She directed a hot glare toward the governor from beneath her lashes as the man launched into another one of his long-winded speeches about Dahlia Colony's needs and his "doubts" over whether or not trade with Jor'y's valetik would adequately supplement their needs. Vanessa clenched her jaw so tightly that it popped. It was all just bullshit. A giant ruse to attempt to manipulate what he wanted from Earth Gov's representatives since his other methods had already failed. Expressing doubts in the valetik's production had been expected, however. She nearly applauded as Jor'y met his criticism with facts and statistics regarding their yearly productions and surplus.

The governor's face reddened almost to a purplish color as they continued down the walk leading out to one of the balconies where Jor'y claimed he had a surprise for them. Vanessa couldn't really imagine what, since the sun was already sinking below the horizon, but she followed, not wanting to be left behind. Especially not when Jor'y's eyes nearly sparkled with excitement when his gaze met hers. She could deal with being around the governor's unpleasantness for whatever surprise he had waiting for them.

Jor'y stopped and gestured to the set of doors in front of them, a warm smile brightening his face. His eyes held hers for a heartbeat, and she felt an electric pulse of excitement run up her spine. It sadly did not last long before he fixed his attention on his guests once more.

Nearby, Da'yel hugged Lucy close beneath his wing, his expression bright with happiness for what was to come. At least his mate looked as clueless as she felt, and that was comforting. Lucy met her eyes and shrugged, smiling as she leaned into her mate's side. Vanessa looked away and back to her own mate, determined not to let jealousy creep back in and sour the moment.

"Guests and friends, these doors lead to the western balcony," Jor'y addressed them in a soft voice, though the silence that suddenly surrounded them carried his words easily. "The sun is nearly gone, and there is a special tradition for the eve of Hashavnal that I wish to share with you. One that I feel is appropriate for some of your own seasonal observances. On the eve of Hashavnal, we kindle the lights of our hearts to remind us of the hope in the darkest of days."

He strode to the doors, and they slid open, admitting them onto the balcony.

Vanessa walked out cautiously and was relieved to see that all of the ice had been melted away, making the stone safe for humans to walk. She took up the rear as everyone filed out, eyes searching the darkness slowly descending all around them. In the distance, riding the crest of the mountains, there was a flushed strip of pink and orange marking all that was left of the setting sun. Her eyes followed the retreating light until Margaret's exclamation drew her attention east, from the side of the estate where the valetik descended down the slope.

Her breath stilled as she stared in wonder. Rising into the skies were hundreds of Aturians, their white wings catching the waning sunlight and the glow of the orb-like lanterns they carried suspended from chains on long poles in front of them. Everyone watched quietly. Even Bradshaw and his men seemed to at least be feigning interest as they politely watched the ceremony.

Wings beat the air, echoing over the mountains as up and west they flew, setting the rhythm for the song they sang. Though she couldn't make out the words clearly, the long, sweet notes of the melody moved her heart and tears sprung to her eye.

Warm wings folded around her, hugging her close, and she leaned back into Jor'y's embrace. She hadn't even heard him come up behind her, but she smiled, glad that he took advantage of the small window of opportunity while everyone watched the valetik.

His voice whispered in her ear, his hot breath fanning the cold skin. "They honor the descending darkness and sing in memory of the coming light. First Mother return to us, First Mother be with us, end the darkness and brighten the light. First Mother bring life on your wings as you crest the mountain, subduer of the great ek'thanak. Chain him to the place beyond the northern mountains and return to us, most noble one."

"That's beautiful," she whispered.

His wings rustled and he hummed softly in agreement before their warmth withdrew and he was gone again, returning to his guests who had not noted his absence. Everyone watched as the Aturians reached the edge of the nearest mountain and disappeared over its edge.

Her heart hurt at his sudden, silent withdrawal but she pushed the feeling down, reminding herself that it was necessary.

Bradshaw turned as Jor'y stepped closer to his side and raised his eyebrows. "Where exactly are they going?"

"There is a place just on the other side of the mountain peak where they will kindle the fires. It is not the shortest flight, but like all things we take seriously, we are dedicated to it and never fail to carry out this important part of the ceremony."

"I see. Wasting time on foolishness then when they could celebrate in the warmth and comfort of their own homes. I guess that should be expected of beings who, for all their technology, are uncivilized," he scoffed.

Jor'y shifted closer to him and leaned down a little closer to the governor while the representatives watched on with interest. Even Dahlia's representatives, although they shot hateful looks at Jor'y, silently observed rather than come to their governor's defense.

"It is a matter of dedication," Jor'y replied. "This mountain is life for us, and so we never fail to give the proper respect and do what needs to be done in order to show respect for that. In turn, we will be happy to share our bounty in peaceful trade with the human colony because our gods provide us surplus gifts. However we may appear to you, this at least I can assure you."

Representatives Thomas and Margaret at the other side of Bradshaw glanced over and shared a look between them, nodding.

Thomas smiled kindly. "Representative Avery and I are in complete agreement. We have been in favor of this trade alliance for these last few days and are more than suitably convinced." He gave Bradshaw a pointed look. "We're prepared to return to our ship tomorrow to report back to Earth, leaving our good hosts in peace for their Hashavnal."

"But, Representative Thomas, surely you don't…" Bradshaw hastily objected.

"I am as well," Bartholomew agreed, interrupting the governor. He straightened a sleeve that had gone askew in the wind. "Moreover, it is well past time to return to Earth. We thank you for your hospitality, Jor'ytal… and for yours, Governor at Dahlia." The latter was said with the tiniest grimace, making Vanessa wonder just how miserable the visit truly had been to earn even that minute amount of distaste from the typically stoic man.

"I see," the governor replied stiffly. Vanessa suppressed a smile as she glanced over at her a'talyna proudly, affection warming through her.

Gods, she wanted to claim him right now at the height of this moment. If only the governor and his cronies weren't there. They were the only ones who kept the words from her lips, declaring that she would remain there with him forever. Governor Bradshaw still had authority over humans on Aturia and could very well decide to try and "save" her from herself and arrest her, causing an interspecies incident in Jor'y's home. Instead, she tried to convey all of her love and pride to her mate through her eyes while all attention seemed focused on him.

At her left, Da'yel leaned down and whispered something in Lucy's ear. She craned her neck back to look up at her mate, a teasing smile lighting her face. Vanessa didn't know how long she stood there watching them, wishing that Jor'y was at her side too. However long it was, it was too long to notice that she wasn't the only one watching.

Her gaze shifting away from the couple, she met the eyes of Dahlia's Darvel Representative Arthur. Gray eyes narrowed on her speculatively before shifting in a telling manner to Lucy and back to her again. A sweat chilled her back as she returned his stare, her mind racing with dread as a number of scenarios popped into her mind. His lips pursed thoughtfully, suspicion lighting his eyes as his gaze darted over to the governor.

Her stomach dropped.

That was it. If they weren't suspicious before, they would be now. Her time was running out. Her fingers curled into fists at her side, and she managed to look away with a feigned expression of disinterest. She doubted her apparent unconcern would fool any of them for long, though it was possible it would give her a little time. Out of the corner of her eye, she caught Lucy looking over at her, her brow knitting with concern. Ducking out from beneath Da'yel's wings, she walked over to stand at Vanessa's side and raised an eyebrow, giving her back to their guests.

"Is everything okay?" she whispered.

Vanessa glanced over at the representative from the corner of her eye and frowned. He had already made his way over to Bradshaw's side and was leaning in close, speaking urgently in a low voice.

Fuck.

"I don't think so. I believe things are going to get very bad any moment now," she replied in a quiet voice.

Bradshaw straightened his robe, his eyes narrowing on her and then Jor'y before striding importantly over to the team from United Earth.

Oh no. No.

"My assistant representative Arthur has just brought something important to my attention that makes me want to urge you to reconsider your position." He glanced over at Jor'y scornfully. "It seems that his cousin is not the only one with a taste for human flesh. I have reason to suspect that Miss Williams has been engaging in an inappropriate relationship with the valmek or is on the verge of doing so. If we cannot trust a valmek to host one of our women without attempting to seduce her, we cannot trust them as trade partners. For her safety, my men will be removing her immediately, and Dahlia will not be engaging in any trade agreements to avoid the risk of losing any more of our women to these scoundrels."

Vanessa shook her head, her feet carrying her forward. "That's not true. He hasn't done anything wrong. We fell in love." She took a deep breath, then scowled at the governor. "You heard that right. I love him and want to stay. I told my mother as much this morning. It's as good as done. You can't penalize him for something that's my decision!"

Jor'y's head snapped toward her, his golden eyes brightening with love and delight.

"A'talyna… you honor me," he murmured. He dropped his head in a small bow, his hand resting flat over his heart.

"This is absurd!" Bradshaw protested. "He obviously has coerced her to say as much!"

Margaret raised a hand, silencing the governor. Her eyes that communicated that she wasn't exactly surprised as she looked over at Vanessa.

"Is this true? You truly wish to remain here and give up all citizenship rights? You are from a prominent family. You're aware that you will lose everything."

Vanessa met her mate's eyes and smiled. Lifting her chin, she looked back at Margaret. "I've never been surer of anything in my life. Nothing I had there is worth losing him and spending the rest of my days without him."

"And he didn't seduce you?" Thomas asked, less successfully hiding the delight shining in his dark eyes.

She snorted and shook her head. "He was always very polite. He indicated his interest but nothing more. I was the one who initiated the relationship from there. We're as good as mated by deed if not by Aturian law. And that too was completely my choice."

That admission alone could land her in prison, but at that point being taken away from him forcibly felt no different. She had to make them see that she wanted this. She couldn't sit by and allow even a shadow of a doubt remain that this mating was her choice and had nothing to do with his trade agreements with the Dahlia Colony.

Jor'y smiled over at her, his feathers puffing out and wings ruffling with delight. "All that is left is to sign the legal documentation at the capital," he affirmed. "It is only a technicality. Vanessa is my mate."

"I see," Margaret murmured. She straightened and drew her coat tightly around her. "Well, in that case, I don't see what that has to do with any of us, nor that it is an obstacle to United Earth's trade agreement between Dahlia Colony and the Mirfal valetik."

Bradshaw blustered, his face darkening. "I am the legal authority on Aturia. I'm the governor. You may represent the interests of United Earth, but I am the law here. They are not legally mated, and so her illegal actions fall under *my* jurisdiction."

He raised his comm, prepared to issue an order, but was stopped by a clawed hand closing around his forearm. A loud metallic crack was heard as Jor'y squeezed, his upper lip peeled back in a snarl, baring a series of sharp teeth and long fangs. His wings spread wide as he yanked the governor's arm up, drawing the man closer to his threatening snarl.

"Do not so much as think of removing her against her will from my estate," he growled. "Neither you nor any of your males will so much as lay a hand on her."

Bradshaw cast a panicked glance around him. "Somebody, do something! This creature is going to kill me!"

There was a flurry of movement as everyone seemed to act all at once. Vansago shouted as he tried to help the governor only to be batted away by one of Jor'y's massive wings. Margaret could be heard arguing with Thomas as the man tried to talk some sense into Bradshaw and talk down the Aturian holding him. Then the guards came barreling in with blasters and were immediately met by Da'yel and the few Aturian guards who hadn't yet taken flight over the mountain to join their kin. The sound of weapons coming online filled the air, mingling with the shouts of humans and Aturians alike.

The excitement on the balcony was enough that she didn't see the gray-robed figure until it was too late. Arthur raced toward her, the hard glint in his eyes the only warning before he hit her with the full force of his weight, driving them both toward the edge of the balcony. She yelped as her back hit the railing, and then the next moment her breath escaped her altogether as she was pitched over the side.

Through a backdrop of white ice and snow, she fell through the air, the jagged mountainside, so far below, rushing up little by little to meet her. Vanessa opened her mouth to scream but no sound came out as she plummeted, Jor'y's infuriated roar following after her.

CHAPTER 29

*J*or'y's heart stopped. His breath stopped. The world stood still as he watched his very heart, his a'talyna, go over the side by the hands of the human. Representative Arthur spun around, his face pale despite the smile widening his mouth.

"Save your mate if you can, beast!" he taunted, greeted by Bradshaw's cruel laughter.

A roar of rage thundered out of him, his feathers bristling out, his wingspan extending to its limit. Da'yel attempted to scurry over, but stopped, his wings spreading wide in defense of his own mate as humans sprung forward. Everywhere, Aturians who turned to assist were ambushed by humans.

A shudder ran over him, his mouth bowing with a killer smile. Reaching up, he grabbed Bradshaw's face in one hand, ignoring the orders hurled at him as, with a jerk of his arm, he snapped the male's neck. The male was no better than ek'thanak and was destroyed just as easily.

The body fell to the ground at his feet, and, with a few powerful flaps of his wings, he rose into the air. He was aware of Margaret gaping up after him, Thomas's arms wrapped around her, keeping her tucked safely against him. He was sorry that they had to see that, but nothing mattered more than his mate as he raced off the side of the balcony, folding his wings to freefall toward his beloved a'talyna.

Below him, as she dropped, she seemed almost suspended in the air, both beautiful and terrible all at once. She had closed her eyes, her face deathly pale as she spun through the air, her clothing fluttering around her, encased in moonlight and a scattering of snow either carried on the wind or dislodged from the balcony during her fall.

Jor'y folded his wings tighter against his body so that his bulk dropped faster, speeding toward her. The brown hair fluttering around her face and arms brushed his fingers and his hand as he reached out for her. Gripping her arm in one hand, he managed to wrap the other around her waist as he drew closer. His first hand joined the second until she was fully in his embrace, their bodies spinning together in nothingness.

Her eyes parted, ice-frosted eyelashes parting to meet his gaze. Gold-speckled brown eyes met his, and her lips, colorless from the intense cold of the rushing air, parted in a gasp. He answered with a smile, crushing her smaller body against his chest, allowing his heat to warm her, and brace her body against his. His wings unfurled, the air catching at the feathers, slowing their fall enough to where he was no longer afraid to harm her by pulling her out of her freefall.

His wings snapped out wide, and a current drove them up. He felt her fingers curl against his crown feathers, and a tiny shriek escaped her. Tucking his hand firmly behind her head, pressing her cheek against his chest, Jor'y flapped his wings, driving them up higher, his body angling his flight back around toward the estate.

As much as he wanted to take her and flee, to hide his mate from the humans, he also knew that his responsibilities as valmek prohibited him that luxury. Gritting his teeth, he gained altitude and wheeled toward the same balcony they had dropped from. The representatives from Earth squinted up at him, and Thomas waved him in. Though their expressions at his distance appeared withdrawn and stern, none of them paid any attention to Bradshaw, who still lay on the stone. He hoped that was a good sign. He liked those humans and did not wish to have conflict with them, but if they sought to take Vanessa away, he would do all that he had to. No one was taking her from him.

Further down the balcony, against the wall of the estate, he spotted the governor's guards. They were gathered in one corner, arms raised in surrender as Jor'y's guard surrounded them. Some pointed blasters, while others had holstered the weapon in favor of the traditional ki'thwan. He counted every one of his guards present there. All except Da'yel.

Concerned, he immediately sought out his cousin, his eyes searching the balcony until he saw Lucy's golden head. She was the first she saw. And then he saw Da'yel. The male held Representative Arthur up by the neck, dangling him over the edge while Representative Bartholomew stood a short distance away. Though the male's voice was too low for Jor'y to catch at his distance, it appeared that Bartholomew was trying to dissuade his cousin from killing the wretched male while Lucy rolled her eyes in a recognizable human expression of disgust.

Winging his way over to his cousin, Jor'y shifted his grasp on his mate to touch down carefully on the balcony. Even after his feet touched the floor, his wings flapped for a moment, steadying them before he allowed her small body to slide down his front until her feet touched the stonework beneath them.

Lucy caught sight of them immediately, and her expression brightened.

"Da'yel, look! Holy shit, he caught her! Vanessa is okay!"

Her mate glanced his way, relief plain on his face as

Bartholomew also turned and let out a sigh.

"Thank the blessed ones," the human uttered reverently, his eyes briefly tracking up the star-speckled skies above before returning to Vanessa. "I'm pleased to see that this miserable idiot's attempt on Miss William's life failed. Now, perhaps you can persuade your cousin not to kill him so we can see to it that Earth justice is served." His expression turned frosty as looked at the Darvel representative. "I can assure you they will *not* be lenient. Especially not once her mother gets involved."

Jor'y scowled, his wings snapping around Vanessa protectively. "He attempted to kill my mate!"

The male nodded. "For which he will be punished. Death is too kind for what they've been doing on this planet, inflicting abuses upon the non-gratas as well as Aturians hired to work at Dahlia. And that doesn't include what they had planned in seizing and stripping as much of the planet as possible for Darvel's profits. His companion," he gestured in the direction of the other human from Dahlia Colony, "has already admitted to all manner of very illegal activities—ones that are illegal on United Earth and strictly punishable by the Alliance as well. United Earth is required to personally deal with the problem, try the culprits we still have remaining to us, and present it to the Alliance with a reformation plan."

Vanessa prodded at his wing, gazing up at him earnestly when he dropped his chin to look down at her. She smiled up at him, and when she spoke her voice was clear and carried over the balcony, drawing the attention of everyone who had been observing the standoff with interest.

"He's right. This is the best way to make sure that Representative Arthur pays for his crimes and to discourage anyone else at Darvel from blatantly flouting Earth and Alliance laws. Remember, Carthy's team has also collected evidence here."

His eyes shot over to the few humans who stood alongside his guards with their weapons turned on their fellow humans. Carthy nodded back to him in agreement. He did not like it, but he could concede that they had a point. His jaw worked, the muscle tightening and loosening as he considered the matter before he let out a solemn breath.

"Turn the human over to the custody of Representative Bartholomew," he ordered. "Since he asked for the male's life, he is now responsible for him and anything else he does on Aturia." He narrowed his eyes at the hapless human held tight in Da'yel's claws. "If I had my way, he would lay beside Bradshaw. Monsters destroyed. But as the First Mother did in her wisdom, this ek'thanak will be chained with the other." He looked meaningfully at Representative Vansago, and the male swallowed, flattening himself against the wall.

Representative Thomas straightened and took several steps toward the other male, his head lifting proudly as an Aturian valmek. "I will see to Vansago personally."

Standing alone once more, Representative Avery cleared her throat and nodded. "I have already begun filing reports with United Earth. These men will be punished, as would have been..." She trailed off as she gestured to the remains of Governor Bradshaw.

"I will not apologize," he growled despite the twinge of unhappiness in his heart. As a valmek, he knew that he had to kill to protect, but it still never set right with him.

His mate's soft hand brushed against his chest in an understanding caress, and he hugged her to him. Only his a'talyna understood his struggle. The bond, though faint between them at the moment was still present even if she did not realize it, and through it she saw into him better than any other. She was a true gift from the gods into his life. Perhaps from the First Mother herself.

"I would suspect not," Avery agreed. "It puts us into a bit of a tight spot, but we will manage. The man was clearly hostile and a serious threat to Miss Williams... uh, your mate, that is. I will explain that to our superiors. And I know Ashlan will back me up." The latter she seemed to address to Representative Thomas, who nodded curtly.

"As will I," Representative Bartholomew added.

"I still say we should flatten him for trying to kill Vanessa," Lucy muttered, earning her a fond look from her mate as he lowered the human and surrendered him to Bartholomew.

"My bloodthirsty mate," he purred, sweeping her up into his arms, making the female squeal with laughter as he playfully nipped her neck.

Jor'y smiled at the pair, content himself now that he had his mate beneath his wings once more. The last few days had been misery, but now it was over.

Da'yel stretched his wings and plucked his mate from the ground. "I think we should go join our brethren in greeting Hashavnal. Don't you agree, a'talyna?"

"Definitely," she laughed, hugging Da'yel's neck as he let out a triumphant shout and leaped from the balcony with several powerful beats of his wings, carrying his mate over toward the mountain.

Vanessa turned in Jor'y's arms and smiled, her hands sliding up his chest though at their height difference she was too low to the ground to wind her own arms around his neck as she obviously wanted. He leaned down and brushed his nose against hers.

"Do you wished to go as well, or would you prefer to return to our quarters?"

Her smile widened. "*Our* quarters?"

"What is mine is yours. You are my a'talyna and my mate," he murmured.

Her eyes danced as she made a show of thinking the matter over. "You know, as wonderful as that would be to get... reacquainted," she murmured, pressing her body into his so that his cock, already thickening, suddenly surged against her belly, "I think it can wait until after the celebration. I would love to see it and to spend our first Hashavnal as it should be spent. With our valetik."

He groaned painfully, his wings hugging her tighter against him. "They would understand."

Muttering profanities that came to mind under his breath, making his delightful mate laugh, he reluctantly withdrew his wings and lifted her high against his body, giving her the opportunity to wrap her arms around his neck. He glanced over at Carthy and paused when Tackert grinned and elbowed the male.

"Don't you worry—we've got this!" Tackert yelled. "We'll make sure that they're set up nice and comfy."

"In the dankest cell we can find," Carthy added in agreement. "And we'll get this," he grimaced at the mess on the stone, "cleaned up for you. Stephens and Fowler would be delighted to help."

"Fuck," muttered Stephens, and Fowler chuckled.

"Well, at least it's cold. Everything should hopefully scrape up easily enough," the other male replied.

Jor'y smiled in gratitude, swinging his female up into his arms.

"Just make sure to do all the things I could only dream of!" Tackert shouted after them, drawing laughs from his companions.

"And congratulations, Vanessa!" Representative Avery shouted after them, delight ringing in her voice echoing behind them.

Ignoring them, Jor'y smiled and nuzzled his mate. "Let us go then, a'talyna."

A delighted gasp left her as they took to the skies, her arms tightening around him. She burrowed her face against his neck for many minutes at their rapid ascent, as if afraid to loosen her grip.

He ran a soothing hand down her back and pressed his cheek against the top of her head, her hair tickling his nose.

"My fearless mate, I have you. I will never let you fall again," he whispered against her hair.

The tension drained out of her body, and she leaned back just enough in his embrace to meet his eyes. He gestured ahead with his chin.

"Look, the valetik awaits. They are lighting our way even as they light the way of Hashavnal and the return of the First Mother."

Vanessa's head turned and she gasped. "Oh my gods," she whispered.

It was a sight, one that never failed to kindle happiness in his heart. Now, with his mate in his arms, that joy swelled, filling him until a tear slipped down one cheek and then the other. Just the two tears, but their presence made him smile. The mountain was all aglow with the flicker of lanterns and bonfires, and Aturians danced on both land and air, by foot and by wing. Cups of steamed o'jar were in many hands as celebrants drank, sang, and celebrated life.

At their approach, Sa'tari broke free from Gal'ythron's embrace to wave eagerly before the male collected her back into his arms. Lucy laughed as Da'yel swung his mate around in dance, his wings flaring out around him in an expression of delight. Kin of his valetik called out to them, welcoming them, and in his arms, happiness like none he had ever seen radiated from his mate. She laughed and waved as they dropped down among them, happily accepting the cup thrust into her hands.

Smiling at his mate, Jor'y took his own cup and allowed himself to truly feel at peace, folding his wing around his mate affectionately as they mingled until their cups were drained and he could not resist sweeping her up into a dance that carried them up into the starry sky.

Vanessa laughed, the sound of her pleasure filling his ears and the heavens around them as she leaned back in his arms and let go of his neck, trusting him completely as she stared up at the stars dancing around them. His heart nearly burst from his chest as he increased his speed until they swept higher, and his mate's laughter grew wilder.

"This is amazing!" she shouted, her voice sparkling with laughter. Her eyes dropped to him as her laughter died, and they softened with a love that stole his breath and heart all over again.

"Not as amazing as you. You gave everything up for me. For this life here that is so different from everything you know."

"For us," she corrected. "And I would do it a thousand times more. Now take me home."

She ran her fingers through his crown feathers, her lips curving sweetly. Drawing his head toward hers, she captured his lips. His long tongue slipped into her mouth, tasting of her love, and never was there a flavor sweeter.

Wheeling through the sky, they departed from the merriment as the sky began to lighten on the horizon. Hours of celebration and the rise of the sun all faded away with their kiss and the heat of the bond rising between them. With one claw, he slit the material of her pants between her legs, enjoying the way she wiggled and moaned into his mouth. He could not wait a moment longer. Opening the seal on his robe completely, he dragged down the band on his knee length pants so that his cock jutted out proudly between them.

Bending his body just right, his knees tucked under her bottom, he drove deep into her, capturing his mate's cries on his tongue. He rutted into her with every beat of his wings, his tail controlling the direction of their flight as they mated through his breeding heat, their bond rippling between them, feeding on each other's desire. They only just barely made it to his private balcony as the sun crested with the Hashavnal morning, their bodies landing across the bed as the passion exploded between them in waves of ecstasy. He drank deep from her and fed her just as deeply from his own energy, the cyclic transference making him shudder with new vigor, the joy mounting in his heart.

Lifting up, he looked down at the female beneath him, unable to believe what he had gained. In the darkest hours of his life when he had lost hope, Hashavnal restored it to him.

She stroked his crown feathers, smiling up at him. "A joyous Hashavnal," his mate whispered.

He nuzzled her nose with us, a grin breaking out over his face. "It truly is. A most happy and blessed solstice to you, a'talyna."

Their lips sealed together in another kiss, their tongues mating until a new fervor was struck and the bond vibrated between them once again. They mated all through the morning, their cries echoing through the room all around them, and quite possibly down the halls as well. All of the estate no doubt echoed with cries of love and passion, and for the first time he didn't feel severed from it. It was as if they were part of something rising in the air all around them, greeting the day as it was meant to be welcomed.

Sometime later as they lay in each other's arms, Vanessa turned her face up to his and pressed a kiss to his chest before her mouth opened wide in a loud yawn.

"Before I nod off and forget, I just wanted to tell you one thing," she murmured.

He pressed a kiss to her brow, his wing folding around her lovingly. "Yes, a'talyna?"

She yawned again. "Never have I enjoyed solstice more. Dick tree and all," she chuckled.

He buried his face against her neck, his wings folding around her as he laughed.

Joy was restored to the estate, and it seemed that for him and his mate, the joys of the season were theirs once more.

EPILOGUE

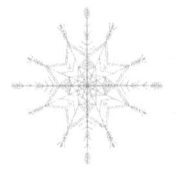

FOUR MONTHS LATER

Vanessa lay back against her mate's chest, his arms cradling her as one large hand cupped her expanding belly. Breeding season had certainly done its job, she was carrying not one but two younglings, which had Jor'y constantly fussing over her. She didn't mind it at all. Even now, as she played with the feathers of one of his wings that were already pinkening with the return of spring, he stroked her belly and hips, relieving the tension that had been accumulating there. Lifting her datapad in her other hand, she read over the message commed to her pad earlier that morning. Her brows furrowed, earning her a gentle tap on the hip from one of his large fingers.

"What is making you frown, a'talyna? Do not tell me that it is your mother again. I will go to the systems room and speak to her directly if I must. I will not have her upsetting you."

Thankfully, it wasn't. She hadn't spoken to her mother since the solstice, when she had once again attempted to talk Vanessa into hopping the next transport back to Earth, unable to accept her mating with Jor'y, but Vanessa was confident that sooner or later her mother would get over the shock. The woman was resilient like that.

Turning her head back, she blinked and grinned up at him.

"Actually, no. It's from Katherine."

He tipped his head, his crown feathers flattening. She was a bit confused herself. She had known when she rejected her citizenship to stay with Jor'y that it would terminate all of her connections on Earth. She hadn't expected to hear from Katherine at all, since her friend was based out of United Earth rather than one of the colonies. It would make working together, while not entirely impossible, very difficult. So this comm was an unexpected surprise. His wings fanned around her just enough that she knew that he was prepared to jump into battle at the word.

"Is this good or bad?" he rumbled.

Her lips pursed. "I don't know. Guess we'll find out."

Running her finger over the message, the screen was suddenly filled with a letter. Vanessa read over it her eyes widening. Jor'y stilled behind her, his hand returning to her belly, anchoring her in place.

"Did you receive something unpleasant?" he murmured, concern filling his voice.

She shook her head, her mouth working silently for a long moment as she struggled to find the right words. She choked a bit on the sentiment filling her throat. There was not only a letter from Katherine but hundreds of little notes from her fans attached to it. Tears filled her eyes as she read through him.

"A'talyna?"

"I can't believe it," she whispered. "Katherine said that this digibook has sold better than any other I've written, mostly on the underground… and they're begging me to rewrite the ending." A tiny sob escaped her. "There's even one from Margaret Avery saying that my heroine deserved the happily ever after that I got."

Margaret and Ashlan Thomas had been approved to take over running Dahlia Colony, announcing their engagement just weeks later. Word was already spreading quickly over Aturia at the new interrelation breakthroughs happening and the opening of the colony to courting among those humans open to it. Even the non-gratas, much to Lucy's surprise and delight.

Although some humans were still scared of the outer rim Aturians, barriers were breaking down and some of the Aturians in the capital cities were beginning to let their feathers along their bodies, calves, and feet grow out. A few were even managing to recover tail feathers, though not everyone was so fortunate. There were even rumors of Aturian lawmakers who were trying to push for eliminating the surgical removal of wings from infants.

That was the third time Vanessa had ever seen her mate overwhelmed enough to cry tears of joy. The first time was after she agreed to remain with him, and the second just weeks later, when it was confirmed that she was pregnant with twins.

She laughed tremulously, swiping tears from her own eyes as she lifted the datapad to show him. "They all love the romance and want the ending changed. All of them!"

He rumbled happily, his wings closing the rest of the way around her. "The world is changing bit by bit, a'talyna. Love is what moves the cosmos and the joy in the heart."

Vanessa snuggled into his embrace, sighing contentedly as she allowed her datapad to fall against her chest. He was right. Lucy and Da'yel were expecting their own little one to arrive any day, and Sa'tari was eagerly preparing nurseries, exclaiming on how next Hashavnal she was going to try for a youngling with Gal'ythron.

Love moved everything, from the darkest night into a new dawn. How fortunate she was that her shuttle crashed there on that mountaintop. That solstice changed her life in ways she never could have imagined.

Kissing her mate's bicep, she rested her head against his chest, allowing the rhythm of his heartbeat to sing to her of their solstice a'talynal gift and bond.

ATURIAN GIFTS OF YULE

A Darvel Exploratory Systems Short

CHAPTER 1

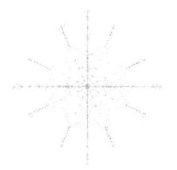

Lucy grimaced as she wiped away the last bit of sweat and bodily fluids and tried to avoid meeting the eye of the Aturian standing just a few away. Even after all of that, the male was still eyeing her hungrily, and not because he was actually interested in her. Over the last several months, she had made a point of educating herself on Aturian mating, because that was ultimately what she was there for—to find a mate. If that meant "kissing" a few frogs to get there, so be it. That didn't mean she was going to give any of them anything more than what her contract stipulated.

Everyone who signed on with the production company had an unbreakable legal document that guaranteed all parties that they would never have to "engage with" a partner more than once. The contract was worded that way to protect everyone involved, males and offworld females both. It protected women who were only there hoping to be eventually discovered by a male. Since it was a viable way for males who failed to find a mate among their own people to find a compatible offworld mate, the arrangement typically worked pretty good for everyone, giving them an opportunity to meet and test compatibility in a way that was also financially profitable for them.

She couldn't pretend that money wasn't part of the appeal too, though she preferred to focus on her long-term goal of finding her mate. Until that happened, however, the reality was that she depended on Aturian Erotica Productions to survive. The company also made quite a bit of money selling the erotic vids. It was only right that the males and females who uprooted themselves to live in Av'kanthal, one of the largest metropolitans of the Aturian Western Continent, were provided adequate funds to offset expenses.

Not that she was living a life of luxury, but it was a far cry from her life in Dahlia Colony. As a non-gratas, she had risked everything on bribing an Aturian goods transport to escape the southern continent. Her life there had been one of brutality, barely able to survive on the scraps that the corrupt Darvel governor allotted to the non-gratas workers. Between hunger and the regular beatings that were doled out for even the most minor infraction, it had been worth the risk.

She had been fortunate that she learned about the production company from a Ugursi female who had found her own mate there. The director had taken one look at her, clucked his tongue in a strange chirping noise, and immediately advanced her enough credits for lodgings and a few months of steady meals to fill out her emaciated body with the curves she had once possessed. He then proceeded to make sure she had a complete medical screening done, made sure that she knew exactly what protections her contract provided, and had personally given her some excellent advice about watching out for some of the males who might take advantage of a lone female.

And because of that advice, she sure as hell wasn't giving any freebies out to Vor'morat. Other women might have swooned over him for his muscular physique, but with his shaved crown feathers that puffed around his head ridiculously, and the silly smattering of stray feathers that sprinkled his neck in a manner that he obviously considered attractive, the male reminded her of a poorly plucked rooster whenever he strutted around the set.

He had been the last male on the planet she wanted to be paired with, but it had only been a matter of time before she was assigned to partner with him. Now that it had happened, she was glad it was over. With his lack of finesse and selfish approach to sex, it had been one of the worse screenings she had endured since starting there nearly a year ago. And yet Vor'morat was practically preening now as he looked down at her with dark orange eyes.

"Lucy Michaels, there you are! I am pleased I did not miss you before you left me forever in the bitter cold. Instead, I insist that you join me for third meal. I know the best spots in Av'kanthal. I have the ability to treat you to an exceptional night that you will never forget," he purred.

She wrinkled her nose and only just resisted rolling her eyes. *Yeah, no.*

Not only was she not a fool, Lucy also paid attention to gossip and knew that every word he spoke was the same line he used on every female, verbatim. More than one female, human and alien both, had ended up on her back, and led on until he got bored and moved onto the next female who caught his eye. She was definitely not looking for that.

Presenting him with a tight, polite smile, Lucy shook her head, slamming her hand on the panel of the storage unit as she collected her belongings from it. She certainly had no plans on being the "lucky woman" who had the honor of satisfying his needs during Hashavnal and his winter breeding season.

"I don't think so, sorry," she said with feigned cheerfulness. "I'm pretty busy with Yule coming up. But I hope you enjoy your Hashavnal."

He tipped his head, his short horn stubs making him appear almost owlish, and not in a cute way. "Ah, your Yule. A human tradition. And this is more important than enjoying the pleasures of courtship with a male."

She shrugged in a pretense of apology and pushed by him, hurrying out of the building. It was only when she was a few blocks away and a glance behind her confirmed that there was no sign of the male on her tail that she was able to draw in an easy breath. She grinned victoriously and turned around again only to get smacked in the face by something large and feathery in a blinding sheet of white.

Sputtering at the feathers brushing her mouth, Lucy struck back at the twitching wall that slapped at her with a force just shy of painful for a moment before withdrawing completely.

"My sincerest apologies," a deep voice rumbled some distance overhead. "Did I harm you? Please say that I did not."

She looked up at what had to be the tallest Aturian she had ever met, a lovely medium hue of violet... and fluffy, with feathers! Everywhere she looked, she saw glossy white feathers, from the long, thin ones that fell down his back and over his shoulders from his head to the thick collar of feathers around his neck... and wings! Wait, wings?

She gaped at the large wings folding and unfolding restlessly behind him. Her mouth dropped open further when she caught a look at the rest of him. His body was taut with lean muscle, with a massive chest and shoulders no doubt the product of the enormous wings on his back. Green eyes stared down at her, of such a lush color that they reminded her of her mother's gardens in the spring before any flowers even bloomed. And his amethyst coloring made her finger itch to reach out and touch him to discover he felt as luxurious as he looked.

He paused, his lips parting as his eyes seemed to widen and

his pupils dilated. He shook his head, his wonderfully full lips pulling down at the corners.

"I did hurt you."

"What? Oh, no. No, I'm fine," she quickly assured him, a blush climbing to her cheeks as she straightened her clothes. "I may want to die of embarrassment, but I'm good. Gods, this is a bit humiliating," she mumbled.

His head tipped to the side. "Why would you be embarrassed? I was the one who wing-swiped you. Completely unintentional, of course, but living here even a few revolutions has not made it any easier for me to navigate the tight confines of the street."

"Why not just fly then?"

A lopsided grin appeared on his face. "You are quite new here, yes? The people here in the capital would be very upset if they saw me fly." He leaned forward, lowering his voice conspiringly. "I am not certain if you have noticed, but wings and feathers are considered uncivilized. It is difficult enough to live and work here without drawing attention to my wings. I would not provoke anyone by flying."

She blinked again in surprise. "Well, I personally think your wings are lovely."

His smile widened, his wings fluffing out around him as he lifted them in a display, obviously preening. "Do you think so? In winter, they are drab, but once spring returns my feathers will begin to return to brighter coloration."

Her eyebrows shot up. She had seen enough Aturians in the summer with their butchered crown feathers a shockingly vivid fuchsia. As she studied the male in front of her, noting the collar of feathers peeking out from around the top of his robe and the feathers on his bare feet in addition to the wide sweep of his wings, she tried to imagine them bright fuchsia, and she was struck by how incredibly beautiful he had to look.

Heat began to crawl up the sides of her neck, down her chest and into her cheeks once more. She had little doubt that she was already turning beet red with the direction of her thoughts. Her personal curse.

She cleared her throat, searching for a safer topic of conversation. She glanced around, noting everyone giving them a wide berth, Aturians sneering at him as they passed, doing everything they could to avoid touching him, and in turn not running her down in their attempts to circle around him. She wrinkled her nose.

"People don't seem very nice to you. Why do you even stay?"

He shrugged his wings, drawing her attention to them once more. "It is not always so easy to find a mate in the outer rim—the wild mountains regions far from the capital cities," he clarified. "That is home. I miss it, but I wish to find my a'talynal first."

That piqued her curiosity. She knew that males and females both looked for mates that appealed to them, but it was the first she was hearing of a'talynal.

"What is that?"

His grin turned impish, the corners of his eyes crinkling. He extended a hand to her. "Would you like me to show you?"

She gave his hand a skeptical look. "I don't know. I don't even know your name."

"I am Da'yel of Mifran valetik."

Shyly, she placed her hand in his. "I'm Lucy Morfalk"

As his fingers closed around hers, a shiver ran up her spine, flooding her blood with a desperate sort of heat that had her nearly panting, her pussy soaking through her panties at a shocking rate. Da'yel's eyes brightened, and a rumbling purr escaped him.

"That," he whispered, a look of blissful pleasure spreading over his face, "is the a'talynal."

Holy shit.

CHAPTER 2

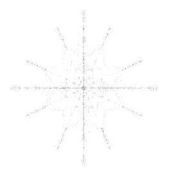

Da'yel trembled with ecstasy at the touch of her hand. The exquisite pleasure of the a'talynal rushed through him, carrying every thought away except to breed his female. Another shiver swept through him. It was so close to Hashavnal and the beginning of his season, it was no wonder he was reacting so strongly to the proximity of his mate. Just her touch alone made him need her with a desperation that even his imagination had failed to equal.

He finally understood why so many males volunteered to make the vids of intimate pleasures. Although he had always been of the opinion that the vids cheapened the full scope of the feelings of the exchange between a pair enjoying union, now he understood the temptation. For a male who had limited opportunities to touch an unrelated and available female, the chance of finding one's mate by any such means would be a powerful incentive.

If he had known, he would have done so himself if it had meant finding his a'talyna even days earlier. Perhaps then it would have been his scent coating her and not an unpleasant mixture that made his feathers stand out aggressively, his wings instinctively flapping around her in a show of mate guarding that had other Aturians on the street giving them an even wider berth. He knew it was unnecessary, but the need to do so rose defiantly within him, as if other males were going to attempt to exert their own claims.

Logically, he knew it was serious. The scents, even though one was fresher than the others, were of only the brief encounters that the production company offered. He certainly did not hold that against her either, since many humans who managed to illegally make their way to the capital eventually found employment there for the same reason that drew males, where they could find a match without the knowledge of the human colony. It was safe for them and provided monetary support. He was glad that his female had been well taken care of, but now that he had found her it would no longer be necessary.

"Come," he murmured softly as he drew her beneath one wing. "It is the hour for the evening meal. You must be hungry."

A nervous laugh scaped his female, and she ducked her head, her cheeks pinkening somehow even further than what the cool bite of the air managed to do. "Yeah… I suppose I am."

Da'yel's chest puffed out. He couldn't deny that he was pleased to begin his courtship. Feeding his female would be the first of many things he could do to prove to her that he would be a good mate. And, of course, give him time to confirm his own instincts and develop deeper feelings for her. He suspected that, with how dull human senses were, it would take even more time than it would for him. He was already falling under the spell of her sweet, clean scent enveloping around him once he was able to isolate it from the others.

Tucking his wing snugly around her so that she was drawn even closer to his side, he struck off for an eating establishment that he had often heard praised. He did not eat out much, typically, preferring to keep to himself when he was not on shift at the docking port, but he would not settle for anything less for his female. Ignoring the eyes that followed them, he led her down the street, the snow crunching beneath their feet drowning out the whispers that greeted them. A quick glance at Lucy assured him that she had not heard the unkind remarks regarding the fact that she was keeping company with an outer rimmer.

Instead of shrinking back with embarrassment, excitement gleamed in her eyes as she took everything in. To his pleasure, her gaze often strayed up to him as if she could not resist looking upon him, and not because she viewed him as an oddity. If he wasn't mistaken, given her fascination and the musk of interest in her scent, she was as taken with him as he was with her. A happy, rumbling croon vibrated through him.

His Lucy was perfection and a feast for his senses. As they approached the nearest shopping and dining districts, the seasonal decor brightened the night in a cheer that echoed the happiness building within him. Even more wondrous was that everywhere bright lights and baubles glittered in festival spirit. They sent a rainbow of hues scattering over her, highlighting her fragile human beauty that drew admiration.

He pretended that he did not notice. With his wing tucked around her, only the boldest of males would dare to approach her. That she did not seem to pay them any attention in turn did much for his confidence as well. He nearly came undone, however, when he felt the brush of her hand against his side, her fingers knotting into the fabric of his tunic. That small, uncertain gesture as they neared the front of the restaurant made him want to yank her up into his arms protectively. That urge became even stronger with the hostile look they were greeted with by the male at the reception.

Although entirely featherless aside from the ridiculously

cropped crown feathers, the male bristled, his crown feathers puffing as little as they could.

"Filthy outer rimmers are not welcome here. I insist that you and your... companion... leave." He gave Lucy only a sparing glance, although it conveyed volumes in its mixture of dismay and disgust. It was a look saved for any female who dared to join with a male like Da'yel.

He felt his own feathers puff out in anger, shamed as he was in front of his female. The fingers gripping his tunic tightened and twisted as they gave a small yank, drawing his attention down to his female. He did not want to look, fearing what he would see there, but another sharp pull had him looking down into his Lucy's eyes.

She was angry, not embarrassed. And it was not directed at him. Her blue eyes glittered fiercely as she glared over at the establishment's host. Her warm body brushed against his as she nudged against him.

"Come on, Da'yel. I don't think I want to eat here anyway. If they think you're filthy, then I don't trust their definition or distinction between what's clean or dirty. Doesn't sound like a place I would trust not to give me a good case of food poisoning. We'd probably be safer eating off my kitchen floor."

The offended gasp of the host would have made him smile if his female's comments had not already done so. Beaming down at her, he nodded and turned away, dismissing the establishment immediately as unworthy of his mate.

"As much as I would gratefully eat anything you offered me, Lucy, I think I can offer better than a kitchen floor," he teased in a low whisper, delight filling him when his female responded with the sweet sound of laughter he had longed to hear.

"I think it would be far safer, since I'm not sure how much I can vouch for the state of the floors," she choked out when she stopped to draw a breath. Wiping a tear of mirth from the corner of her eye, his Lucy grinned up at him. "But I am intrigued as to what you might have in mind."

Leaning down so that she might hear him better, he whispered, "Do you trust me?"

"Only a foolish female would completely trust a male she just met," she answered.

His heart sank a bit, but he could not deny the truth of her words. Still, he clung to hope as her lips pursed thoughtfully. The sideways glance that she gave him was considering, but, in the end, her lips quirked with the adventurous spirit shining in her eyes.

By the First Mother, she was glorious!

"Oh, what the hell? I didn't get this far by playing safe. Besides, I just have a feeling that there's nowhere safer for me than by your side."

Although amusement filled her voice, perhaps at herself more than anything, Da'yel took them to heart, his wings and feathers fanning out with pride.

"You can be certain of that," he agreed, his voice a quiet rumble so not to be heard by anyone other than his a'talyna. "No being is safer in all of the world than a male's a'talyna." He stooped and swept her up into his arms, exactly where he wanted her. "Now, hold on, Lucy," he murmured. "It will be quicker from here if we fly."

Her arms covered flung around his neck, pressing her small breasts against his chest in a way that was more than a little distracting. It was only with considerable willpower that he was able to ignore it and hop into the air with a snap of his wings. Surprised curses from the land-bound Aturians followed them into the air, but they fell back quickly as Da'yel advanced through the air with great sweeps of his powerful wings, carrying him and his mate further away.

It did not take him long to make his way to the outer city

limits where the outer rimmer housing was erected, far away from polite Aturian citizens. Workers lived their solitary lives there in cramped rented spaces. There were a few females there as well, those who had not opted for surgery to be accepted and look for a mate among the citizens of the capital, preferring to work hard among their peers and earn credits. Even fewer were the small family units that had begun among single males and females. Although conditions were far too cramped for families, for most of them it was a short-term solution until credits could be saved for passage back to their valetiks.

It was to one such family that had befriended him and took him in soon after his arrival to the capital that he made his way. As he often ate with them, he always gave them a good portion of his wages, and he knew that the food would be plentiful and the atmosphere hospitable for his female.

In truth, his friends would be delighted to see that he had found a mate.

El'valmay and her mate Ta'twathan were more than delighted, as it turned out. No sooner had he introduced her as his a'talyna than Lucy was pulled out from beneath his wing to receive the welcoming pat of hands from the couple, as well as their two small younglings who were eager to join in. Rather than seeming overwhelmed among the company of Aturians far larger than the wingless ones she was accustomed to, Lucy met it at all with amusement and genuine delight. She even spent half of the meal with one of the younglings tucked into her lap, eating around the little one with the expertise of one accustomed to children.

"You are a natural with the little ones," El'valmay remarked casually to Lucy, throwing an amused grin and knowing look in Da'yel's direction.

No doubt the female was imagining Da'yel with a nest full of his own little ones. The thought sent pleasure running through him. He suddenly wanted that more than he wanted anything. First Mother will it.

"I'm the oldest of eight myself," Lucy admitted as she evaded a sticky hand and quickly mopped it with a wet towel before enjoying another bite of her own food. "I was nearly grown when the youngest four arrived, so I became accustomed to babies very early and helped my mother until... well, things changed. I'm sure they're half grown by now and probably don't even remember me."

A distressed look tightened El'valmay's features as she shared a concerned look with her mate. "I do not wish to pry, but I do not understand. If you did not wish to leave your family, then why are you here? The Aturian capital is not safe for humans, given your illegal status here. You do not have the legal protections that even outer rimmers enjoy."

Lucy's answering laughter held no humor. "Trust me, it's better than Dahlia Colony. I grew up on another human colony and had hoped I would be assigned there permanently, but I was reassigned to Dahlia. I had no choice, and anything is better than that place."

El'valmay crooned comfortingly, her one wing extending to lightly brush Lucy's shoulder as she exchanged another look with her mate. "Do not be distressed. You now have family with us for as long as you need until Da'yel can get you to his valetik."

Ta'twathan nodded in agreement, though his gaze was appraising when he met Da'yel's eyes. "Be grateful that you met your a'talyna so early while you still have credits from your valetik. You will be able to return to your valetik sooner than many families are able to."

Da'yel lowered his head in agreement, his gaze drawn helplessly back to his mate, whose expression had once again relaxed as conversation turned to more pleasant topics. Her gaze slipped back in his direction and her smile widened as their eyes met. He could not help himself; his wings fanned out and snapped around her, dragging her into his arms. Her startled laughter faded into a sigh as he tucked her against his chest and held her against his heart.

Yes, he was very fortunate.

CHAPTER 3

Lucy stared out at the snow falling in fat, fluffy flakes on other side of her window. She had done the unimaginable. She had called out from work for the first time since being employed by the production company. Oh, it wasn't like she worked that often, despite how generous her pay was. It certainly wasn't a daily affair, but she had called in and let the producer know she would be unavailable entirely until after the holidays.

The male had been shocked but had rambled out several assurances that her job would still be available when she was ready to return and that she was welcome to come in at any time if she changed her mind.

She wasn't about to share the fact that she had no intention of changing her mind, especially not now. For one, she couldn't bear the idea of being touched by any other male while she was already so entranced with one, and for another, it felt disloyal to Da'yel when he was so earnestly courting her. This was what she came to the capital for, and the whole reason she joined Aturian Erotica Productions. Granted, she had stumbled across Da'yel on her own by some blind luck, but she had what she wanted: an Aturian who made her pulse race and her heart fill with so much happiness that she could barely contain it.

But there was plenty of worry to go along with that. She worried about him now while he worked on shift at the docking port. She worried about being caught by Darvel's authorities before she and Da'yel had a chance at a life together. Yet, when they were together, those worries faded into the background. He made her feel safe and cared for even after only a few days of knowing him.

She smiled to herself as she prepared a cup of steamed o'jar. She had become addicted to the spiced drink soon after arriving at Av'kanthal. She had considered it her only real pleasure she had living on Aturia, until meeting Da'yel. He had already surpassed it.

How strange that she felt so close to him already. The a'talynal was unusual as far as human experiences went, and far more alien than she would have ever realized when she had considered mating outside of her species. Not that she was complaining. A shiver skittered up her spine in reaction to the memory of his touch and the way he seemed to draw the reaction from her.

Gods, if a touch did that, sex was going to blow her mind. Not that he seemed to be in any hurry to share that experience with her. He had dropped her off at her building with nothing more than a chaste press of his lips against her brow and a promise that he would return the next day. She had been so surprised that she had not even considered trying to tempt him until he had already taken once more to the air, leaving her gaping after him.

Oh, her neighbors would disapprove if she managed to get him to her bed. She knew that already. She had caught a few disapproving looks from some of the other residents who happened to witness it.

Well, she didn't give a fuck. Being a non-gratas, she had no patience for classist bullshit. She encountered enough of that in her life to tolerate seeing it practiced against someone else, especially not a male as sweet and wonderful as Da'yel.

What if that was why he left? Maybe he didn't want her to be on the receiving end of any sort of stigma for being intimate with him. Well, fuck that. Before he came along it was shaping up to be a cold, lonely Yule. Now that she practically had a mate of her own, she wasn't going to waste a single moment with him. She wasn't going to let anyone deter her.

She was just going to have to communicate that fact to Da'yel. Even if that meant seducing her courting male.

A grin lit her face at the thought, imagining his big amethyst body responding to her every touch. She never considered herself particularly seductive, but they would figure it out together.

Her mind turned to plotting when a chime from the entrance interrupted. It was a single chime rather than a double chime, so it wasn't a visitor. That was a relief because she really had no interest in having any guests dropping in on her when she was eagerly waiting for her male. A delivery though? She hadn't ordered anything.

Her heart leaped with excitement. Perhaps it was a gift sent from Da'yel. She had no idea when he would have even found time to do such a thing, but perhaps there was some small thing he saw on his break that made him think of her. That alone would be better than even the most extravagant gift as far as she was concerned.

Face warming with pleasure and a lightness in her step, Lucy hurried over to the door and opened it, stepping out in front of the package receptacle unit. Nearly half her size, the unit built into the right of her door seemed a bit overkill in her opinion, but then she had no doubt that there were those who made large purchases. Without such a large unit, there was a risk of theft, apparently an issue that the owners of her building took very seriously when it came to their residents.

Pressing her hand on its panel, she squealed in surprise when it opened and a small gold and red delivery sphere darted out to hover right in front of her.

Lucy's eyebrows went up as she stared at it. It certainly looked fancy, far more than she would have expected from Da'yel. Not when a shuttle back to his valetik in the outer rim would cost a considerable amount of credits. Lifting her hands to accept the sphere, she frowned down at it as it settled into her cupped palms. She would have to have a discussion with him about this. She understood that courting was important in Aturian culture, but a regular delivery sphere would have been more than suitable. Or even better, he could deliver it to her himself.

The sphere opened on contact, the top lifting off to reveal what was nestled within. Her mouth parted, rounding in surprise as she stared at the large glittering necklace coiled within it. The metal very near to gold was sprayed with an array of diamond-like clusters set into the pendant's starburst design.

She grimaced, holding it away from her, nose wrinkling.

It was clearly expensive... and hideous.

Did Da'yel really think that she would get pleasure out of something like that?

She groaned inwardly. As far as she knew it could be a cultural thing, though she didn't recall seeing El'valmay wearing anything so gaudy. All the same, she didn't want him to feel like she was rejecting his courting gift either. That meant that she was going to have to pretend to like it too, especially because she had no doubt that he had spent an obscene amount on it.

She didn't want to embarrass him at all. She would just have to find a way to suggest a preference for smaller, more intimate gifts over gifts that she would never have an opportunity to wear anywhere. *Or would ever want to wear it at all for that matter*, she mentally added.

Clasping it around her neck, she also noticed that it was just as heavy as it looked, the metal clasp and chain biting into the tender skin of her neck. As tempted as she was to rip it right off, she resolved to keep it on at least until after Da'yel had the opportunity to see her wearing the thing.

Somehow, it just seemed to get heavier throughout the day. She was nearly ready to tear it off when she heard a flurry of wings just outside of her balcony window. Although the conditions were too slick now for her to risk setting foot on her balcony, she laughed as she spun around and raced toward it, excitement filling her that not even the painful drag of the chain around her neck could dull.

Tapping a hand against the privacy plate covering the balcony, her face lit up with joy when she spotted Da'yel perched on the railing. He spotted her immediately, a relieved smile stretching across his face as he dropped down to the balcony, something wrapped in cloth clasped tightly in his hand. She gave it only a passing glance as she initiated the opening sequence for the door and was promptly swept up in arms and wings the moment Da'yel had enough space to clear the entrance.

A soft laugh escaped her, and he emitted a happy croon as he nuzzled her cheek and neck fervently.

"I have missed you, a'talyna," he murmured against her skin, his lips caressing a sweet spot just behind her ear before lowering her once more to her feet so that he could step back and grin down at her. "I could not wait until I could return to you. And to give you this."

He lifted the small bundle up, and she truly looked at it for the first time. It wasn't fabric but some kind of green packaging material tied off with a bit of twine. It was the complete opposite of the extravagance of his earlier gift, so much so that for a moment she was struck speechless as he placed it in her hands.

"Another gift?" she asked, perplexed as she pulled the twine loose. The packaging material fell away and opened up to reveal a small carved opaline gemstone that had the appearance of an unfamiliar flower. It was so delicately carved that it took her breath away. It would have made such a better pendant, and far more pleasant one to wear, than the one that was currently pinching her neck. She winced at a sharp prick at the back of her neck.

Oww! Damn it!

She slapped a hand over the back of her neck, feeling something curiously warm, and slick, and then froze.

"Another?" Da'yel echoed, his mouth pulling down into a confused frown. "I did not give you any other gifts, a'talyna." He drew in a breath and then he too stilled. "Why do I smell blood?"

In less than a heartbeat, he gently pulled her hand away and hissed, grabbing the offending chain. The snap of the links was quick, and before she knew it the awful pendant was dangling between them, pulled free from where it had fallen into her sweater. He glared at the offending jewelry, his eyes darting up to her in confusion.

"I do not understand, a'talyna... Are you accepting gifts from another male?"

Lucy's mouth dropped open. "What? No! I thought that this was from you?"

His head tilted, his eyes narrowing. "From me?" He sighed. "Lucy, it would take more credits than I could spare to buy you a gift like this. That," he nodded to the stone flower still clutched tightly in the hand she held pressed against her chest, "is what I can manage. I am not a wealthy male. Perhaps..." He trailed off, looking away as he extended the ugly necklace back toward her.

He swallowed. "Lucy, if you want a mate who can shower you with fine gifts, I cannot be that male, no matter how much I wish to be."

She stared at him and then the pendant. It hadn't come from him?

Oh, thank the gods.

An incredulous laugh left her that had him lifting his head. Gently, she pulled the pendant from his hand only to toss it to the floor.

"Trust me," she whispered, "that hideous thing is the last thing I want." She grinned sheepishly up at him as she cupped his jaw with her spare hand, marveling at the small spurs there. "I don't want fancy shit that doesn't mean anything. In fact, I was trying to think of a nice way to ask you not to send me gifts like that," she admitted with an embarrassed giggle. "This, though," she murmured, holding his gift between them, watching the way his eyes went down to it and seemed to glow when they returned to her face, "is perfect. Thank you."

Grabbing a handful of feathers, she dragged his head down to brush a kiss against his lips. He shivered, a deep, purring croon leaving him that had her smiling against his mouth. That smile turned to a gasp when he became the aggressor, his tongue sweeping across her lips. The moment her mouth parted, his long tongue invaded, filling her with his intoxicating spiced flavor. It was like sucking on her favorite cinnamon candy, and she craved more. A disappointed groan left her when he suddenly tore his mouth away, and she squeaked as she found her head carefully tipped to the side, exposing the damaged skin to Da'yel's hardening gaze.

"I am not a valmek, but I would happily kill the male who has harmed your delicate skin with his gift. He is unworthy," he sneered.

Lucy cupped her hand against his and frowned. "I can't imagine who would have sent it. Like I said, I honestly thought it was from you."

The growl that rumbled from Da'yel's chest sent goosebumps over her skin, and she leaned into him when he dragged her close into his embrace, his warm wings wrapping around them.

"He will show himself eventually," he grumbled. "But we will not give him space in our courtship." Drawing back a little, he tipped his head and smiled down at her. "Now, my Lucy, you were right about one thing. There is another gift, though one I have not yet presented to you. Would you care to see one of my favorite sights in all of Av'kanthal?"

Excitement jumped in her chest, accompanied by a warmth knowing that he was sharing something special with her. This was what she had wanted more than anything.

"Sounds like the perfect gift, and like I'd better put something warm on then," she added, ducking out from Da'yel's wings despite his protest and the warmth of his chuckle following after her.

Gods, she was hopeless. She loved the sound of his laughter, or the way he crooned at her, or even just simply speaking. At that moment, she had no doubt she was grinning like a fool as she pulled on her heavy coat, hat, mittens, and scarf. The old her never smiled so much. Never had a reason to. It felt frighteningly unnatural, and yet, at the same time, she just couldn't help herself. Being with him and feeling that special connection growing between them made it hard for her to not be happy. Even as she went about her day, no matter what she was feeling, a little spark of that happiness had remained within her. And that was almost hard to believe.

Part of her suspected it was all some cosmic joke, or to find out that it was nothing more than a strange psychological conditioning. It felt too good, and with her history, she just didn't trust things that felt too good to be real.

"I am real, the a'talynal is real, and this will only grow stronger if you allow it," Da'yel whispered suddenly from behind her.

"I didn't realize I said that aloud."

He chuckled. "More than spoken. Along the a'talynal bond forming between us, I could feel your doubts and wonders sliding into me with our physical contact. This," he whispered, "is only a taste of what the bond will be like fully blooming between us when we are joined. The a'talynal is coveted for a reason."

She glanced at him curiously over her shoulder and turned to face him, her fingers trailing over the heavy tunic as she marveled how he never seemed to need more than that despite the cold outside.

"Why wait then?"

He scooped her up in his arms, and his low groan vibrated through her. "Do not tempt me. Not yet, a'talyna."

"All right. Give me my second gift then," she whispered.

A tremor racked him, and he exited onto the balcony, this time with Lucy secure in his arms. A small hop and a heavy beat of his wings and once again they were airborne, flying away from her building. Everything within her quickened with excitement as they rose higher, and she was grateful that the heavier snowfall had tapered off into flurries. Through the light snow, she could see patches of clear sky within the clouds, and still alien stars winking down at them.

Da'yel carried her higher and farther than before, and when he finally set her on her feet again, she sank straight to her calves in the snow. She grimaced as snow filled her boots and her male growled and yanked her back into his arms, turning her in his embrace so that she was looking out away from him. All questions died on her tongue as she stared out in wonder at the sight laid out in front of them.

They were on a snowy uprise that overlooked all of Av'kanthal, the capital stretching out beneath them in a glory of lights. Not just the customary lights that she had seen before from a distance when the shuttle she had bribed passage on as a stowaway had passed over the city, but with a riot of hues and all manner of lights in celebration of the winter festivities.

There were large structures made of nothing but lights and glass baubles that bounced, reflected, and transmuted that light into a sparkling wonder of swirling peaks lifting up like thousands of hands entreating to the sky.

Her brow furrowed. Maybe not hands. The shapes were too irregular and more like chaotic spirals of voices lifting up. Yes, that was how she decided to think of it. Music visually rendered into light, lifting up to what divinity or divinities the Aturians honored. Although they were too far away and the night had descended, she knew that among those spires there would be cascading garlands of vibrant berries and brightly painted baubles of all kinds, especially in the downtown district where so much of the brilliance was concentrated. She felt a pang of envy that she couldn't personally see that. The downtown area was where the citizens lived.

"Hashavnal brings out the best in Aturians," Da'yel observed quietly, interrupting the silent wonder that had stretched out between them. "Never will you see our people happier, nor our cities reflect so much joy of spirit."

Lucy nodded. "I think that is a cultural similarity shared between our people. Humans love this time of the year, though we have many names for it. My family celebrates the twelve nights of Yule, and I can't remember a happier time than when the festival came around. Even when you have little, it feels like much more than it is at that time of the year."

Da'yel glanced over at her curiously. "What do humans do for your Yule?"

Nestling closer against him, enjoying the intense warmth of his body, she smiled. "Well, food is shared and enjoyed, special things that are cooked that Mama doesn't bother with the rest of the year because it's too much work. That's one of the few times that non-gratas are truly given exemption from our duties with paid bonuses, and so Mama would smile a lot as she baked sweets and shared drinks with other adults. We exchange small gifts, and there are decorations everywhere. Sometimes Daddy would try to catch Mama under the mistletoe because old Earth tradition says that a couple beneath the plant should kiss. There would be carols sung and games played. Everything is warm and cheerful, no matter how dreary or miserable the rest of the world is. It was always my favorite time of the year."

"It seems we have many traditions in common." He paused, his wings shifting around him with uncertainty. "I am not a great singer, but if you would permit, I would be delighted to sing for you, to celebrate this season with a traditional song of hope and the return of light and joy. And the hope of love and joy eternal with one's mate," he added hesitantly.

She grinned at his unexpected shyness and snuggled against him, her arms wrapping around him. "I'd love that."

His voice rose then, a deep cascade of notes falling upon each other that her translator struggled to decipher. But she didn't need the words. His melody ensnared her heart, carrying her reverently along as his song rolled out over the landscape. To her wonder, the lights below seemed to bow and dance to it, and she could have sworn that she caught a few echoes of song lifting up in response, but she couldn't be certain. If they did, it wouldn't have surprised her. What Da'yel sang was both a song and a prayer, one that she felt deep into her bones. Even the stars peeking out above seem to shine a bit brighter for it.

In his arms, she surrendered completely, welcoming the rush of tender emotions that ran through her in response to the beauty of the night and the pure love and joy reflected through his song as his wings surrounded her in his embrace.

CHAPTER 4

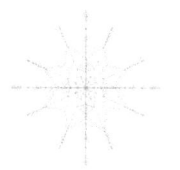

Da'yel was eager to return to his mate. Although the interloper had not made his presence known, several more gifts had arrived over the last few days. At first, he had been embarrassed by the meagerness of his own gifts in comparison until his mate sufficiently assured him that she did not care for the fancy gifts that this unknown male showered on her. Every one of these "inappropriate gifts" Lucy kept together in a box to return to the male once he made himself known.

Personally, he would be all too happy to shove them down the male's throat. The fact that another male pursued his Lucy did not set well with him, but it was strange that the male was being so secretive. Worse was the gifts came in a way that let him know that the mystery male was watching his Lucy, like a male on the hunt rather than courting. A male courting would have divulged his identity, not continued to hide in shadows waiting for the moment to strike.

It made him want to cleave all the closer to his mate to assure himself that no harm would come to her. The idea of a male trying to approach her when she was alone made his feathers rise on end. With this being Hashavnal, most Aturians would not give the presence of strangers a second thought as all manner of individuals wandered freely among the buildings, visiting friends and families.

Truthfully, it made him homesick for his valetik. Soon his kin would be gathering at the estate to share food and stories with each other after the midnight welcoming of the Hashavnal day. He missed it so fiercely that he felt like an idiot for ever leaving—but then he remembered his a'talyna and was reminded of exactly why he had left. He had wanted the opportunity to prove himself away from his kin, who knew his every transgression and rebellious acts as a youngling, and to find his a'talyna.

Young males leaving to find mates was not strange among their people, but few dared to venture as far as the capital like he did. The city was not as safe, and the celebratory fervor seemed to take on a wildness that didn't exist in the outer rim celebrations. For all that the citizens of the capital sneered at their outer rim members of their species, it was in the heart of the capital and large cities that posed the most hidden danger despite the extreme pacifist nature of most Aturians there. Of course, humans and Aturians were not the only species who made Aturia their home, and unlike humans, these others preferred to live among Aturians within the capitals.

These strangers added greater levels of uncertainty that made Da'yel want to hide his mate deep within the mountains of his home. With all the beauty, warmth, and joy of the season, it created a dark layer beneath it all that disturbed him. One that heightened on the eve of Hashavnal.

This would be their last revolution in Av'kanthal. By next Hashavnal, he would make certain, one way or another, to have his female far from there.

In the meantime, he had a special gift to deliver and a promise of an evening watching vids with his female. He had grown quite addicted to curling up with her, holding her in his arms and wings as they watched old human films and shows. He especially enjoyed old Earth depictions of aliens. *Star Trek* he found especially humorous and enjoyable, and his female claimed to have found a holiday episode that he might enjoy that showed a Christmas celebration, which she said was a lot like Yule but with a different spiritual context.

He found that idea intriguing, since Aturians held some similar beliefs. There were variations between regions, but there were certain commonalities as far as he was aware. Or perhaps those commonalities were all that existed after the unifying of their planet. It made him wonder if Aturia had been a lot more varied once rather than just merely separated between the flightless citizens and the outer rimmers.

With another energetic flap of his wings, he soared over the tops of several tall buildings, his special gift tucked securely against his breast. He couldn't wait for his mate to see it, to watch her eyes brighten with pleasure. A bloom of fire sparks drew his attention to find a small band of younglings entertaining themselves in their celebrations. Casting a misgiving look upon them, he made an anonymous report via comm and continued on his way. For all that the local Aturians looked down on him, he wasn't going to let any part of the capital burn down around him —at least not while his mate was there.

My mate. The very thought of her warmed his heart and quickened the beats of his wings so that he shot forward in the waning light, making his way with to her residence.

Unlike the other balconies of her building that were left ignored by Aturians who could make no use for them during the bitter cold months, his Lucy's balcony was draped with colorful Aturian garlands and lights, a warm and welcoming beacon.

Extending his wings to soften his drop, he landed lightly on it, puffs of snow falling off the rails at his impact. Shaking the lingering snow from his wings, he grinned as the privacy shield slid away from the door to reveal his mate standing just behind it with a welcoming smile upon her face. Tonight, she wore a sheer lacy covering with a pale floral print that just barely concealed her form beneath it. Her nipples were visible, as was the shadow of her mons, making his cock harden within its sheath.

Their games of temptation had increased over the last few nights until he felt like he was about to burst. Tonight, however, he felt his resolve weaken. He loved his mate. Her loyalty, her ferocity, her compassion... Free and genuine affection, bravery, and empathy made her all that he had could have ever desired. More than that, she brought out the best in him. He wanted to shelter her beneath his wings not just to selfishly keep her all to himself, but because he truly needed her sweetness and light in his life. She was like everything that the First Mother ever promised to her children.

Tonight, he would reveal the depth of his feelings for her and pray that they were returned.

Ducking inside, Da'yel plucked his mate up off her feet and hugged her against his chest.

"Happy Yule Eve, a'talyna," he purred.

"Happy Hashavnal Eve, my love," she replied breathlessly as she returned his embrace.

He could have kept her there in his arms forever, but she gave his chest a little pat, indicating that she wished to be put down, and so he set her on her feet again reluctantly. Amusement danced in her eyes as she stepped out from beneath his wings, and she gave one of his wing claws a little flick.

"There will be plenty of time for that later, but first I need to check on dinner. I managed to get some Earth-reared pork imported from the Dahlia Colony, thanks to El'valmay, as well as some sweet potatoes and fixings for a few of my favorite dishes.

It will be just like Yule back home." She gave him a shy look beneath her lashes. "I'm so excited to share this with you."

"A gift of your heart is the best gift a male can receive," he purred reverently, making the color in his female's cheeks brighten.

"That won't be your only gift," she retorted with an amused shake of her head. "There are gifts for you over on the table that we'll open later on. But first, dinner, and then we'll watch some holiday vids and you can share your customs. After that, we can perhaps play some games... however the spirit moves us," she added with a mischievous smile that made his cock press against the seam of his sheath eagerly.

He certainly hoped that one of his gifts might be a certain game for two. He could imagine a few that he would like to try. Nothing from any of the vids. He refused to even so much as look at them, not even for a bit of inspiration on what a human female might enjoy. He had not wanted to chance seeing his mate with another male in one just to make certain that he was not suddenly possessed by the need to hunt down his faux rival. His imagination and his own past experiences were enough to conjure more than a few things he wanted to try with his female if she were agreeable.

A snort of amusement nearly left him. Lucy was spirited and quite adventurous. He had little doubt that she would take to any of his ideas and probably match him with several of her own that could make him wish to do the human blush.

He was greatly looking forward to it.

As she waved him off to the common room, he took a seat, setting Lucy's gift on the table by the others, and listened as she moved around her kitchen. He did not know exactly what she was doing in there, but delicious smells perfumed the entire abode, making his mouth water. Temptation to investigate nearly overwhelmed him when a strange double chime echoed through the unit. He frowned, cocking his head. He had heard of the chime alerts, but his quarters, like most in the buildings where outer rimmers lived, had nothing of the sort.

From within the kitchen, he heard his female curse. "Who the hell could that be?"

His feathers ruffling, he strode toward the door, keeping his steps light as not to alert whoever waited at the other side of the door of his presence. From somewhere in the building, there was a crash and laughter as Hashavnal merriment got underway and someone who drank too much fermented juices likely obliterated some piece of furniture. Or a door. As long as whoever it was stayed far away from his mate's abode, Da'yel would not care, his sole focus on whoever lurked just outside waiting for Lucy.

He heard his mate come up behind him, and he fanned a wing out, gesturing for her to be silent when she opened her mouth to speak. It snapped closed again, and she nodded as she dropped behind him. She did not hide but grabbed a metal pole from a nook beside the door and gave him a hard look. Pride welled up within him that his mate had his back, conflicting with his own panicked need to have her far from any danger. Swallowing back his own desire to stow her someplace safe, he gave his mate a sharp nod. He turned just enough to give Lucy room to place her hand on the security plate for her door and waited with menace as it slid open.

A male with a ridiculous tuft of feathers on his neck and short, spiked crown feathers gaped at him for only a second before Da'yel wrapped his hand around that neck and dragged the male inside. If he was going to kill him, he did not want to do it where there might be witnesses, even if it meant profusely apologizing to his mate and enduring a long cleanup afterward. All through the building, Hashavnal melodies rang out, providing a festive backdrop as he slammed the male against the wall to the ode to joy and light, pinning him in place with one large hand, his claws pressing against the vulnerable flesh there.

"Who in the dark nights are you?" the male wheezed, his claws scrambling pitifully against Da'yel's grip.

"I think that would be my question," Da'yel replied menacingly. "You are the one who has turned up at my mate's home without invitation or permission."

"Mate? Impossible!"

The male's pathetic squawks were eroding his patience as the male sputtered denials and called out for Lucy.

My Lucy. Fury had him tightening his grip, cutting off the male's air until Lucy pushed against his side, making room for herself, a scowl on her lovely face. That scowl turned to a surprised expression that didn't make him feel any better. Clearly, she knew him. That was confirmed immediately by the first words out of her mouth.

"Vor'morat? What the hell are you doing here?"

The male turned his eyes toward her, a look of offense tightening his features subtly. Thankfully, Lucy was accustomed to being around Aturians enough that she did not miss the look and her own demeanor turned icy.

Da'yel snorted. It was a ridiculous name. He could not imagine any parent willingly naming their offspring "beautiful one rising at the dawn," after the goddess of the day, Vor'morlay.

Lucy tapped his arm, dragging his attention back to his small mate.

"Da'yel, not so tight. I want to hear his excuse for coming here."

Grunting, he eased off. Perhaps he was closer to his valmek kin than he thought. As an Aturian, he would have no problem shedding blood to protect his kin, yet most Aturians would not derive pleasure from it who were not valmeks. He was feeling all too much pleasure at holding the male helpless beneath his grip, eager to tear him apart at the threat. He tipped his head in consideration as he eased off the smaller male, completely releasing him for the time being.

Vor'morat coughed, his hand going up to his throat as he cast Da'yel a venomous look that made him want to choke the male all over again. The male sniffed and rose gracelessly to his feet, his short crown feathers in such disarray that Da'yel took a particular delight in it as the male attempted to preen in front of Lucy, addressing her with a haughty expression.

"It was meant to be a surprise," the male mumbled. "Any female would have been delighted to be courted by me. But, of course, not you. Not when you are taking up with outer rimmers." He sneered at Da'yel. "That explains why you were so often gone at night. The only time I had a chance to watch you was during the day if you happened to leave your residence at all. I am shocked, Lucy. I never would have thought you would have preferred the likes of that to me. Not when I gave you such pleasure."

His eyes narrowed and met Da'yel's. "Did she tell you about me? I was the last she performed with. It was exquisite. The moment I tasted her cunt I knew. Have you had that pleasure?" He tipped his head, his lips curving in a cruel smile as Da'yel instinctively recoiled in disgust from the male. Not for what Lucy did but for the words dripping from his mouth, sharing his private thoughts. "No, I thought not," Vor'morat purred. "I knew then that she was to be mine, especially when my cock fit inside her so perfectly and she keened beautifully beneath me. Didn't you, Lucy?"

A quick glance at his mate affirmed the truth of at least that part of the statement as her face reddened, her eyes cast away in shame. It infuriated Da'yel. *The loathsome male!*

The idiot, however, kept talking.

"When she didn't return to work, I knew she had to be waiting for me and so I sent the courting gifts. It timed so perfectly with Hashavnal that I couldn't have planned it better. My female allowing filth into her residence... Be grateful, Lucy, that I am willing to forgive all of this."

"I have no interest in your forgiveness," she shot back, her color still alarmingly high in her cheeks. "I told you then that I have no interest in being with you. If I wouldn't share a meal with you, what makes you think I have any desire to be your mate? That's just insane!"

The male's eyes lit as he tracked Lucy's movement, his own reaction broadcasting something that made Da'yel bristle in turn. There was something not right about the male, something that was festering in so many of the wingless ones. A stench of madness that made Da'yel's claws itch to strike out.

"But you are interested in *this*?" Vor'morat demanded shrilly, drawing out the beginning of a displeased rumble from Da'yel that the male chose to ignore. "What can he give you that I cannot. Doubtlessly he is larger, but you know for yourself I have a fine cock. I can take care of you far better than this outer rimmer could ever dream of! He could not give you even a portion of what I have offered."

Lucy's lip curled with disgust, and Da'yel almost expected her to strike the male with her metal pole—even hoped for it.

"Oh, yes, your gifts... the ugliest things I've ever set eyes on. Designed purely with the intent of trying to buy a female rather than show her any amount of true feeling or value outside of what you can pull out in credits."

She stormed over to a sealed box and plucked it up. Carrying it over, she thrust it at the male. "Here. I kept them all safe for you. You can see if they'll buy you a 'finer' female somewhere else, because they don't impress me in the least."

Fury filled the male's gaze as he lurched forward at such speed that had Lucy stumbling back in surprise. With a sweep of his wings, Da'yel thrust himself between them, a growl rising from him loud enough to startle all three of them. With a flurry of his giant wings beating at the male, he drove his rival back toward the door. As much as he wanted to use his claws, he kept his hands off of Vor'morat, relying solely on the bruising force of his wings.

It was enough. Wing beating rivals was a non-lethal way for Aturians to deal with unwelcome males who approach females. Brothers and fathers would defend sisters and daughters in that manner. As expected, Vor'morat had little defense against the wings slapping mercilessly at him, his shouts drowning out all music and celebration. Still, Da'yel did not stop until he drove the male out into the hall. Distantly, he could hear doors opening and the gasps and murmurs of other residents as they swarmed out into the halls to watch the spectacle.

"Da'yel, I think he's had enough," Lucy called out from behind him. "Let's return to our celebration of Hashavnal and leave him to his humiliation. I don't think he'll bother us anymore. I've already commed the authorities about being stalked and harassed by him, and I have witnesses from the studio who I know will back me up."

A tremor ran through him and he let his head drop warily, his eyes fastening with dark intention on the male defensively curled up in front of him.

"You will leave her alone?"

The male's head jerked in agreement with a whimper, and Da'yel felt his aggression drain out of him as he glanced around at those staring at them. The proud, strutting male had been shamed in front of an audience. He doubtlessly would not make an appearance again, even without the threat of the arrival of the authorities. This would be a good lesson that Vor'morat would not soon forget.

A sigh leaving him, Da'yel turned and followed his mate back into her home, the door closing behind them. As expected, a short time later they were questioned by males who viewed the pair of them suspiciously. Thankfully, eyewitnesses and security vids backed up their story. As did the vid feed around the property that showed the male stalking Lucy and initiating delivery drones just outside the building. All of this the authorities confirmed begrudgingly before leaving them to their private celebrations long after the other residents resumed their own festive activities.

The faint hum of Aturian music was soon replaced when Lucy initiated the recording stored within the modest residential AI systems of her quarters. To his surprise, a human song full of merriment filled the room, singing of bells and snow. This was followed by an Aturian favorite, and then by another from Earth in a blend of their cultures.

It was perfect.

Heart lightening once more, he felt closer to his mate than ever with her efforts to join their customs into one celebration. The bond thrummed between them, and his heart swelled with greater love and devotion as he sat down to last meal with his a'talyna and enjoyed the human feast set before him. The savory flavors that met his tongue were incredible on their own, made all the better with the knowledge that they were provided by his mate's own delicate hands.

Despite how much he loved the meal she made, he knew that, truthfully, she could have made the plainest dishes that humans were notorious for enjoying when eating among Aturians—something he thankfully never witnessed with his own mate—and he still would have adored every bite just knowing that it was a gift from his mate's hand.

Love was glorious, the light and true joy of Hashavnal as every adult Aturian came to know eventually. Never had he understood it clearer than he did now, the way that it cut through the darkness and stirred creation.

First Mother and all the gods knew that he was stirred to attempt creation the moment he could get his mate beneath him. Da'yel covered a groan with his fist as he eyed his mate beside him at the table.

He could not wait to begin their next round of celebrations.

CHAPTER 5

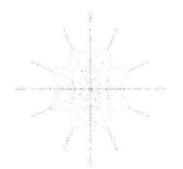

For what had to be the thousandth time, Lucy glanced at Da'yel from beneath her lashes. Gods, the way he had dealt with Vor'morat had turned her on more than she wanted him to know. Aturians were generally such a peace-loving species. She didn't want him to know just how much she enjoyed it. Instead, she contented herself to stolen glances when he was not looking all throughout dinner.

And she sure did love watching him enjoy her cooking. It gave her a certain domestic pleasure she had never felt before, knowing that her clumsy attempt to follow a recipe had created something he ate with obvious relish. Even she had to admit that it turned out surprisingly good. Dinner at least was a nice distraction. Now that it was over, she wasn't sure where to look or what to do that wouldn't give away just how much she desired him.

Watching the vids was almost torture, even though she loved listening to his commentary over the series that Da'yel proclaimed as his favorite. She never would have guessed an alien would be a *Star Trek: The Next Generation* fan, but Da'yel had a way of surprising her with his easy, relaxed humor that was so contrary to the image of a large, intimidating outer rim Aturian male in his prime. It was no wonder that he had found work easily down at the docking port. Few would guess from looking at him that he was genuinely a very sweet and caring male. It was something, however, that he hadn't been shy to show her from the beginning, which made her fall in love with him faster than any gift or gesture could have.

A tiny sigh passed her lips, and Da'yel's head tipped toward her, his green eyes focusing on her as if she were all that truly existed for him, the holiday vid that was playing now completely forgotten.

"A'talyna?"

"Maybe we should go ahead and exchange gifts," Lucy blurted out.

Although he gave her a surprised look, he nodded and reached for the gift he had brought. Like the other gifts he had brought to her daily while they were courting, the package was small, but she knew it would contain something meaningful. Aside from the carved flower, he had brought her a small collection of Aturian spices she had expressed interest in during one of their conversations about food, a little bouquet of luminous blue flowers that he said reminded him of her eyes, a gold feather from an exotic alien species that he purchased from a trader from the port all because he wanted to see how it looked against her hair. He had proclaimed that her hair was even lovelier, which made her adore the gift even more. And around her wrist was a thin band of tiny polished yellow stones that he said represented the joy that filled his heart whenever she was near. She wasn't sure how he was going to even top that one, but she knew that, somehow, he would do it. Her Da'yel was a romantic.

In comparison, she really wasn't, and she had the sinking feeling that her meager gifts wouldn't come close to anything he gave hers. In truth, she was pretty sure that her gift giving skills sucked, and she dreaded disappointing the male she wanted to have as her mate.

Nervously licking her lips, Lucy reached for a gift. It was okay, she had no reason to be nervous. She just had to remind herself that it was Yule, not begging him to express his commitment. It wasn't a competition.

Taking a deep breath, she smiled and thrust the little package at him. "You've given me so many gifts already. You should open yours first."

Da'yel looked down at it and smiled as he carefully took it from her hand, mindful as always of his claws. "Very well, a'talyna. I would be honored."

His claws made quick work of the wrapping as she fidgeted in place, the paper and twine falling away to reveal a small box. She had painstakingly engraved a feather and a flower into the lid. He traced his claws delicately over the design and glanced up at her.

"I made it," she mumbled, feeling the heat creeping into her cheeks. "Flowers and feathers make me think of us together. It's a bit silly, I know, but I figure the box can be useful to store little things that are important. It has an old-fashioned latch on it too. You can start with this if you'd like," she added, blindly shoving another gift at him, unable to meet his eyes.

There was nothing for a long moment, and she was certain that she would die on the spot from embarrassment, but then she heard his claws tear away the wrapping on the second gift and his little gasp. She peeked over at him and watched as he stared down at the intricately carved imperial jasper pendant in his hand. With the surprise painted so blatantly across his features, she could not tell whether or not he otherwise liked it. Damn Aturian poker faces.

"It's nothing special. Well, it *is* special to me," she amended, and his gaze turned once more to the pendant, "but it has no great monetary value. Green jasper is pretty common on Earth. I admit that the roses carved on it aren't very manly. After all, my great grandfather gave it to my great grandmother because he could not afford to buy her the actual flower. Outside of specialized growers who charged large sums of credit for cut roses, most roses went extinct with the bee collapse. Scientists restored bee populations, but roses never really recovered once their growth was privatized." She winced. Oh, gods, she was rambling. "Anyway, Grandmother loved it so much that it was one of the few things that not only made it to the colony but remained in our family. My father gave it to my mother, and before I left, Mama gave it to me with the hope that I would find a love like theirs."

His eyes shot up, meeting hers, his green eyes gleaming as if flushed with light.

"You love me?" he whispered.

She nodded. Swallowing back her nerves, she reached over and traced a rose, her fingertip gliding against his claw. "Roses mean love in all its varieties, even as they once came in numerous hues, as well as a promise of hope and new beginnings." She licked her lips again, meeting his eyes. "Those are all things I feel and want with you."

His gaze softened, his eyes shining with barely contained happiness. "And that is the best gift of all," he whispered. "I love the box, knowing that it will hold our memories, and I especially love the pendant and will wear it proudly because of the history behind it and all that it means to you. I do not understand 'manly,' but I understand love and hope, and these are things I would be happy to wear as a symbol of our union. But it is your love that cannot be measured against any possession." He looked chagrined. "I admit that I did not wish to tell you of my heart until I gave you your gift, so please take it now."

Curious, she pulled it into her lap. The bundle had a bit more weight than usual, which was curious. Unwrapping it, she found a small tin box contained inside. She gave Da'yel a curious glance and opened the lid. Her lips tipped as she looked upon numerous chocolates nestled within colorful papers. Old Earth romance spelled out with sweets. She couldn't believe it.

"How?" she murmured.

Her intended mate winced, but he utterly failed any kind of shamefaced expression as a willful smile crossed his face. "I may have bribed a supply runner who was stopping over for repairs to sell me something special enjoyed by human females. I wanted something that would convey how much sweetness you brought into my lonely life… and how much I love and adore you, a'talyna. My Lucy."

Her lip quivered with emotion. "Really? You love me?"

His smile grew rueful. "I believe I came close to killing a male for you and would have done so happily. I would have thought you realized my feelings from that alone."

She choked out a laugh. "I think I was too focused on just how hot I thought that was."

Da'yel's head tipped again in inquiry. "Hot?"

"Sexy," she clarified with an embarrassed giggle, and a grin lit up his face.

Moving with the speed of a panther, Da'yel quickly crawled over the short distance separating them from the floor where he had been lazily crouched on the couch with her, his large body hemming her in as his wings folded around them. A crooning purr rumbled through him as he stroked one claw down her neck, and her breath caught in wonder. His lips trailed against her throat, his breath fanning her skin as he whispered reverently.

"You feel the a'talynal, and you love me. This alone is precious to me. So, I ask you now, will you allow me to make you mine and honor me with this granting on the holy Hashavnal?"

She didn't have to glance at her comm to know that the hour was late, and it was well past what was considered the midnight hour in Aturia. It was technically Hashavnal and Yule morning, even if the sun hadn't risen. What could be a more perfect gift to celebrate the return of hope, joy, light and love?

"Yes," she whispered, and with that one word sealed her fate and the a'talynal between them.

Mouths interlocked, tongues twining, unspoken words of love and adoration flooded through them, quaking along the bond she could feel expanding between them with every questing flick of his tongue and every stroke of his hands as they rid her of her clothes. Bliss flowed over and through her, and into him and back into her. It was like some strange exchange of ecstasy that had only been hinted at in what she knew about humans and Aturians. But now she understood. The a'talynal, that perfect chemistry, was created from that bond, fed to greater heights by the love between them.

That combination was everything. It was a madness that swept between them carrying every pleasure and every need, heightening them all tenfold.

So great was the ecstasy that, when Da'yel broke away, she would have cried out if she hadn't been silenced by the slick heat of his tongue tracing over her skin, restoring that connection, feeding her hunger, energizing her. She knew he felt it too. She could practically feel him drawing every bit of the sexual heat from her flesh into himself, his moans and growls echoing in her ears as his tail stiffened, the fan of feathers along its length spreading wide behind him as if he were a snowy peacock.

His hot tongue circled her nipple, and she gasped and was surprised when a milky chocolate was pressed into her mouth, against her tongue. She bit down, the sweetness of the cherry within bursting on her tongue as his tongue trailed down her belly to seek out the hidden nub of her clit. With the sweetness flooding her senses, her body shook at the first lap of his tongue, her hips canting up off the couch. Growling, he drew her in tighter, tasting of her like she was a favorite peppermint stick until she was practically mad with desire.

Grabbing one horn, she pulled his head away and met burning green eyes, his lips pulled back from his teeth in a fierce grimace. It didn't frighten her at all. There was no hostility in his face, just the raw lust and adoration that flooded their bond.

"Let's take this to the bedroom, shall we?"

With an audible snarl, he snatched her up into his arms, his wings closing around her. The scrape of his claws against her floor was the only sound outside of the rushing of her pulse in her ears. The festive carols had faded away. Even the vid they had been watching had reached its end, leaving nothing but a blessed silence in its wake interrupted by the soft plop of her body hitting the bed where Da'yel deposited her. Eyes glowing with desire, he watched her as he stripped. She eagerly devoured the sight of each inch of amethyst skin he exposed and the silence lengthened and deepened, creating a new pulse between them that heightened every moment.

As the silence of night birthed new beginnings, it seemed appropriate then that there was nothing but the sounds of their need between them, the world around them rendered to nothing but a vast dark silence in the depths of the night. If there was any commotion anywhere, it didn't reach them. She was aware of nothing but the rasp of his snarl, the deep croon of his song rumbling over her, the huff of his breath, and the slide of bare flesh against bare flesh as he joined her on the bed. His wings snapped around them, and his tail fanned as their bodies undulated together as mouths and hands worshiped lover's flesh.

And how she loved him.

She could feel it swell within her, that love. It wound desire around it in a tighter coil. With a whispered demand, Lucy pushed Da'yel flat on his back and grabbed his fuchsia sex in her hand. Its girth seemed to thicken in her palm, and tiny threads along the top of his shaft vibrated searchingly in an instinctive demand to be snug within her pussy.

She shivered as she stroked her fingers over them, the small knobs on his cock releasing a sweet, spicy-scented scented lubrication with every pass of her palm. He groaned and canted into her touch, his wings trembling with desire that she could feel flooding into her. Feeling particularly powerful in the moment, Lucy leaned down to sample his flavor, the familiar taste of cinnamon candies bursting on her tongue as she lapped along his length, teasing the tripart head weeping with precum. She barely had the opportunity to suck him into her mouth when Da'yel roared and pulled her away, his cock popping free from her lips. A tiny gasp of surprise left her in the next moment as he yanked her bottom down toward him, sending her flat on her back so that he could crawl over her like some kind of dark, alien angel.

If angels had the sinful cocks of demons.

Yes, her alien was a mix of both and all hers. The sweet and the sinful, the loving and playful, and the brutal territorial male. And she loved all of him for it.

Pleasure rushed through her as he mounted and breached her, impaling her slowly on his length. Her breath rushed out in a sigh that was silenced and captured immediately by his mouth on hers. He swallowed her every moan and cry as his hips rocked against hers in a primal rhythm. It felt like some ancient, wordless worship, calling back life on the longest, darkest night of the year. As if the power running between them along their bond was fueling something greater than themselves as one small orgasm tripped into another.

It could all be fantasy, but at that moment she felt as if they were one with the heart of Aturia, their bodies moving together as his pace grew more frantic and her hips rose to meet him. His claws scraped against her thighs and ass, adjusting his angle to rut into her, his season coming upon him. She could feel the difference the moment the change came, and her body wept for it with a desperate need that she had never felt before. His cock thickened within her, his hips snapped, grinding deep, coaxing moans from what felt like deep within her soul.

Her fingernails bit into his back as she felt the brush of his teeth on her shoulder. Her breath stilled, wondering if he would bite. Did that make her kinky if she wanted it? She moaned and pressed against his mouth, but he licked the flesh there instead and pumped deep until she felt something tap so deep that her sex spasmed. He pistoned ravenously, his wing claws digging into the bedding at either side of her and his hunger pulling at her until she moved with wild abandon against him, drawing from him in turn. With the passing of one moment into the next, his cock seemed to swell more. The vibrations of the little whip at the top of his cock increased until the entire girth of him felt like it was vibrating with every thrust.

Lucy panted, her head thrashing with the ecstasy running full-steam through her blood until the bond seemed to engulf her, her orgasm detonating through it with such strength that she barely heard Da'yel's roar over her own scream. His cock jerked hard with every deposit of hot cum sprayed, each triggering another orgasm in her as his release flooded through in a golden blast until she lay entirely spent and boneless beneath her mate, and the deep hunger within her completely satisfied. She lay blissfully in his arms and wings that had gathered her up to hold her close, their hearts beating in tandem.

She was quite certain that somewhere the sun was rising, spreading the glory of its rays over Aturia.

His claws brushed through her hair, and she smiled, leaning into the touch.

"Happy Yule, a'talyna."

"Happy Hashavnal, my love," she whispered, her heart content.

AUTHOR'S NOTE

I hope you enjoyed Vanessa and Jor'y's story (as well as the short for Da'yel and Lucy). Originally this was meant to be a holiday novella while I worked on Serpents of the Night (which is yes still coming but has been moved back to early 2022 because its taking a bit longer to write and this book ended up being over twice the length I intended to be starting out) but there story was not quick telling. And then I fell in love with Da'yel and Lucy and just had to give everyone a special little insight into how they met and their whirl wind courtship.

As always, a huge thankyou to my alpha and beta readers who really go above and beyond in helping me get all of this done, and a thank you to all of my readers as well for taking the time to read another one of my romances.

Happy Holidays!

SJ Sanders

OTHER WORKS BY S.J. SANDERS

The Mate Index
First Contact

The VaDorok

Hearts of Indesh (Valentine Novella)

The Edoka's Destiny

The Vori's Mate

Eliza's Miracle (Novella)

A Kiss on Kaidava

The Vori's Secret

A Mate for Oigr (Halloween Novella)

Heart of the Agraak

A Gift for Medif

The Arobi's Queen

Teril's Fire

A Winged Embrace

Monsterly Yours
The Orc Wife

The Troll Bride

The Accidental Werewolf's Mate

The Pixie's Queen

The Unicorn's Mare

How to Claim a Human Mate

Trick or Orc

The Troll King (coming soon)

Sci-Fi Fairytales

Red: A Dystopian World Alien Romance

Sirein

Ragoru Beginnings Romance

White: Emala's Story

Huntress

Origins (coming soon)

Ragoru Romance

A Mother's Night Gift

Warrioress (coming soon)

Dark Spirits

Havoc of Souls

Forest of Spirits

Desert of the Vanished (coming soon)

Dark Spirits Fairytales

The Mirror

Matchsticks

Glass Slippers (coming soon)

Shadowed Dreams Erotica

The Lantern

The Mintars

Librarian and the Beast

The Atlavans

The Darvel Exploratory Systems

Classified Planet: Turongal

Serpents of the Abyss

Snows of Aturia

Serpents of the Night (coming soon)

Mist World: Asylum of Graelf (coming soon)

Eternal (coming soon)

Argurma Salvager

Broken Earth

Pirate's Gold

Sands of Argurumal

The Argurma Chronicles

Argurma Warrior (coming soon)

ABOUT THE AUTHOR

S.J. Sanders is a writer of Science Fiction and Fantasy Romance. With a love of all things alien and monster she is fascinated with concepts of far off worlds, as well as the lore and legends of various cultures. When not writing, she loves reading, sculpting, painting and travel (especially to exotic destinations). Although born and raised in Alaska, she currently is a resident of Florida with her family.

Readers can follow her on Facebook
https://www.facebook.com/authorsjsanders
Or join her Facebook group S.J. Sanders Unusual Playhouse
https://www.facebook.com/groups/361374411254067/
Newsletter: https://mailchi.mp/7144ec4ca0e4/sjsandersromance
Twitter: @monsterlyluv
TikTok: @authorsjsanders
Website: https://sjsandersromance.wordpress.com/